THE LIGHTNING PEOPLE PLAY

A NOVEL

TIM CUMMINGS

Black Rose Writing | Texas

The author grants the final approval for this literary material.

First printing

ISBN: 978-1-68513-619-2 (Paperback); 978-1-68513-656-7 (Hardcover)
PUBLISHED BY BLACK ROSE WRITING
www.blackrosewriting.com

Printed in the United States of America
Suggested Retail Price (SRP) $21.95; (Paperback) $26.95 (Hardcover)

The Lightning People Play is printed in Garamond Premier Pro

*As a planet-friendly publisher, Black Rose Writing does its best to eliminate unnecessary waste to reduce paper usage and energy costs, while never compromising the reading experience. As a result, the final word count vs. page count may not meet common expectations.

PRAISE FOR THE LIGHTNING PEOPLE PLAY

"The narrator is sarcastic yet sweet, the plot funny yet scary. There are hilarious theatre kids with crushes on each other and villainous bullies roaming the halls. There are kinda heroic teens confronting mysterious symbols from the other side (maybe?). In other words: *The Lightning People Play* has absolutely everything you'd want in a YA novel, and then some."

–Josh Berk, Edgar Award nominee and author of *The Dark Days of Hamburger Halpin*

"Tim Cummings weaves vivid, gripping tales filled with heart and irreverent humor, and told in an electric, irresistible voice. They're pure fun to read and *The Lighting People Play* is a perfect showcase for his talents."

– Jeff Zentner, Morris-award winning author of *The Serpent King* and *In The Wild Light.*

"This book is sheer magic. The magic of the theatre, the magic of community, the magic of being one's truest self all shimmer from the page like stars. Tim Cummings writes with such authenticity, such power, such charm, such vision, such heart. This book will change lives—it's a breathtaking celebration of creativity and neurodivergence and connection and the messy beauty of being a human in a world filled with both pain and possibility. *The Lightning People Play* will forever sizzle inside me."

–Gayle Brandeis, award-winning author of *The Art of Misdiagnosis* and *My Life with The Lincolns*

"A dazzling, kinetic and bewitching journey of navigating the family we are born into, the family we choose and the inexhaustible worlds of carnivals, theatre barns and backyard forests that connect them all. I fell in love with acerbic theater nerd, Kirby Renton, as he drew me through his complicated, heartbreaking and agonizingly hilarious life – never knowing if he is going to triumph or burst into flames from page to page. Oh, the aches and pains of those teenage years. Sigh. *The Lightning People Play* is both an otherworldly delight and a touching homage to the underappreciated wisdom, resilience and devotion of an upcoming generation of humans. It is a way better planet with resplendent author Tim Cummings and his waggish and courageous crew of misfits on it. You should definitely spend some time with them."

–Kim Maxwell, Ojai Playwrights Conference Co-Founder & Youth Program Director

"This novel is a beautiful, poignantly-written depiction of the lengths one teenage boy will go to save his brother. Kirby, Baxter, Heddy the dog, and the rest of the cast—through theatre and seizures and sacrifice—evoke themes of brotherhood, sonship, and the healing power of art all while facing trauma, self-doubt, abandonment, and neurological disorders. Like lightning, Tim Cummings strikes to the core of what it means to love—and what it means to be a young person—during a time in life when the perils of adulthood threaten to keep us grounded. With the sentiment of John Green and the wit of Andrew Smith, *The Lightning People Play* celebrates what makes each of us special as well as the bonds that connect us as friends, as families, and as individuals."

–Nathan Elias, author of *Coil Quake Rift* and *The Reincarnations*

"Tim Cummings forms ice sculptures out of words—but *The Lightning People Play* is more than beautiful prose. Through Kirby and the ragtag band of thespians, stagehands, and mentors who aid him in helping his brother Bax, we experience family, enchantment, and the miracle of live performance. It's a book about those momentous first steps toward a life in the arts, with all their accompanying rapture and sorrow."

–Ari Rosenschein, author of *Dr. Z and Matty Take Telegraph* and *Coasting*

"In Tim Cummings' captivating YA novel, *The Lightning People Play*, fourteen-year-old Kirby will stop at nothing to help his little brother, Bax, who has epilepsy. Determined to raise funds for a seizure dog that could change Bax's life, Kirby enlists his theater friends to create a mesmerizing play that reflects the other-worldly portal that Bax seems to enter when having a seizure. Kirby's voice resonates with raw emotion as his synesthetic experiences draw him (and us!) deep into the complexities of his brother's condition. Lyrical prose mirrors the magic of the story, beautifully intertwining serious themes with a unique, well-paced, and often humorous storyline. This is a tender yet powerful tale that serves as a reminder that with compassion and courage, even the youngest among us can make a difference."

–Kimberly Behre Kenna, award-winning author of *Jett Jamison and the Secret Storm*

THE LIGHTNING PEOPLE PLAY

"The seller of lightning rods arrived just ahead of the storm."
–Ray Bradbury, *Something Wicked This Way Comes*

"What would this world be like without dogs?"
–Mary Oliver, *Dog Songs: Poems*

"I won't eat any cereal that doesn't turn the milk purple."
–Bill Watterson

THE LIGHTNING PEOPLE

My little brother Baxter sees things he calls 'the lightning people', but he will not tell me who or what they are. It's driving me up a rat pole. I don't even know what a rat pole is. I think I saw it in a dream, or maybe one of Bax's video games? But, it sounds like something that I, Kirby Daniel Renton the 1st, would be driven up.

About a month ago, Pop abandoned us and disappeared.

Dad asks me not to say that. "It's not true," he says. "We've separated for now, and he's in Texas with Granbuela, and that's all there is to it."

Yeah, but still, I tell him.

"Don't 'but still' me," he says. "There is no 'but still'."

Yeah, but still.

After Pop abandoned us and disappeared, Bax started having seizures, usually in the middle of the night. The darkest part of the night, that's when they happen, that's when he sees things. Monsters, or aliens, or people, or witches—I don't know exactly—who slink down from the lightning in a dark purple sky full of puffed-up clouds.

He says they show him things.

"What things?" I ask him, and get all fidgety, probably from nerves. "Tell me."

But he refuses. "They're not yours," he says. "They're mine." He wants to keep them to himself. He'll be eleven in a few months. He one-ups everything constantly. The other morning, I got more marshmallows than him in my bowl of Lucky Charms. He tossed his spoon across the kitchen island and stormed off.

I want to know about the lightning people because I kinda have this thing with my brains. Dad calls it my 'magic', but I've heard others, like my teachers, say it might be 'mild OCD', or 'symmetry OCD. OCD is obsessive compulsive disorder, a lot of 's' sounds, like a snake is about to uncoil and bite you in the face and suck out your face juices. But, it actually means you like to be orderly. Or at least that's what it means for me. For some people, in severe cases, it's pretty high-key, as in buying 250 toothbrushes and throwing them out after using them for a milli-second because germs get on them so they can't use them anymore. A milli-second.

We saw the doctor about this, years ago. But, I am not diagnosed. He told us that if it was not impeding on my day-to-day life in a negative way, then not to worry. It could be OCD, or something else, or a million other things. Or it could just be me.

I organize stuff. Not just books and boxes and junk drawers. It includes people, and feelings, too. I see people's feelings, as if they were colors, and I want to organize them. Feelings look like colored pencils that need to be put next to each other in the right way in the colored pencil box. When I see colors, I move them around. No one really knows about this stuff. No, I mean, my best friends Rockford and Ellie know, but they're all, "Whatevz, we love you." And Thaddeus Krasinski—he heads up YOUTHEATRE, our theatre club at Weirville Junior High. And yes, we call it 'youth eater' all the time. ('Theatre' is the act itself while 'theater' is the space where it happens. Krasinski is particular about that 're' versus 'er' thing.) He knows about my brains 'cause I told him after I rearranged the plays and books on the shelves in his office. Beige Blue Green Orange Purple Red White Yellow. Alphabetical by color. Colorbetical.

I need to know the lightning people are not going to hurt my brother, but it's hard to figure out 'cause I can't go up inside his brains while he's having a seizure. Doctor-of-Brains (the Neurologist dude) told us that the electrical pathways in the brain get mixed up for epileptics—that's the condition that causes seizures. Epilepsy. Bax was placed inside a monster X-ray machine that looked like a giant robot butthole so Doctor-of-Brains could figure out what was going on. He said Bax was an anomaly for being able to remember anything that happened during a seizure. He said that was not normal at all. Usually, people go unconscious. All I wanted to know, and all I kept asking, was, Why? How could this all just *happen*? What is it? Where did it come from? Why did it pick Bax? Stuff doesn't just *happen*. But the doctor said, "Well, yeah, actually, it does."

So, I told Dad my theory: that it's his fault Pop left. Hear me out: Pop is Bax's favorite person in the whole world, and the fact he could leave us—leave Bax—is what made his brains explode inside his head and that's what's causing the seizures. After I told Dad this very wise theory of mine, that it was all his fault, he grounded me for the summer. Okay, a few weeks, maybe three, but it felt like the entire summer, 'cause during summer, when you're free, every day's a huge day. To have twenty-one of them robbed from you—for telling the truth—it may as well have been all seventy-five. Drove me up the rat pole, I swear.

And now Bax is changing. I see it. He's growing younger.

Bax has always been the smartest kid in any class. He likes to dress like a professor. Dad and Pop would buy him suits and nice shoes to wear to school. He doesn't like to look like other kids. He likes to look like Charles Xavier from X-Men. Always put together. Even though he's a little maniac and plays football and freeze-tag during recess. In the suits. We are used to this, how dirty he is when he comes home, so we don't worry. Other people think he's lit: the nice ties and big expressive eyes and shock of hair combed nicely with pomade. But, ever since Pop abandoned us and disappeared, and Bax's seizures started, he now wants to look like a stick of Fruit Stripe gum. He wears T-shirts with colored stripes on them, bright sneakers, and his hair is a mess. He looks...normal. But, if this is normal, it's the weirdest normal ever. And the real question, anyway, is: How do I get him to tell me about the lighting people? I need to know who they are and what they want.

Here's the thing: I won't let anything bad happen to Bax.

FREAKCITY

It's the Weirville Carnival tonight, best thing to happen all year. Rides, games, a giant labyrinth like in that scary movie with the maniac writer guy in the snow at the haunted hotel chasing his son with an axe. Except this labyrinth is normal. I think. Cotton candy, hot dogs, lemon-ices at the sock-puppet show. Motorcycle brigades. I could own a carnival someday. Maybe I'll fill my carnival with tall rat poles all in a row. I don't know. Something weird.

Tonight, YOUTHEATRE is raising money for the fall play. We don't know which one we'll do yet, it's still being decided, but last year we did *The Curious Incident of the Dog in the Night-Time*, a play about autism. I played the lead role and won this big acting award. When I accepted the award, I laughed, even though the Mayor of Weirville and the Principal of my school gave me the award at this fancy awards ceremony. I said, "Why am I winning an award? It's playing—why do people win awards for this?" It was a big deal for the adults. And Dad and Pop went nuts. Pop picked me up and spun me like I was a five-year-old on the playground.

Tonight, we'll do some scenes and songs on a stage off the thoroughfare. But *before* that, we will arrive early and ride rides and mash hot salty cheese into our faces. I might accidentally puke on someone's head down below while I'm hurtling above them on a ride, screaming my head off.

The Carnival down at Kerryville Grange takes place every year during the last week of August. Kerryville sits at the bottom of a valley and driving past Downtown Weirville, which we call DoWe, and into the open spaces is EEM. (Dad: "What does EEM mean?" Me: "'Enjoy every moment.' Keep up, Dad.") As you approach the valley from above, you can see everything down below. It's one of my favorite parts of the carnival, seeing it glowing and flickering in the distance while the sun sets all dark-blue, orange-pink, and purple-gray. The Ferris Wheel rises up, blinking its lights. I lean out the window to take pix with my phone and Dad yells at me not to fall out of the car and get splattered all over the street, and we laugh. I smell cotton candy, hot pretzels, hay. Also, the smell of a dead skunk on the road, what a funky stink. I hear old-fashioned carnival music. I think it's called calliope. It sounds all warped as it rides the wind, almost like a scary movie.

As we head down toward the carnival, Bax sticks his head out the other window and screams 'cause he's so excited. I smile, my face tingling. I can't wait to go on the Zipper ride that throws you up, down, over, to the side, backwards, forwards, spinning, lurching, jerking until you yack chunks all over. I hope I don't fall out and tumble down and crack my head open, but if I do, I hope hot pretzel cheese oozes out instead of blood. EEM.

After we arrive, we bolt straight to the ride, but the line is too long. We look up and see the machine, a big metallic colored centipede, its P-shaped carriages flipping around as the spine of the ride spins in a wide circle. Everyone is screaming. "Shake It Off" blasts from the speakers. The two girls in front of us are Swifties, never missing a beat, lightning on their feet. I tell Bax to wait, sprint to the front of the line to see if anyone we know is up there. Hoping to see Ellie and Rockford. Nope. Rats.

While dashing all the way back to Bax, to our place in line, I turn my head and see an entire stretch of carnival taken over by some buildings that say **F R E A K C I T Y** across the top in bright red letters. I stop, staring at it. I have never seen this attraction here before. It looks like its own little town. There is *Mirror Maze Way*, in a building with a giant mirror for the front, reflecting everything that moves. Beside that stands *Dunk Tank Drive*, and you can see through the glass of that building to all the dunk tanks lined up in a row. The little rooms are flooded with red light, and the dunk tanks themselves are painted with spirals, and thorns, and evil-long clown faces. Next there's a ride called *Freekout.* It looks like the gigantic hand of the devil holding four huge seating machines. It lifts them, rocks them, spins them, and flings them back and forth. It keeps moving up, up, up toward the sky, then it drops back down. I think I see vomit chunks flying out of it up near the top and I'm not kidding. Flying yackchunks.

Last in the row of buildings and rides is *Haunted Estates*. It is a purple and orange mansion, very Halloween-looking. A mini train-track for the carriages runs out front. The carriages, with bat wings painted on the sides, take you in the house through double doors inside a giant witch's mouth. She opens her huge jaws right as the carriage is about to go through, and she cackles. The little car disappears, and the doors go THWACK THWACK with a loud crack of thunder. This looks scary. I'm definitely riding this.

I hop back to Bax, grab him. "Zipper's too long of a wait. Come see this FREAKCITY." I take his hand for some reason, the way I did when we were little kids, and at first, he's okay with it as he shoves pale blue cotton candy into his face. But after a minute, looking around at the teenagers and the carnival ride operators in their leather jackets and thick mustaches, he yanks his hand free. I tap him on the back, just letting him know how much I love him, even though he gets annoyed by that.

Suddenly I feel a hard SHWAT on the back of my head. It hurts. I whirl around to find DeSean Riggs and Jeremy Jameson smirking at us. DeSean holds a bag of popcorn, all greasy, which is what he used to whack me. They're 10th graders.

"Heard one of your dads split," DeSean says.

"Flattened by the Pride float?" Jeremy says.

"Splattered in the street where they belong," DeSean says as they skulk past.

I swallow, anger boiling all the water in my body. Bax's cheeks flood blood red and he lunges after them, but I stop him and place my hand on his chest to calm him down. Sometimes I think that some of the people who live in Weirville belong back in Texas. That's where we moved here from.

Dad and Pop didn't want to leave Texas. They met there, got married after five years, and used a surrogate for me and Bax. But some of our neighbors made life difficult. One day, we arrived home after soccer practice to find neighbors on our lawn with shotguns screaming Bible verses and Devil curses. Pop confronted them, and Dad shoved us back in the car and drove like 90mph to the police station. I felt so scared Pop was gonna get shot. Bax screamed in the backseat the whole way.

We considered moving to Austin, but Pop said it was too pretentious. I think that's the word he used. Los Angeles was too far; Pop wanted to stay close to our Granbuela. New York, too expensive. Vermont was a possibility until we visited in winter. Then came an opening in Weirville, America's 'beloved rookie city' northwest of Pittsburgh and southeast of Cleveland, on the border of Pennsylvania and Ohio—but no one could move there because it had, like, filled up. No houses available. No new building happening for a little while.

But then a house came on the market, a dark-blue Craftsman, which both my dads wanted, really badly. After some finagling, we got it, moved here, and we love it. Weirville is 'America's freshest city, impeccably curated and designed, an imagined *Subtropolis* for the 21st Century.' That's on a plaque at school, and on the bridge downtown, too. It's on every landmark here. My dads say Weirville, as it turns out, isn't that innovative, not that different from other American cities. "America will always be America," they say. Pop says he never knows what decade we're in here. "Weirville is out of time—no one knows if it's the 80s, 90s, 00s, or 10s. It's an era-blender." I think it's a cool place to live. Except for craptraps like DeSean and Jeremy, who make it stink here like the squashed skunk we smelled on the street.

I pat Bax's chest to make sure he has chilled out and turn his body around so that he's looking directly at FREAKCITY. "Whoa," he says. "A haunted house ride! Let's go!" He bolts for the ride, flies up the steps, flashes his neon bracelet at the conductor, and nearly slams into the people in line in front of him. The cotton candy has had its way with him.

The Haunted Estates ride has a long wait, too. I mean, I think there's only two or three carriages that go through it, and only two at a time in a carriage, and it must be huge inside there because it takes so long for them to come back out. Dad's waiting across the thoroughfare with some friends, sitting on bales of hay, eating street corn, corn dogs, and burgers. I only recognize one of his friends: the guy who looks like Ant Man. His dog peed all over our house at Dad's birthday party last year. They're sitting close to one another, I see that, and a fizz zizzles through my chest. I sigh, but it's more like a hiss. I miss Pop. A lot.

Bax's sugar crash makes him fall forward *into* me with a groan. I wrap my hands around his little head and give him a shake. *Grgrgrgrgrgrgrgrgr*, and he laughs out loud.

"Love you, Kirbz," he says.

I grin.

Then he farts.

I shake my head.

"Oh. Look," he says, and points.

I turn my head and see painted creepiness: bats, ghosts, ghouls on the long wall of the front of the ride. Purple witches dance with black cats around a giant totem pole of lightning.

"That's like my dreams," he says all slow and quiet.

I feel twitchy in my belly, like weird little spasms. I swallow. "Your dreams?"

"You know," he says, "My see-thingies."

"See-thingies? You mean seizures?"

"Mmm."

"You think they're dreams?"

He looks away.

Looking at the witches, I shudder. They look so mean. I say, "So, are those witches like the lightning people?" I regret it, waiting for him to kick me in the wiener for even asking.

Instead, he yawns, "No, but I've seen them do that," pointing to their dancing. "But, it's different. They're not really dancing. They're just...."

I wait. "What," I say. "You can tell me."

"Shut up."

"Okay," I say, and turn away, feeling little kicks in my belly as if I am carrying a baby witch in there.

After a minute, he says, "They show me things, that's all, okay?"

"That's so cool. What things?" A million questions run through my head, a million possibilities of what they might be showing him. The secrets of the universe? The existence of God, or ghosts, or Santa Claus?

"Things. Um. Symbols."

A shiver chills my spine. *Symbols?*

"What do they look like?" I ask, but as nonchalantly as I possibly can (even though I'm freaking out that he's actually finally telling me). "The lightning people. Are they, like, human?"

He shrugs. "They're outlines."

"Hmm?"

"Sillyheads. Uh. How do you say it?"

"Sillyheads?" I see aliens suddenly, the way some of them have gigantic heads.

"Sillyheads. When light comes from behind and makes an outline."

"Silhouettes!"

"Oh. Sillyheads is way better."

I cannot believe he is talking about it right now. What changed? Maybe we need to go to more carnivals? Was it the *sugar?* I wait, my head buzzing, needing to know more, but he doesn't say anything else. We shuffle up to the front of the line and the conductor goes, "Heh heh. You boys are in for a real treat." Why do they all have mustaches? Is it required that you have one, and tattoos, and a leather vest, to operate rides? He says the ride is brand spankin' new, created by designers who worked for Disneyland, so the effects are aces and the ride is super scary. Cool. Go, Weirville.

A carriage pulls up beside us, and the conductor gestures to the little gate, which opens so we can hop in. Bax sits on the right, and I take the left. I smell tropical bubble-gum and a sweet perfume, the kind all the girls in 8th grade wear, like fruity chemicals. The lights overhead dim and we're about to go in. I turn to Bax and say, "You can tell me anytime, okay? I promise I won't say anything. If you don't want me to. About the see-thingies and sillyheads."

But he's too excited now and doesn't care, clapping his hands excitedly. I join in, pumping my fists. A breeze that smells like salt and sugar ruffles my hair and face. The carriage lurches forward. Right as we're about to get sucked through the doors, a sign lights up in creepy orange letters:

NO SMOKING. NO VAPING.
NO LIGHTERS OR MATCHES.
LEAVE YOUR PHONE IN YOUR POCKET,
IF IT FALLS, WE CAN'T RETRIEVE IT.
KEEP YOUR HANDS INSIDE THE CART.

WARNING: THIS RIDE HAS—
JERKY MOVEMENTS,
CLOUDS OF HAZE,
LOUD NOISES,
STROBE LIGHTS.

Wait—did Doctor-of-Brains say that flashing lights are bad for Bax and could set off a seizure? But how many? How does it work? And how many strobes will there be on this ride? "WAIT," I yell, turning around and waving to the conductor. "Let us off!" Bax swats my arm, like, 'What are you doing? Stop.' The conductor doesn't see me though, and can't hear me either, because the witch's mouth opens to let us in. She cackles, and the crack of thunder is so loud, our faces vibrate. As soon as the doors close behind us, it's pitch black and all I hear is the sound of water dripping, echoing through the space.

"Bax," I say, "You can't look at strobe lights."

"What?" he says.

"If flashing lights come on, you have to cover your eyes."

"Why? Just shut up."

Strobe lights flash. Hundreds of them. They light up an old-fashioned drawing room or something, as if we're in Buckingham Palace. The room is filled with royal reds and golds and dead queens and princes and kings and their Spaniels sitting on velvety couches and fancy furniture. Cobwebs crisscross the space, the strobes flickering maniacally through the threads. I immediately clap my hands over Bax's eyes, but he claws them away.

A sign lights up: THE ROYAL DEAD, and we hear people laughing, people who sound very rich or something. Snooty laughter. The carriage lurches left suddenly, and another set of doors opens. Kitchen doors, the kind that swing in and out, and we move through the space, which is brightly lit so you can see all the pots and pans and spoons and dishes and utensils. Animatronic bloody-faced werewolves wear chef's hats, moving their robot arms and legs back and forth, as if they're cooking. Little forest elves with freaky ears pop out of steaming pots and pans as we pass by them. They are holding severed heads up. That's what's for dinner, I guess. It looks so real. It's amazing.

I watch Bax. He seems okay. He's looking around at everything, pointing, laughing. The carriage lurches right suddenly, and another set of double doors cracks open: THWANK-WHACK. Now we are in a giant dining room. It's all candle-lit, warm and dim. A fake fire burns in a hearth against the wall. Eerie piano music plays. Little rat robots dance along the mantle. They have red eyes. Fake bats fly overhead, wings flapping. Fake spiders drop from the ceiling and scurry back up again. The long dining room table is covered in dust, and all the people, sitting and eating, are dead. Skeletons. Mummies. They hold forks and knives and look at their plates, which have bloody eyeballs and fingers on them. Gross—why are they eating eyes and fingers? Dead things eat fingers and eyes?

We move through the dining room toward another set of doors. These don't fly open though, because they already are, as if welcoming us. Soon as we go through, the carriage lurches left again—Bax yelps—we both grip the metal bar across our laps to steady ourselves as the lights go out. It's pitch black and smells chemical-sweet, the smell of the smoke haze. Everything starts to glow.

"Cool," Bax says. "Look, Kirbz."

Walls. I think it's a labyrinth. The carriage moves on through it, but every few seconds, a wall shifts, blocking us, until another one opens and lets us through. Some of the walls move toward us quickly, and we yell out, but before they hit the carriage, they stop and then retract. When we finally make it to the end of the maze—no wonder this ride takes so long—big glowing purple words appear above: WITCH'S LABO-RAT-ORY.

The carriage enters a mad scientist's lab with cauldrons and microscopes, bulbous glass containers, trays of tools, and jars stuffed with squishy creatures. A witchy voice rings out: *"Eeee-heee-heee, now deary, you'll make a fine addition to my experiments. How about a nice warm bath? Yes, a bath—IN MY BUBBLING CAULDRON. HA HA HA."*

Suddenly, a panel on the floor slides open. Haze and green light fill the room, and a huge witch, maybe ten feet tall, rises up slowly from under the floor, her pointy hat tall and glitter-black, a dusty broom in her warty hands. A screeching animatronic rat prances on her shoulder. She makes the Wicked Witch of the West look like a Barbie doll. Her skin glows green and her eyes blaze orange. She mechanically jerks her head toward us in the cart, then lunges aggressively as the lights pop off once again.

Strobe lights start flashing and pumping by the hundreds, thousands, millions. I yelp and cover Bax's eyes. He wrestles free. "Bax, no," I say. "Don't look."

I can't see properly. Only flickers of things between the strobes. It's...it makes me feel dizzy. The witch's long black arms are outstretched, and she reaches for Bax. I try to grab him. Everything looks slow and choppy because of the strobing. And between the flashes, I see him slump forward, then back, then forward, then side to side, and I can't tell if this is...if is this part of the ride. Is he doing this?

No.

He's having one right now.

My heart flip-flops in my chest, playing witchfrog with my other organs. I feel it down in my stomach, thumping and jolting.

Not sure what else to do, so I yell, as loud as I can. I scream out. "Help us," but no one can hear me. Not over the sounds of bubbling, and cackling, and thunder, and scary music. I throw my whole body onto Bax's, trying to stop the thrashing. I hear moans garbling from his mouth. He does this when he has seizures. Doctor-of-Brains says it has to do with his brain trying to get itself working again, like when a hose gets a kink, and you unravel it for the water to flow.

Tears shoot out from my eyes. My hands are shaking. *Bax, no.* I've only been at home when he's had a seizure. Dad has always been there. This is something else, and I might throw up. The giant evil witch finally retracts into the floor, hissing as she melts. The lights come up again, and the car jostles forward to the next part of the ride. I'm holding onto Bax so hard. I feel wetness, can smell pee. I nudge my fingers into his mouth to make sure he doesn't swallow his tongue—they told us this would happen and to never put anything in his mouth during a seizure, but the thought of him swallowing his tongue is too scary. But he's out, as if he's fainted. I'm sweating. I can feel the warm droplets in my eyelashes.

The car moves through a few more rooms, but I can't pay attention to what's happening. I'm trembling so much, my teeth chatter. I'm yelling at the top of my lungs, but no one can hear me. I try to text Dad, but there's no signal inside this stupid ride. I keep shaking Bax to wake him up, but he won't wake up. I put my ear to his chest to make sure he is breathing. He is.

The little car jerks and lurches along on its tracks as we move through some other...what's this? I look around: wait, a bathroom? Ghosts appear in the mirror and disappear again. Almost like the people in the Harry Potter portraits. The faucet turns on and off suddenly, filling the sink with steam. Overhead, hazy light flickers on and off. The walls are a pale green, tiled. A werewolf reading a bloodied newspaper sits on a toilet in the corner, lets out a loud howl.

My hand is clamped hard over Bax's eyes even though he is unconscious, but I'm so scared that he might open them again right as more strobe lights go off. I keep shaking him, hoping he'll wake up. I can smell his orangey shampoo. Hugging him, I squeeze my eyes shut and say,

"Please God, get us out of here." I've never said 'Please God' in my entire life.

A second later, the carriage rises on the tracks and clunks through a tube that is basically like the inside of a car wash. Gigantic, colorful fabric strips flail around, whipping and slapping me in the head and face, which would be fun if I wasn't freaking out. I keep Bax covered, protecting him from these weird, heavy blankets thrashing us around. Otherwise he'd be thrown clear out of the cart. My entire body is trembling, I can even feel it in my small toe.

BLAM! We are back outside, in the front, down the line from where we started, a cool rush of wind on my face, and blinking lights, and the smells so strong right now. Pretzels and bubble gum, perfume and hay, beer and hot cheese. I stand up in the carriage and yell out for Dad. He hears me, standing out in the thoroughfare with his friends, turns his head and sees me, smiles and waves.

"No," I yell, "it's Bax. It's bad."

He stares at me for a second, adjusts his glasses, then his face goes slack. He says something over his shoulder to his friends and they all jump up suddenly and run over, fast, shoving people out of the way as they cross the crowded thoroughfare. I sigh, my shaking hand on Baxter's dampened head.

Tears stream down my face.

In the distance, the warbly old-fashioned carnival music prances on the air as the horses on the carousel bow and curtsy, bobbing and diving. A sea of colored steel mares that glide up and down, around and around. Why do they paint such scary faces on carousel horses?

PLAYS and GLOW-STARS

I'm sleepy, but I stay awake to watch over Baxter. He's right across the room from me, sprawled in his bed, snoring. We came right home. I did not perform for the fundraiser. Dad said I could stay if I wanted, but there was no way. I was so freaked. I can't stop seeing that giant witch reaching for us in the slow throbbing flashes with her creepy eyes and Baxter thrashing in the cramped carriage.

I turn my head to my bedside table. The plays I need to read for YOUTHEATRE wait for me, spines glowing in the light of my bedside lamp. School starts soon and I have to know these plays. Plays make me feel better. I like the way the words appear on the pages of plays. The format is different from regular books. The words of plays feel more organized. I grab the first one, *Romeo & Juliet*, flip it open and start to read. I already know what it's about. I've seen scenes from it before, but I've never read it from beginning to end. Krasinski told us not to get tripped up by the language, just keep going, take in what we *do* understand, and we'll discuss what we don't later. So, the very first words of the play:

Two households, both alike in dignity,
In fair Verona, where we lay our scene,
From ancient grudge break to new mutiny,
Where civil blood makes civil hands unclean.

Uh. So. Two rich families in Italy who have been fighting forever are going to keep fighting, but this time it's gonna get really bad? K. So far, so good. There are so many things I don't understand in the play, but it's pretty clear what's going on and I actually like the language. I mean, there are times I laugh out loud—did people really talk this way to one another back in the 1600s? Even when they were shoving swords through each other's guts and spilling puddles of blood all over the streets? The language feels too pretty for cursing and fighting and so much death, but 'whatevz', as Ellie would say. 'I think that's the point', she would say. Romeo and Juliet, when they're together, make me think about her, and then my insides feel like eels.

Then there's stuff that's cool, like if you say, "*Thou possesseth my vital-motht organth, a mound of thumping muscle filleth to the brimeth with bloodth,*" (that's not in the play, I am just mimicking Shakespeare), you're really saying, 'I love you.' Or, like, 'I'm obsessed with you and I'm gonna stab myself in the heart if I can't have you.' What I like best about reading Shakespeare is the way the words drop down the pages like little black word-waterfalls.

I get halfway through, get a little frustrated, and switch to the next play.

The Crucible starts with a little girl half-dead in a bed who they think has been bewitched because girls were found dancing in the woods with a woman from Barbados who was doing spells and flying over rooftops. The Devil is in Salem, vengeful spirits. This play scares me because...witches. Why are they after me so much tonight? Leave me alone, witches.

In Texas, in 4th grade, before we moved, this kid named Dustin Brisco said the reason I don't have a real mother was because my fathers pulled me screaming and bloody out of a witch. Dustin was dirty and smelled like spoiled milk. He would draw pictures of witches and leave them on my desk. One picture was of a witch cradling a baby and he wrote my name over the baby and behind the witch stood two demons in the fire. He wrote, 'Kirby Dads In Hell' over the demons. He forgot the apostrophe, so I fixed it for him, and gave it back: *Kirby's.*

The drawing was good, really good, like a movie poster, like Dustin Brisco is probably gonna be a great artist someday. I never told on him or anything. Not my teachers, my dads. People in Texas are like that. I mean, it's in their DNA to be like that. Not *everyone* who lives there, obviously. Take my dads, for example. They're not dumb. That's why they got out. And took us with them. Thanks, Dads.

But the thing about *The Crucible* is most of the girls and some of the boys in YOUTHEATRE are gonna scurry happily up rat poles 'cause of all the screaming and crying and crushes and dying. And Krasinski doesn't make boys only do boy scenes and girls only do girl scenes. If we want to play a role that is not written in our gender, we can. We are encouraged to bring our own cultural heritage to any character, any narrative. If we do not feel it fits into a play originally written for a certain type, 'cause most are, then we're encouraged to write our own scenes. A lot of kids do.

Krasinski chose this play last year at his professional theatre company in the Burgh-of-Pitts (that's what I call Pittsburgh ha ha), because he said everything is so weird in our country right now. He played John Proctor, the main dude. He said that theatre is really powerful if you know how to wield its power to help people, change their minds, alter their perspectives, and make them feel. He's big on that. "Feel, feel, you have to feel, and you have to feel the need to feel, but more importantly *they* have to feel," he says, gesturing out to the seats in the auditorium. He said the writer of this play, Arthur Miller, was trying to do that when he wrote it in the olden days. He said a play can change the world if you want it to—but you need to know what you want to say.

I wonder what I would need to say if I were to write a play....

Krasinski said that when he was young, when he was our age, doing theatre was the most un-cool thing in the world. He'd started doing it out of spite, to be a rebel, to make people angry. He said they used to call him 'Hideous Crapstinky' instead of Thaddeus Krasinski. He used to get beat up for doing theatre. I don't know why anyone would beat him up, he's so nice, but he said 'nice' doesn't get you through life. "Nice helps you get people around you who help you get through life," he said. His theatre people are his family now, his 'chosen family', and most theatre people, most artists, create chosen families because the ones they come from are often broken or because they don't understand you and never will.

I wonder if I'm one of those people now?

Now that Pop has abandoned us and disappeared and proved some of the people in Texas right—we will burn in hell for our sins. That sounds so stupid, oh my god. Or Ellie, and how her dad left her mom because he fell in love with her sister, Ellie's Aunt Nance, and now she refuses to talk to him but misses him so much and I think that's why she dances. I think in her heart she is trying to dance her way back to him invisibly. Or Rockford, whose parents are demanding. They make him have a tutor, so he'll get all A's, make him take ninjitsu (I mean at least he loves that) and compete in all the tournaments (he kinda hates that), join the math club, cook at their restaurant downtown, and help his mom make videos for her YouTube cooking channel that has like 500,000 subscribers.

But does all that mean you are from a broken home?

Doesn't it just mean everything's totes norms?

What's a *not-broken* home?

I look over at Bax. Still snoring. Looks peaceful. His face looks red.

I swallow a lump in my throat, remembering his thrashing and the lights flashing.

I check my phone: yup. Pop called and texted 20 times.

I put down my phone, put down *The Crucible*, pick up *Our Town.*

I like *Our Town*. I think it's sweet and weird and sad. To die and come back and realize you didn't appreciate life. I wonder what it would be like to have Emily Webb as a mom, but that's kind of cringe because she dies giving birth. I love the scene at the end where she starts to let go of her humanness while she watches her husband cry at her grave, and when she says, "They don't understand, do they?", a fizz runs through my heart. I think about Baxter and the lightning people. Not sure why.

It's late, I'm like a full-on high schooler staying up past midnight. Outside, the summer night stays close. I toss the plays onto my bed. I like books open and splayed all over. I check on Bax one last time. He seems okay, and I turn off the light and nestle down into my covers. When I close my eyes, the witch is going away, back in her cage under the floor of that freaky ride in Freakcity. But she feels near. I can still hear the echo of her cackle in my brains.

* * *

At 3:30am, I wake to weird noises. Moans, gulps, backwards un-words. A strange smell hovers in the air, something metallic, or like rain. I feel pressure, like a storm's about to hit. I can't swallow. I can't move. The dark swirls around me like a Dementor sucking my breath away. I can *feel* the thing across the room: like walking into a house where you can tell that a television set is on even though you don't hear it or see it. There's this kind of invisible frequency in the air. That's what it feels like in the dark.

This is bad, the worst of them so far, anyway. Worse than the one on the ride.

A sliver of pale light spills through the window and shines directly onto a spot on the wall above Bax's bed. It looks like a silver door, almost diamond-shaped.

I can tell by the sound he's making, all garbled and spitty, that I need to turn him on his side. Doctor-of-Brains said to do this so that he doesn't swallow his tongue, which is what he's doing right now. I can hear it. It's bad, it's so, so bad. My heart rabbits hard against the inside of my chest. There's a weird taste in my mouth, as if I drank blood.

Get up, Kirby.

I can't.

I am stuck.

I try to move, but my muscles are locked down.

I don't know how much time passes. I am somewhere else.

Finally, I feel a little explosion inside my head, and something snaps, gives, releases me. I throw the covers off and scramble out of bed, reach to flick on the lamp. But, in my weird state, I miss it, and knock it over instead. It hits the floor with a crash and the bulb under the shade POPS in a bright blue-white flash, and goes out, the sound of breaking glass like Christmas day when an ornament falls off the tree. The room is thrown into complete blackness. Bax keeps making the moans and un-words.

I fly across the room to flick the overhead light on instead. The room fills with light, and it takes my eyes a second to adjust. When they do, I see that Bax is thrashing in the bed, his fingers curled into themselves, his body tensed and bent and stuck. I can't move again! Tears fill up my eyeballs so fast and spill down my face hot and salty. Doctor-of-Brains also said to 'time the seizure' but my phone is over by my bed. I don't have time to grab it because suddenly Bax flies upward, like something invisible is lifting him, yanking him.

I dive onto the floor, as if into a pool. If he lands on the floor, he's going to land on his head so hard. I'll make a pillow of my body for him. I land on my stomach, and he falls a little short, onto my wrist and forearm. I hear a weird snap, like *KRRCHKK* and then a sharp twisty burning, a deep stinging. My arm was kind of twisted a bit when I hit the floor, so when he landed on it, I think it *double*-snapped.

He's twisting, almost in slow motion, like when you pour salt on a slug, the most horrible thing you could ever do. I saw that once. It should be outlawed. I'm on my stomach, and he is on top of me, but his head is hanging off the side of my left shoulder and it starts banging against the floor, hard. I shimmy my body over to protect his head, but Bax is heavy, I can barely move. The arm he landed on, my left one, throbs against the floor, the pain shoots both up and down at the same time, which is so weird. It feels like being electrocuted.

I cry out for Dad, I yell for help, not knowing what else I should do. I close my eyes tight and see weird colors bleed down like the rainbow wax at the carwash dribbling down the windshield. I use all my might, all my strength, to jam my body over and protect his head. It works. Now he's just banging it between my shoulder blades. He's still making that tongue-swallowing sound. I take my right arm, the good arm, and I flip it up and over behind my neck so that I can steady his head and once I do that, pressing him hard against my back, I wiggle my fingers around until they meet his mouth. I nestle them inside his lips, feeling for his tongue, but I don't have enough slack to grab it. I'm not supposed to do this, but I have to. He bites down on my fingers so hard, I think I feel his teeth go through them. His teeth are clamped down, I can't pull my hand out.

Oh my god I hate seizures so much.

I wish Pop would walk into the bedroom right now and after lifting Baxter gently off me and laying him down in the bed and tucking him in, he would turn and hug me, but you know what? He can choke on a hot crapball. He can eat 80,000 steaming balls of smelly crap in stupid Texas, 'cause he left us and I'm on the floor and it feels like Bax is dying on top of me.

I feel warm wetness against my lower back.

I cry out for Dad again, as loud as I can. I bang my free fist against the floor to make noise. Suddenly, he's here. He lifts Bax off me and I feel a release, like my bones, crushed against the floor, are flying up to heaven like souls. I roll over onto my back and look up to see a milky spread of glow-in-the-dark stars, comets, and planets spread across the ceiling. We put them up when we were little. Pop had brought a ladder up and let us climb it with him so we could peel the little plastic pieces away from their adhesive and then stick them perfectly to our ceiling sky.

I hate him so much right now. I miss him so much right now.

Dad's pulling a clean pair of pajamas from the dresser, and he sniffles a few times and when he turns his face toward me, I see his eyes all red and wet, his cheeks pink. He sighs as he dresses Bax. "Can you grab me a wash towel from the linen closet and wet it?" But I can't get up. I mean, I can get up, but I can't push against the floor with my wrist to help myself up. "Kirby," Dad says, "What's the matter? You're shaking like a leaf."

"It's my wrist."

"What? Oh jeez, and you're bleeding."

"I'm okay, Dad. But I think I broke it."

"Come here," he says.

He's cradling Baxter in his arms, sitting up in his bed with him. I try to get up but it's too hard: my wrist hurts too bad on one side and on the other, my fingers are mauled. So, I just plop back down onto my back and stare up at the stars. Saturn's rings on these little plastic pieces glow differently, not just the normal dayglo neon green. The rings glow pale pink, pale blue, and pale orange. I remember being little and feeling comforted that things glowed in more than just normal dayglo color. I guess I still feel that way looking up at them now.

Dad lays Bax down and gets out of the bed to help me up. When I'm on my feet, he pulls me in for a hug. He smells like sleep: sour-hair and soap and the detergent of his sheets. His shoulder feels very wide and soft where I cradle my chin. I open my eyes and look at Bax lying in bed. Is he still my little brother? *The witches got him.* It all seems so off now.

I can't help but wonder while Dad hugs me, if Baxter saw the lighting people again. That's all I want to know. If he saw them, did they help him? Or hurt him? Who are they, why are they here, and what do they want?

Two crazy seizures in one night. It's getting worse. What does this mean?

I'm scared.

That line from *Our Town* repeats in my mind: "They don't understand, do they?"

SYMBOLS

Doctor-of-Brains says Bax is sick. It could be as harmless as a cold, but, we didn't see anything. He wasn't sniffling, coughing, feverish, nothing. He says, "Sometimes the sickness might be forming, and when an epileptic's immune system is weak, or weakened, intensified seizures occur." That, he says, might explain the two really bad seizures in a row. Looking at the splint on my wrist and my badly bruised fingers after I explained to him what happened in our bedroom, he sighs and nods.

"Have you considered a seizure alert dog?" he asks, taking his glasses off and cleaning them with the corner of his white coat. "There are dogs specially trained that help epileptics and their families with seizures."

Wait, what?

When we get home, I sit at Dad's desk in front of his massive iMac that he uses for work. He owns a graphic design company called Nate Renton Designworks. NRD for short (as in 'nerd' ha ha, but Dad's not nerdy, only a little nerdy). I type in his password, HARVEYMILKSHAKE, my dads' cat who died last year when he was nineteen years old. I google "seizure-alert dogs."

So. Much. Info.

But then, it *is* the internet.

I find a national organization that breeds dogs and trains them to be epilepsy companions. They have a few chapters around the country. One of them is in Washington D.C. That's not very far from us.

Seizure dogs can supposedly *smell* a seizure. Scientists and doctors once collected samples from epileptics during EKG testing that allegedly contain the smell of a seizure. Basically, the dog knows when one is coming on from the weird smell of the hormones that the body gives off. The dog can alert the epileptic, or the epileptic's family, friends, or spouse. I watch a video that shows a woman having simulated convulsions on the street and her sweet-faced gray Pitbull pup sliding its muscular body underneath her head so that she doesn't knock it against the cement. The pup looks so happy and yet so concerned, and after the woman is finished with her 'fake' seizure, the dog stands and smiles and looks proud. Then the pooch nuzzles the lady's hand just to make sure she is okay.

My eyes fill up with hot tears. Is this really happening? Seizure-alert dogs?

We have to get one. I mean right now. I don't want Bax to die. I want him to be okay. Come help us, happy epilepsy pup. The website says: *There are three main ways of obtaining a seizure dog. Some seizure dog training programs require the recipient to fundraise for the organization, and you receive the dog after reaching a specific fundraising goal. Or, you could go on the waiting list to get the dog reduced price, or free. However, the average wait time on these lists can range from one to fifteen years. Lastly, you can purchase the dog, with the average cost ranging from $7,000 - $50,000.*

$50,000? For a dog?

Plus, the cost of caring for them. That's totes bread.

"Dad?" I call out and he comes up from the basement and joins me at his computer. He's holding the hamper, and it smells like lavender and vanilla. He goes nuts with the fabric softener. "Can we afford seven to fifty thousand dollars for a seizure dog?"

"That's a vast range, seven to fifty."

"What about somewhere in the middle?" I ask, "like, $21,500?"

"Nice math skills, kiddo," he says. "Are they covered? Isn't it a medical expense?"

"You can raise funds for the organization, and if you reach the goal, you get the dog."

"Okay, well, that sounds hard, especially for us right now, and to answer your question, no, we don't have seven or fifty or even twenty-one thousand dollars lying around. At all." Dad sighs, looks down, and shrugs. He adjusts his glasses, then shuffles away. His shoulders are all slumped.

"I didn't mean to upset you," I call after him.

"You didn't," he calls back, but he's upset. I can tell by his shoulders.

A pile of mail, all messy, sits next to his computer. The edges are pointing out in all different directions. Nope. I pick up each envelope and place it down neatly on top of the next, so that by the end, the stack looks straight. I slide it over so that edge of the mail pile matches the edge of the computer monitor. Most of the mail is white, so I don't have to colorbetize it. Once it looks the way I need it to, I feel better.

Then, an idea. A perfectly clear idea, like blue-green vacation water you can see through.

I see it in my brains like a red flower opening in slow motion at nighttime. The way you see it on nature programs sometimes. I saw one about lotus flowers. They grow under the water.

I check my phone: Ellie and Rockford texted that they're on their way over. Sweet. School starts in one week, and we need to rehearse the scenes from the plays we read over the summer. I bookmark the seizure-alert dog info on my dad's iMac, click it off, wipe my face, and go check on Bax.

I head to our room, though he's probably in the basement playing ME & MY SHADOW online with his friends, wearing his VR headset on his face and swinging around the controller wands. Dad calls it 'insidious' and doesn't want him playing it. Most kids call it 'Game of Clones' because the story is about people who have to find the clone makers, The ShadowBirthers, who make any number of clones of you, depending on how many talismans you gather on the way to finding them. Then your clones are tasked with things, some of it good, like farm-building and social work on the moon and Mars. Some of it is bad, as in clones sent back to earth to make sure it stays uninhabitable for The ShadowAborters, beings who can only thrive in fire, but safe for the ShadowBreeders, who live in these giant pods filled with weird milk.

I'm not into video games or virtual animated interactive worlds. I'm into theatre, which is a different kind of interactive world, when you really think about it.

I guess the big question now is whether it's safe for Bax to play VR video games because of his epilepsy. But, if we try to make him stop playing, he will pack his bags and hit the road.

I move toward Bax's side of the room. His bed sits against the wall where the door is, and I listen, to see if I can hear the game playing on the TV down in the basement. That's when I notice something that looks like a black sketchbook, the kind that artists use, with spines of coiling metal. Kids in school who draw carry them around. For some reason, there's one peeking out from beneath his bed. It looks like some creature that lives under there is pushing it out for me to see.

I lift his blankets and look under there and speaking of creatures: holy rat pole. My heart fizzes, my fingers go icy, it's hard to swallow, I feel pressed down like a house landed on me. I can't believe Dad would ever in a trillion years allow this kind of mess. I want to yank everything out, and order it, re-order it, order it again. I close my eyes and breathe.

Messes are hard for me. Especially fixable messes.

I slowly slide the sketchbook out, sit cross-legged on the floor, and open it. I flip through the pages, looking at his drawings of rabbits with horns, beetles with dragon nostrils, other weird monsters, Marvel characters (he loves Wolverine and Rogue) and a few of me, Dad, Pop, Ellie, Rockford and the little girl who lives down the block, Bree Jones, who is blind in one eye.

Bax is a good artist. I guess I didn't know how good, but I haven't been looking at his sketchbook, especially because he's been hiding it in the bloodbath under his bed. He's pretty secretive, though. No wonder he and Pop got along so well. I feel weirdly betrayed. Maybe because I don't have any secrets. I don't hide sketchbooks.

Wait—*do* I have secrets?

I flip the pages. The more recent drawings are of characters from his video game, the liquidy people, the ShadowBirthers and ShadowBreeders. For some reason, he has decided to color these pictures in with colored pencils. Not sure why, because every other drawing up to this point is in black and white, mostly pencil, but sometimes black ink. I wonder if the shift to color happened after he started having seizures? Weird. I flip the page.

My guts go CHWOOP, up into my throat. My heart jostles and my face fizzes. Bax's next set of drawings are of the symbols. I think. The symbols that the lightning people show him. I found them. Here they are.

The symbols. I think.

I do a quick check to make sure he's still down in the basement. Then I swallow hard, studying them, wondering what they are, what they mean.

The first drawing looks like a small pod, with a little crown on top. It has spikes, little purple spikes. Weird. Is it supposed to be big? Or little? Is it a weapon? Is it a flower? Is it *food?* What is this?

The next one is a weird blob of glittery-looking material. I think he used a metallic marker to color it. I lift it to my nose. Yes, it smells so strong, just like one of those markers. Is it a plus sign? Or an X, if you rotated it? It's not specific, but it feels important. A lost key to a lost world. What is this material? Glass? Silk?

The third symbol is a curly tangle of slimy creatures. Snakes? Eels? Maybe they are octopus tentacles without suckers. I don't know if these creatures, if that's what they are, are alive or dead. Are they roads? Maybe this is a map!

Food, a key, a map.

No, that can't be right, that's just what *I* see. But is that what they are? *Is he going on a journey*? I wipe at my forehead; I'm sweating. The symbols make my insides feel plucked like a spider pulling threads as it weaves its web. Maybe I just need to go to the bathroom. Did I eat something weird? I sometimes have crazy guts.

I flip the page and I see—I guess—the world they come from? Because Bax has drawn some kind of gateway in the sky, right above our house. A door, shaped like a diamond, sort of, and it hangs over our home. Like a kite, but without a string.

I should get my phone, 'cause I need to snap pictures of the symbols. No, that would be wrong of me to do. He would get so mad. I left it down at Dad's iMac. Nuts. I slowly place the sketchbook down on his bed and stand up.

The bedroom door flies open.

I freeze in place—it's Bax.

I plop down onto his bed suddenly, on top of the sketchbook, as nonchalantly as possible, so he can't see I was looking through it. But I can tell he knows something is up because my face feels pale, and my ears are on fire, and he sees it on me. He asks what I'm doing, why am I on his bed. I shrug, like a loser, like a silly sock-puppet with buttons for eyes. I can't play it off. So much for my Best Actor award. He comes over to his bed and shoves me, trying to get me to move. I have no defense, so I just pull his book out from under my butt and hold it up. He yanks it from my hand, shoves me and yells, "They're not yours, boomer lover!"

"What? Why am I boomer lover?"

He starts wailing on me. I hold my splint up to fend him off. He punches it, and I feel the bones rattle beneath. "They're mine," he yells. "Why are you *like* this?"

"Let me help," I say.

"Shut up, Freaky-Fixer-Upper. You think you can fix everything. And I'm sick of it."

Exhausted, he finally plops down onto his butt and pounds the floor with his fists.

"Stop, stop, Bax. Stop it." I feel that weird twitch in my stomach again.

"You have no right," he says, slowly and quietly, as if he's some grown-up man and this is a serious scene in a grown-up movie.

"Bax," I say, and lean toward him. "Tell me about the lightning people. I think I know how to make them help us. I have an idea."

I expect him to punch me again, storm out of the room, and slam the door behind him.

I expect this struggle to be drawn out. He's stubborn, just like Pop, who also likes to storm out.

Instead, he looks at me, then looks all around the room at our stuff as if taking stock of our lives or something deep and sad, like 'It's the very last time I will see my bedroom.' He sighs, then throws his hands up in surrender. "Fine. You win. Boomer-lover-fixer-upper."

"Bax, c'mon, I'm not trying to *win*. I'm just trying to get you a seizure dog. Okay?"

I watch this information and this possibility spread across his face. A dog. We've always wanted a dog. Not only that, though—a dog that will help him with his seizures. I see it all in his face, in his eyes.

He licks his lips, swallows, and moves closer to me. "Really?" he whispers. "A dog? Like a real dog and not a robot dog?"

"Huh? What's a robot dog?"

"People have them now, okay? I've seen them, okay?"

"Okay, okay, I believe you. Calm down. No, not a *robot dog.* A real dog. I looked it up," I say. "It's a real thing. I swear. Doctor-of-Brains said we should try to get one for you. But, they're...well, I have an idea for how I can get one for you, though..."

"Though what?" His eyes are so big, his hair so stormy, all his littleness so big to me lately with how much space he takes up in my heart and my brains. And in dad's slumpy shoulders.

"You need to tell me about the lightning people. And these symbols you drew."

He blinks, drops his head, shakes it, looks back up at me, sighs, stands, takes the sketchbook, and walks across the room. He turns around and sits on my bed, opens the book to the drawings of the symbols, looks down at them, drops his hands in his lap, and looks up at me.

He finally tells me everything.

FOREST/YARD

I go outside into the air and the light, to the green, and sweet-sour smell of berry-rich bushes. Woods begin where our yard ends. A forest rumbles up a hill on the other side of a big fence that Pop built when we were little. He and Dad didn't want us wandering off and getting lost in the scores of oaks and pines. When we got older, Pop built a big gray gate in the fence and Bax and I made a wreath out of pinecones, twigs, bird feathers, acorns, leaves, flowers, and other objects we found in the ground. Pop nailed it to the gate. Now we look at it when we go into the trees to explore.

Ellie and Rockford live in Hawkweir, the neighborhood beyond the woods, about a half-mile away. When they come over, they duck through a hole at the far end of the fence. They don't like to use the gate. We didn't make the hole. I think animals did? One tree, though—one very big tree—lives in our yard. It's not in the woods. It's in the corner, over to the left if you are looking out from the raised back deck of our house. I don't know why it's not with the other trees. When I was little, I used to wonder if it felt lonely. But as I grew up, I realized that it's like a sentinel, a guard for the rest of the woods. And for us. Now, when we go into the forest, I walk to that tree first and bow to it like it's a King or Queen, and we must ask permission to enter its land.

We named it ORI. QUING ORI, because trees are both queens and kings.

I hear leaves crunching and I know they're approaching from the other side. I hear the ducking and whooshing and rustling. A minute later, Ellie and Rockford come around either side of Ori's massive trunk, at the same time, like they're doing a dance or something. They're laughing, but something weird happens: Were they just holding hands? A tiny needle, so small that you can't even see it, yet it's the sharpest thing in the universe, slides inside my belly and then out again.

Wait, what?

Ellie wears her CHVRCHES T-shirt from the concert we went to last year. CHVRCHES is her fave band. And also, an older band called DURAN DURAN that my dads like, too. I can see the emblem peeking out under her unzipped army-green jumpsuit covered in pockets and zippers and patches. She wears jumpsuits all the time lately. She says she wants to look like a woman who jumps out of planes and parachutes down into the woods to save endangered species from wildfires. She would be good jumping out of planes because of her dancing. She's been a dancer since she was a little kid. Her hair is long and dark-red and wavy. Her eyes are green but sometimes they turn blue and once or twice I thought they were brown. She's a shapeshifter.

Rockford got Doc Marten's for his birthday, and he wears them like they are the most meaningful thing imaginable. And it's weird because your attention always goes to his feet—if his head was on fire and he was butt naked, you would still look at his feet. Also, he has a weird Mohawk-y haircut now. It looks...okay. He's trying to grow it in, I guess. Rockford is tall. His father is Japanese, and his mother is Korean and Mexican American. His last name is Nakano-McKenna. He calls himself a 'Japakorican' and I love that. He calls me 'Walshy' lately because he thinks I look and act like Mikey Walsh, the kid from *The Goonies*, which is his new fave movie ever since he saw it with his dad this summer at Retro

Drive-in. It's his dad's fave movie from when he was a kid. The same actor plays Samwise Gamgee in *The Lord of the Rings*, but, all grown up.

Ellie sometimes feels like she needs to be our mom or something. I think it freaks her out a little that Bax and I don't have one. But then, she is super close to hers. They're like sisters, but maybe that's where her mothering thing comes from. One time I told her to stop treating me like she was my high school babysitter, and she got really quiet. Then she nodded as if she understood. She makes me fizz, makes my middles feel like eels are slithering. It's a deep fizz.

She comes to me, hugs me, and lifts my splint. "Kirbz, jeez. Are you okay?"

I wave it off. "Tell you later. I need to talk to you both and it's important."

"About our scenes?" Roc asks. "Well, yeah."

"No no no," I answer. "I mean, yes, that, too—but something even more important."

We sit in the grass and I tell them the plan: fundraise for the organization that trains seizure dogs by writing a play and performing it here in our backyard. Right here, under the tree Quing Ori. A play about the lightning people and the symbols they show Bax when he has seizures.

"So, when I found the symbols in his sketchbook," I say, "Bax went Bellatrix on me, but I calmed him down—'cause I'm *so* the magic—and after pounding on me, he told me that he thinks the lightning people might be a family."

"How come?" Ellie asks, scooting in.

"He said that two of them look grown-up and one of them looks young. Or at least, smaller than the other two. But, he doesn't know if that means anything. He can't, like, see their faces or bodies, only their 'sillyheads'—"

"Say whaa?" Roc asks.

"That's how he says silhouettes."

"Oh my God I love him," Ellie says.

"And," I continue, pulling up a strand of dark green grass and running the sandpapery side across my thumb, "He said they move like lynxes, like, I don't know, like gracefully and deliberately."

"Whoa, lynxes," Roc says.

"You're a lynx," Ellie says to him, and that little invisible needle does its slide in and out of my belly again. I let it go.

"They approach him, then the symbols appear, glowing in front of them, then they turn and walk away and rise back up into the lightning."

"I just got chills," Ellie says.

"I know," I say. "I'm totes a chill factory lately."

Rockford sighs. "Is he...I mean, is it real, you think?"

"You mean is he making it up?"

Roc nods. Ellie looks at him, chews a nail. I rub the blade of grass.

"He's not that type, though, you know him. Why would be make this up?"

Roc shrugs. "Attention?"

I laugh. "Baxter? No way."

"But I mean like 'cause of your dads."

"Oh," I say. "Oh." I guess I never thought about that. I feel that itchy twitch again imaging myself asking him if he's making this all up, and why, and if it has to do with Pop. I move it out of the way for now. I hop up, a little wobbly 'cause my arm.

Rockford and Ellie stay down on the grass and look up at me.

"Help me write it?" I say. "We can put dances in it, and ninjitsu, and ask others to help. I mean, look, we need that dog. You guys don't understand what's happening to Baxter."

Roc asks why we can't just do a Kickstarter to raise the money.

"We can, I guess," I say. "But—"

"Kinda basic," Ellie interjects. "So much internet time to get people you don't even know to give you money for something they don't care about. You have to send them reward stuff like buttons and T-shirts and magnets and your mother's vegan brownies. I don't know, I'm a stops girl with crowdfunding," she shrugs.

"Yeah," Roc says, "but people raise mad funds for stuff."

Ellie cocks her head. "Actually, you're right. Crowdsourcing saves lives sometimes, because, you know, people who have a terminal illness who need money for medical bills because the health insurance system in this country is so whack, actually get a lot of money. My mom's good friend did when she had breast cancer. Even though she used every cent of it on treatment and then died, anyway."

"Who?" I ask.

"Tessa Sandoval's mom?"

"Oh, right. That was so sad." Tessa Sandoval goes to our school, she's a year younger, and it's so wrong that she lost her mom so young. It makes my teeth hurt thinking about it.

"So," Ellie says, "I stand corrected."

"Can we try both?" I ask. "Cover our bases?"

"We should definitely do the play," Ellie says. She grabs a strand of hair and puts it in her mouth. She does this a lot when she's thinking. It sends a hiss through my body to imagine any part of her being in my mouth, even her hair. "The play. I have a weird feeling about it," she says with finality, looking around the yard as if she's imagining it into being already.

"I do, too," Rockford says, also looking around. Then he shrugs, nods, high-fives me, bear hugs me, fake kicks me, and I laugh. "Let's do this thing, Walshy," he says, and does a molten ninja flip, HOOFWASH, right on the grass. He is *so* the magic, too. He is liquid cool. Ellie flips her finger across her black glass and the CHVRCHES song "Clearest Blue" blasts out. We jump all over the yard at the part in the song where it gets super jumpy.

A breeze blows through the trees in the woods beyond the yard. Toads and snakes and racoons and skunks wander back there. Bears. Owls. Maybe a witch. The breeze feels chilled. School is starting soon. The weather is turning. The light drains from the sky a little earlier each day. We collapse on the grass after the song ends, breathing heavily. Everything smells like grass, dirt, and fallen fruit. Then the air fills with dinner smells as the wind carries the scent of meats and spices and breads all over Weirville.

It's such a comforting smell. That and the smell of dryer sheets.

Above us, in the half-light sky, the clouds make shapes.

I see a dog.

* * *

That night, Dad tries to set up a camera on Bax's dresser, one of those baby monitor things, except a more sophisticated kind. Bax refuses to fall asleep with a camera on him. He throws a tantrum and Dad calmly takes it away. He comes into the bathroom while I'm brushing my teeth.

"After he falls asleep," he whispers, "Please set this up for me, okay?"

"But, Dad, we don't need it. I'm there."

"You are indeed, thank you. Please, though. Just set it up. Extra caution, okay?"

I nod.

I set it up after Bax has fallen into a deep sleep but as soon as I turn it on, he wakes up, as if the camera itself has poked him in the side with a stick. He clambers out of bed, picks up the camera, hurls it against the wall. He goes back to sleep.

Once he's snoring, I go over to his bed, gently nudge him toward the wall and climb in beside him. If another seizure comes for him, it will have to get past me first. I stay awake next to him for a long time, lying on my side, notebook open beside me, resting on my purple splint.

I begin writing the play.

I...I don't really know what I'm doing. I follow the same formula I'm familiar with from reading so many plays in YOUTHEATRE. I studied the script for *The Curious Incident of the Dog in the Night-Time* so much last year, I practically ate the thing. I think about the lightning people, the symbols. I close my eyes, see them hovering in the air. The pod thing, the X thing, the snake-tentacles thing. I start writing, remembering stuff Krasinski has said to us about the awesome power of a play, how it can move people, and change them, bring them together.

And, I wonder, now, with Bax sleeping and breathing beside me, what we'll name the dog. Will it curl up in a ball? Lie on its back with its belly open? Or is it the snout-on-paws kind of sleeper? Maybe it won't sleep at all—maybe seizure dogs stay awake all night, alert and observant, like security guards working the graveyard shift at a bank that holds rare diamonds in its gilded chamber of safety deposit boxes.

What will it feel like to have a dog here lying in the bed with us? Living in our home.

DIRECT IT

After our first week of school, the splint comes off (skin is all white and clammy underneath, like vampire skin, EEM), and we have our first meeting for YOUTHEATRE. We vote on the Council, talk about possible plays for the fall and spring slots, and Krasinski starts matching up scene partners and assigning plays to read and scenes to study.

After it's over—so sleepy by the end of the day—I stay behind so I can talk to Krasinski. His office is in the Arts Wing, at the back of the school behind the auditorium, which the sports guys call the 'Farts Wing.' Other kids are waiting before me to see him, dumping their dramas on him. The kids in our troupe are Extra, especially the newer kids who can be totes needy when it comes to the theatre stuff.

When it's my turn to go in (I make sure I'm last so no one is waiting after me), I sit in his office that smells like black licorice and burning leaves, in the wooly blue chair across from his big, dark desk. I clasp my hands in my lap and gaze at the shelves behind his head, the same ones I reorganized colorbetically last year.

He says, "Kirbaciousness Rentonmeister." He always does something like that to my name, and I love it. "Sorry about your Pop. Sorry about your little bro."

I wasn't expecting this, that he would know what was happening at home, and it takes me by surprise. I swallow.

"Your dad filled me in," he adds.

I gaze at the floor, wondering why and how Dad decided he wanted to fill Krasinski in on the details of our lives. Am I mad at him? A little. I feel like he went behind my back. I know he probably did it out of concern. Sometimes, though, Dad's concern is annoying. Then, Krasinski says, "You can let this place be a sanctuary."

He always says that. I nod.

"Start with that little lump of coal in your chest called a heart, Kirbsauce. Start there."

I grin. Now that he knows at least the basics of what's going on, I tell him the rest: the seizures, the lightning people, and the symbols. I tell him I want to write a play to raise money for a seizure-alert dog. I tell him everything. Even how I feel about Ellie. He runs his fingers through his beard, his brow furrowed, nodding, his eyes alive and maybe getting watery at times.

"Go on," he says.

I go on.

I go on and on.

And on.

This is why I planned to be the last one to see him today.

After I finally stop talking, he stares at me for the longest time, like he's forgotten where he is or has fallen asleep with his eyes open. Finally, he points at me and blurts: "So you'll direct this thing."

My face turns to snow and melts off my skull. "Wait, what? Never. Why would I direct it? I'm writing it—Ell and Roc are gonna help—and I'm playing myself in it. Why would you...even ask that?"

"'Cause you're gonna direct it, Sir Kirbinflakken."

"No. I act. And sometimes write. That's all."

He smirks. "You can write and act and direct and produce and design and sing and dance and anything else you can dream of within the laws of the universe. Don't limit yourself to one thing. Artists are, and should be, prismatic beings."

"No, but—what's prismatic mean?"

"Multi-faceted. Many colors. A prism."

I squirm. I love prisms, even though I want to change the order of the colors sometimes. "But Thaddeus Krasinski, you don't get it—if I tried to direct, I'd fly up the rat pole."

"The what?"

"I would lose my mind. My magic would make my guts explode."

"Your *magic*," he says, "is precisely why you will make an astounding director."

I lean forward and jab a finger down onto his desk for emphasis. "Never gonna happen."

Krasinski chuckles, shakes his head, sits back and pats his beard some more.

"And the main reason I wanted to talk today was to ask you who I *could* get to direct it. I mean, I want *you*, but I know that's probably not—"

He shakes his head.

"Yeah, see I knew that. But, maybe, like, someone you know from Weirville High?"

The theatre kids from Weirville High are no laughing matter. Some of them are legendary. You can't go near them with a ten-foot pole. Or a rat pole for that matter.

Krasinski moves his arms up behind his head. Then he jimmies his fingers through his thick, messy head of hair and chews the inside of his lip for a second. "Lucius Beetlemeyer, Senior now, early acceptance to Carnegie Mellon for directing. Maybe he could take it on. I think his slot this year is in the spring so he's probably free in fall."

"I mean, that can't be his real name," I say.

Krasinski smiles. Lucius Beetlemeyer? Is he a character in a Tim Burton movie?

Krasinski tells me that Lucius directed this GOAT production of *The Seagull* last year that we loved so much. Suddenly I'm one thousand percent on board. I flick at my black glass and find him on Insta and send him a DM.

As I'm leaving, Krasinski whistles. I turn around and he tosses me a book. I catch it and look at the cover: *A Director Prepares* by Anne Bogart. The cover looks like a brown shower curtain with a shadowy hand reaching down. Huh? I immediately throw it back, saying "Tu es loco," something Pop says (said) all the time.

He picks it up, walks it over to me. "It's not solely for directing," he says, presenting it like it's a fancy gold watch or something. "It's a very well-rounded collection about theatre and art. Read it."

"But, it's an *adult's* book. Isn't it?"

"Sorta. It's out of your league—I mean Anne's out of everyone's league—but I wanna know what you make of it. You, the Rentonsiphon, as an 8th grader. Read it. Consider it extra credit."

I roll my eyes, tucking the book into my knapsack.

"Matter of fact, consider it a required assignment—I want a book report on it."

"Aww Thaddeus, not one of *those*. That's so 5th grade."

He smirks and escorts me out of his office and shuts his door.

THISTLE

After the first week of school, Bax gets transferred into classes for kids with disabilities. He cannot focus as easily now. Doctor-of-Brains says that for some kids with newly diagnosed epilepsy, cognitive impairments can occur. Dad tries not to make a big deal of it so Bax doesn't feel bad, but I can tell he is worried. His shoulders have been slumped for days. Doc also said these cognitive impairments can sometimes be a common side effect of the strong medications Bax takes now to keep the epilepsy under control, pills with names that sound like characters from a sci-fi comic book, like Keppra and Valproate and Xcopri.

When we drop off Bax, he asks me to walk him to his new classroom, downstairs from his usual one, way on the opposite side of Weirville Elementary. As we head down the far hallway toward these classrooms, we hear all the kids, and his friends, playing outside the building, goofing off before they get called in to start the school day. But, Bax doesn't want to be out there with them. He's not dressed in one of his little professorial suits, but in a pair of lime green sweatpants and a purple fleece pullover instead. He seems nervous. The hallway smells like cafeteria food, bready and salty and oniony, and craft glue, rubbery and sweet.

We meet his new teacher, Ms. Devika, who wears a sari and has a Bindi. She's so pretty, with eyes like dark jewels, and when you move close to her, it feels as if she has invisible arms that uncoil around you and make you feel calm. So calm. Like, my head tingles when she comes over to say hi to us. Everything melts away. Everything tingles. It's so ASMR. She smiles at Bax. She smells like fruity sandalwood and coconut shampoo. Her long dark hair looks like black water.

The classroom is neat. Ordered. Clean. I like it. Shelves at the back are organized with books, markers, construction paper, stickers, crafts. Gigantic posters hang on the wall: the solar system, the earth, the oceans, the insides of human and animal bodies, all painted in bold, dark colors like navy blue, mustard, and dark red. I would rather spend my days in this classroom than any of the ones I remember from when I attended this school. It's way more alive.

Devika has a vase of fresh wildflowers on her desk. Stems spill up and out, husks and leaves, flowering plants I have never seen before. I spot something in the bouquet, and suddenly hear a pinching high-pitched tone in my left ear. It sears through my brains for a few seconds and then dissipates. Ouch. One of the flowers is colorful and prickly and weird. Bright purple-pink and super spiky. The bud rises from a crispy pod beneath, and the pod has small sharp barbs all around it. I walk to Devika's desk and stare at the flower for a minute.

I can't believe it. It's here.

Bax sees it, too, and joins me. "Oh," he says quietly.

"How could it be?" I whisper.

"They're coming," Bax answers, and nods, as if to reassure himself.

Chills spill. "Who?" I ask.

Bax looks at me.

Devika walks over to us, gestures to the spiky bud. "You like that? The thistle?"

Thistle.

It looks like one of the symbols. It *is* one of them, or practically identical, anyway. I feel my heart slither in my chest, a baby snake crossing a river rock. "Cool," Bax says. He walks away, settles himself in a desk at the back. His backpack slides to the floor, *thwump,* and he looks around at all the maps, diagrams, and artwork on the walls. He doesn't seem worried about this whole thing at all.

Other kids arrive. They do not know me, and so stare curiously. I smile and turn to Devika. "Do you have a lot of experience with teaching kids with special needs?"

"Disabilities," she corrects me.

"Sorry."

"Why do you ask? Are you concerned for your brother?" she asks.

"No, I guess...I just don't want him to feel different."

"But different is good," she says.

I melt from her invisible ASMR tentacles. Her Bindi looks like a little round doorway.

"'Special needs' is a negative misnomer if ever I've heard one," she says. "Special doesn't begin to describe these angels. Their hearts and minds go beyond what you and I and any able-bodied child can comprehend, yet they are deemed slow, problematic, needy. Such dreaded, dire, injudicious words."

Devika comes around her desk and stands in front of me. Her dreamy eyes stare through my soul, and I swallow. "Truth is," she says, "They contain multitudes. The world is too small for their gifts."

I see Bax gazing out the window at the trees. The classrooms at this end of the school face the other side, the woods. All you see when you look outside is a forest with watery dapples of bright sunlight dripping through the leaves. It makes the woodland move and breathe. It feels like a big, living green body right outside the classroom. I can't tell what Bax is feeling. He's a different Bax now. Wearing colored clothes and sneakers.

One kid comes scuttling in, drops his backpack, stops, and points at me: "Heeeey! Christopher John Francis Boone!" (That's who I played in *The Curious Incident of the Dog in the Night-Time.*) I smile. He yells out, "HELLO CHRISTOPHER, CHRISTOPHER HELLO!" He walks up to me slowly, staring at me like I'm royalty. All the kids watch this with interest. The boy gestures for me to lean down to him, and when I do, he whispers in my ear, "It's okay, Christopher Boone. We'll help." He smiles and touches my face. My throat tightens. I feel like I swallowed Fizzy-Lifting-drink. I'm floating in a sky of bubbles. I need to belch to come down or get sucked into a roaring metal fan.

After the kids in the class have settled, Devika looks at me. "There are no *needs* here," she says calmly. "Not for these children. If there are any *needs*, then they're for the people who feel uncomfortable with all the wonder inherent here." She waves her hand across her classroom. I nod. She gently plucks the thistle from the bouquet and hands it to me. I feel her jewel eyes probing my soul. I take the beautiful thistle. It fizzes in my fingers as if it is alive. Feels like a cat's sandpapery tongue. It's heavier than it looks. It appears fragile and light, but it's hefty. I turn it over in my hands a few times.

How could it be?

I look over at Baxter. A burst of morning sun streams through the window beside him, lighting up one side of his face while casting the other in shadow. Him and not-him. He blinks into the light, a pet sunning itself in a patch of warm light on a porch. I can almost hear him purring. I study the thistle in my fingers, and it feels like that's purring, too.

X OR +

Saturday morning, and we're driving to Brussels, out in the country, beyond DoWe. Brian, a guy who sometimes helps Dad with graphic design, is a carpenter. He mostly builds custom furniture and ships it to the nearby cities, Pittsburgh and Cleveland and Columbus. Dad tells me he and his wife don't have kids, but have four dogs. Dad wants to talk to him about something.

I sit up front in the old dark-blue Bronco, leftover from our days in Texas. We barely drive it anymore because it's not in tip-top shape. Pop was always working on it. I like its wideness and roughness. It feels like it might fall apart any second. The seats still smell like Pop, but no one mentions it. Even Bax keeps quiet, sitting in the back watching ME & MY SHADOW vids on YouTube and flipping through his packs of collectors' cards with the characters from the game, and *Pokémon* and *Magic: The Gathering* cards, too.

Brussels is north, with wide-open fields, hills, farms, apple orchards. The little village in the heart of the town is old school stone roads, brick buildings, and small simple shops. We don't come out here much. It's a mixture of folks who lived around here for centuries before Weirville was built and new people who came after. The people who lived here beforehand have mixed feelings about the new people, and about Weirville in general. Pop would say that's how it always is. Dad says to be careful in the outlying areas because people are devout and don't like modern families like ours. Also, they hunt, a lot, so they carry guns. Like to the grocery store and post office.

We drive up the long dirt road driveway to Brian's place. The sky hangs low and lazy blue where the hills rise in the distance. The day looks like a painting, one of those watercolor things you'd find at a dentist's office. Brian is outside watering plants in the front of his old-fashioned farmhouse when we pull up. His wears his long hair down and has a beard and kind eyes. He looks like Jesus. He waves to us. Behind him a barn rises, his workshop. Brian is tall and thin, but his voice is low and deep, as if it belongs inside a way heftier dude.

Bax wants to stay in the Bronco until he finishes his videos, so we tell him to find us in the barn when he's ready. As we're walking back there, Brian's dogs bound out of the house and rumble over, tails wagging. Two Golden Retrievers, smiley and furry. Two German Shepherds, darker and wilier. They follow us into the barn, barking but friendly.

Dogs!

Brian's handmade furniture is scattered about. Tables, chairs, benches, cabinets, and even a child's slide made out of wood. Weird. How can you slide down that and not get splinters? I explore while Brian and Dad talk. Dad's saying, "...something that doesn't *look* like a crib, you know? But that prevents him from flying out of bed. I don't know, something that looks cool but does the trick? Do I sound ridiculous right now?"

Brian says, "No. What if it was built almost like a big birdcage, but horizontal rather than vertical? Could fit a bed in it, but looked modern and cool, not like a crib in any way at all."

"That might work," Dad says. "Can you maybe sketch it out for me?"

"Yeah, let's go up to the house for a second," and they turn and leave.

I wander among the furniture, the smell of wood and polish and sandpaper and sealant tickling my nostrils. Sawdust everywhere. I come upon a circle of chairs, all the same, like for a dining set, but they are all messy, facing different directions. My brains fizz. I shift them so the circle makes more sense to my fizzbrains. I sit down in one of them. Sturdy. Smells like fresh wood. Something *plops* beside me. I look up: the rafters are crawling with birds. They're silent as slithering snakes and they look down at me, darting their little black eyes around. Some of them fly out of the barn, FLOOSH. The sound of their wings flapping echoes in the space.

One of the birds, though, flies over to a huge shelf on the far side of the barn, something I didn't see when we first came in. It takes up the entire wall back there, and it's glowing: Shafts of light streaming in through an upper barn window shine down on rows of glass sculptures. The bird opens its beak and squawks, as if calling me over. I start walking back there, winding through a woody labyrinth of tables, jagged coils and squares of sawdust all over the floor.

"Hey!"

I turn and see Bax silhouetted in the light of the doors.

He raises his arm, pointing past me. "What's all that?"

"That's what I'm checking out," I say. "Are you okay?"

"Yeah, why?"

"I'm just making sure you're okay."

"Shut up, fart eater. I'm not a baby."

"You'll always be my baby brother."

"I'm going to throw one of these chairs at you."

"Don't," I say, "I just rearranged them."

Bax rolls his eyes. (He's getting so good at it. He learned that from me, I guess.)

We continue toward the wall of glass, where the space opens into a small studio. We see metal tables, trays, buckets filled with tools, and a contraption in the corner that looks like a big steam-punk stove-creature or something. A rusted, square-shaped robot.

"I know what that is! It's for glass blowing," Bax says. "Cool."

It's a glass-blowing studio. The shelf against the back wall holds the glassy creations. The top shelf has tall, colorful vases that look like flames, spikes of glass dancing upwards. They almost look like octopuses' arms. On the lower shelves sit orbs, bulbs, spheres, tubes, animals, glasses, cups, all kinds of neat stuff. It smells chemically and sweet. We walk over to the stove-thing. I think this is where they heat up the glass? It's so cool, like a robot with metal arms and legs jutting out.

"SQUAAARW!"

Bax and I startle at the bird, who perches over the shelf at the far end of the wall. "Chill, dawg," I say, imitating Rockford. We make our way over. The bird moves once we get too close but doesn't fly away. I scan the shelves, full of goblets and bowls and vases in blues and yellows and greens, but these pieces look like they didn't become their true selves or something. They look warped, and unfinished, or got messed up in the process, maybe.

In the center of the middle shelf, we notice this one weird object. Bax gently gasps. I swallow. We stare at it, and I squint. I can't tell if it's upright, or on its side. It looks like two hourglasses intersecting that create the shape of a cross, or an X on its side, or a plus sign, a bulbous one. Streaks of color swim through the glass like little colored eels. This thing, like the thistle from school the other day, looks like one of the symbols. Bax looks up at me with wonder in his eyes. "Told you," he says. A bolt of electricity jolts through my face in slow motion. My cheeks fizz like when you throw a bath bomb into the tub.

"Oh, hello there."

Bax and I yelp and whirl around: A woman stands there dressed in a red and brown summer dress. She wears sandals and her long black hair falls across her shoulders. She looks Egyptian or Moroccan, like a goddess from a way cooler world. Her eyes are black and gold, but I think it's just the way they are reflecting the light that shines off the glass objects. Beside her, the four dogs sit silently and stock still like regal sphinxes, two on each side.

Wait, what?

She looks at Bax very seriously, then smiles.

"Sorry," she laughs and puts her hands up apologetically, "Didn't mean to startle you. I'm Dahlia. Brian is my partner. You must be Kirby and Baxter. I've heard so much about you both." She extends a long golden arm with fingers that look velvety. We shake her hand. "Did you meet the family?" she asks and gestures to the dogs. "This is Antho and Theo," she says to the German Shepherds. "And here, opposite them, are Gilda and Rowan."

"Cool names," Bax says.

"Shake their hands," Dahlia says to the dogs. Each front paw rises at once.

Bax tosses his head back and laughs. We lean down and take their paws and say hello, and the dogs place their paws back down and sit beside Dahlia again.

"Is this your glass-blowing studio?" Bax asks.

"Yes," Dahlia says, "It's a hobby, you know, something I like to do. I have started to sell some at local flea markets and craft fairs, though."

"What about this one?" Bax says and turns and points to the intersecting hourglasses.

Dahlia walks to it and picks it up and looks it over. She hands it to Bax. "Brian calls this one 'time distorted'. A mistake, really. When learning how to do it, I messed up on the marver—that's fancy glassblowing talk—and still needed practice with the blowpipe. But something about this one I've always loved. It's so not what it was meant to be, and yet there's a kind of magic in it. So, I kept it."

"Who are you," I blurt out.

She looks at me strangely.

"Leave my brother alone."

"Sorry?" she says. She seems very serious, but then smiles.

I feel the same thing I did when I met Devika. My heart feels like my finger when I dip it into hot wax and pull it out and it's covered with a gluey shell. Bax elbows me suddenly, and I collect myself.

"Sorry," I murmur.

"It's yours," Dahlia says, handing it to Bax, but she's still looking at me. "If you want it."

"Really?" Bax asks, his eyes wide.

"I've had it long enough, time to pass it on. Keep it."

Bax hands me the object. In his drawings, in the center of the intersect, there is an eye, a small eye, but it's actually not an eye. If you look really closely, it's a teeny tiny bridge. This one has no eye-bridge, but almost everything else about looks the same. I wonder if the weird glittery kind of material Bax drew in his sketchbook was *glass.* Chills spill.

"In ancient times," Dahlia says, "Keepers of the technique of glassblowing were considered sacred. Isn't that lovely?"

Bax and I nod.

"I don't feel sacred," she says, "But it's easy to see how working with glass would make people think that. It's an earthy process—the sand, the fire—but creates otherworldly results. Sometimes I think these objects belong to the souls in heaven. They're here as...as conduits."

"A conduit?" Bax blurts out. "Isn't that a French pastry with cream in it?"

She laughs. "I think that's a cannoli. And that's Italian. No, a conduit is, like, a way to pass messages back and forth."

"Oh. Yeah. Like the invisible tunnel," he says.

I look at him.

Dahlia just nods.

The invisible tunnel?

My phone buzzes suddenly, BWARMPH, startling me so bad I nearly let out a fart. I slide it out of my pocket and flick it awake. It's a message on Insta from Lucius Beetlemeyer, the director guy. He wants to talk to me about the play. Nice!

SQUAAARW.

That bird suddenly shrieks again, flicks its beady black eye at me, then lifts into flight, flooshing its big velvety wings up into the rafters and then out through the double barn doors into the sunlight. We watch it go, silhouetted against the sky.

* * *

I find Bax in our basement playing ME & MY SHADOW. The VR goggles are plastered to his face. He is darting, ducking, spinning around the space, lost in the virtual world. The square of light through the upper basement window casts a dusky, purple, dark-pink shadow on the rug. It smells like Jolly Ranchers down here. I make him pause the game and remove the goggles. He is breathing heavily, and little droplets of sweat drip down his forehead.

"What's happening, Bax?" I ask quietly. I don't want Dad to hear. He's making dinner.

"I'm almost to Gætü17, that's what happening."

"I don't know your weird game talk and that's not what I mean."

He plops down onto the floor, cross-legged.

"You said, 'They're coming' and you also said. 'I told you' and it's like you know something and I want to know what it is."

He shrugs, wiping sweat off his brow.

I plop down on the floor in front of him. The rug feels shaggy beneath my butt. Upstairs, Dad sings along to that Ed Sheeran song on the radio.

Baxter scoots back. "Hello? A little space, please," he says.

"Bax, what do they want?"

"I told you everything already."

"I know, but...."

"I told you so you could make the play and get the seizure dog."

"And I will, but don't you *feel* anything about what's happening?" I sound like Krasinski.

"Kirby, you can't move everything around to fit the way you need it to fit," he says. "Just do the play." He's like some little wizard man now.

I nod. "Okay, but—"

"Can I go back in now, please? My team's waiting. Gætü17 is no joke."

"Gimme a hug first," I tell him.

He leans forward and hugs me and it's a good one. He smells like apple shampoo, a sour smell like unwashed hair, and a tangy metallic smell maybe from his seizure medication.

"I'm gonna fart in two seconds," he says, his head on my shoulder.

I scramble up the stairs.

ABOUT

Lucius wants to know what my play will be *about*.

ABOUT is a big word for him. We're standing in my backyard under Quing Ori, the tree. It's Sunday, a colder day today. The leaves are beginning to lose their green shininess. I can smell a fire burning somewhere in the distance. I'm showing him where I want the play to happen. He's looking around at everything, like a detective, making odd gestures with his hands, movements with his arms and head as if he's shifting around imaginary objects, taking pictures with his phone, sniffling a lot. I can't tell if he has a cold, or he's crying, or has allergies.

He's wearing the kind of clothes all the Seniors wear that are a mixture of like eight different decades but always with pants pulled up to their nipples and so much sock. Like their legs are all sock. It's a little worse when it's theatre people because they always throw an extra layer onto it. In Lucius' case it's a white scarf with freaky black fish on it that he keeps whipping around. He talks, for some reason, like The Joker from *The Dark Knight* and kinda sorta maybe almost has a British accent? He's nice, I think, but all he wants to know is 'ABOUT, ABOUT, ABOUT.'

"What is the play *about,* or going *to be* about? I know you're still writing it, but I need to know what it's about, what you're trying to say, and about how long the play will be, and about how long you think we'll need to rehearse it."

I tell him everything I know so far.

Also, maybe I don't know 100% yet what the play is ABOUT (ABOUT, ABOUT) but what I do know is that there are seizures, lightning people, and symbols that I want to show to raise funds to get a dog for my brother that can help him, and us, every time he has a tonic-clonic seizure.

I have this awful vision suddenly, this scary flash of Dad and Pop weeping over Bax's broken body after he's fallen down a flight of stairs after having a seizure and broken his neck or something. I'm not there. Or, I am, but I'm watching it from a distance. I remove Bax and Dad and just leave Pop there, crying over a pile of nothing, suffering.

Wait, what? What is happening?

I erase that image from my mind. Inside, eels slither through my belly. From the phone in my pocket, I feel the buzzing of his texts. He's been calling and texting, but I don't want to talk to him because this is all his fault. No, it's Dad's fault, but it's Pop's fault. It's both. Adult humans confuse me so much. My brains hurt.

Lucius claps his hands at me. "Are you there?" he snaps.

"Sorry," I say. "I went away for a second."

"Yes," he says, "Well, part of my job as a director is to clap people back. Not only audience members who need clapping back from the harsh reality of life, but actors, writers, designers who need to be clapped back to attention from time to time when their mercurial little minds drift off, which they tend to do rather often. More often than you'd imagine."

I nod.

He nods, too.

Why does he talk like this?

"Maybe," I say, "The people who see the play can tell us what it's about rather than the other way around?" He shakes his head—no, no, no, no, no—and lectures me on the purpose and intent and efficacy of storytelling and how 'it needs to exist inside a structure, a frame, or it's like lightning in a bottle, a force of chaos that could destroy the universe.' "Sauron, Thanos, the Night King, Kilmonger, Iago." He turns and wanders toward the gate to the woods and stops to study our custom wreath for a moment. He doesn't say anything. He just looks at it for a minute. I suddenly feel self-conscious of it, something I have never felt about our wreath.

"Kirby," he says, as he's gathering his things and getting ready to leave. "Putting up a play needs to be a brave act of sheer will and most importantly, truth." He fingers the wooly fringes on the ends of his fish scarf. "When you expound truth—and theatre is such an extraordinary expounder of truth—that truth spreads off the stage and into the audience like a flood from a hurricane in a city on the Gulf of Mexico."

I nod. I have a vision of hurricane winds lifting him up and out of my yard forever.

"Something about you," he says, "And what you want to do here, you know, get this dog savior, is suffused with truth. I sense it. I have a good inner barometer for truth—it's why I got accepted on 3/4 scholarship to Carnegie Mellon's inimitable directing program—and you contain truth, young Mr. Renton."

I nod. Inside, I feel young, and squirmy. And annoyed.

"I'm not sure what it is about you, in particular, 'cause I tend to loathe the youngsters in Krasinski's lower classes, they're all so...hormonal and smelly and the boys are so insecure about the fact that they're interested in theatre, but you, you're a paragon. I'm not sure why, but I'm not going to discern. I'll leave it at that."

I nod, not knowing what *dis-earn* means.

I'm just me, Kirby Daniel Renton, Truthful Paragonal Nodder.

"Send whatever pages you have written tonight, no later than 10pm," he says, "So I can see where you're at and based on that I'll make my final decision."

He's bossy. Guess that makes him a good director?

"Do you know what email is?"

I nod. How could he think I don't know what email is?

"Okay, well, I thought you annoying newbs only communicated through, like, infantile apps and sticky perpetual finger-scrollings."

I shrug.

"My email is luciusisconfucius at gmail dot com." He turns back, "You know how to spell Confucius?"

I don't nod.

GRASS DANCE

As Ellie and Roc finish reading the play (what I have of it so far), I keep my eyes on their faces. Rockford crouches on his knees behind Ellie, his hands on her shoulders, reading, his brow furrowed. I can't tell if he loves it or hates it. My jaw feels tense and the space between my eyebrows feels like a canyon, like a long deep crevice is cutting through.

Ellie reads with a finger in her mouth, chewing a nail. A strand of red hair hangs over one side of her face. The shadows of leaves from Quing Ori, above us, dance across their faces, and onto the pages of the play. I watch, feeling nervous but excited. Lucius Confucius Beetlemeyer has agreed to direct the play based on the pages I have written so far. So, it looks like it's happening. But, there is still so much to figure out.

When they finish reading, Ellie gently lays the play down on the grass and reaches for her phone, which she places on top to prevent any pages from blowing away. She stands up, tucking her hair behind her ears—today she wears one of her one-piece jumpsuit thingies, it's eggplant purple—and she walks out into the center of the yard, looking up at our house, hands planted on her hips. Rockford lies back on the grass, his hands behind his head, looking up at the sky through the canopy of Quing Ori's branches and leaves.

Ell turns around, squints, and says, "So. I'm playing the seizure."

"Yes."

"And I'm the lightning people," Roc says.

"Yup."

Ell starts moving around. She moves her body one way, the other way, up, down, in circles, reaching, thrusting, bursting. The ground is wet from some recent rainfall, so she slips a few times but somehow makes it part of the 'dance'. She suicide-dives onto the grass, her back a perfect arc, her body in slow motion as she settles onto the grass, graceful like a crane. She rests for a moment, her chest rising and falling with her breath. I find that my own breathing starts to match hers, because I feel like I know what's coming. This is the calm before the storm. Then, it happens—she starts spasming, jerking, lifting, dropping, twisting, and grasping. Her mouth is open in a big O, her fingers curl into themselves, and her body tenses, relaxes, tenses, relaxes.

My heart races, and beads of sweat pop out onto my forehead.

Afterward, she is still for a minute and I watch her chest rise and fall. She lifts her head, looks over at me: "That's kinda what it's like, right?"

I nod, and exhale, my mouth filled with saliva. I try to find words to describe to them what it feels like to experience this almost every night, but there aren't words, only feelings. Or maybe...maybe the words are in the play already?

Ellie keeps going, saying, "I researched this a lot to get it right."

Rockford walks past Ellie until he's behind her, and he slows down. He begins moving around her, then me, then Ori. He's swimming through the air, a shark, doing his ninja moves. He leaps, punches, spins like he's a creature trapped under ice but knows how to get out. He is fast, slow, gentle, rough, scary, and cool. I watch the two of them become these things, these entities, here in my backyard. Right where we are going to do this. I watch them transforming. She is a Seizure, and he is a Lightning Person.

I swallow hard.

Ellie and Rockford begin dancing together, weaving in and out, braiding, lowering, rising, limbs finding limbs but then moving apart. I swear it's like a National Geographic special about cuttlefish, or jellyfish, or sea dragons, narrated by the old dude with the white eyebrows and posh accent. I'm so happy this is happening, but I wish it were me in there dancing that close to Ellie. I can never be as cool as Rockford, and I can't move like that either. The tiniest and sharpest icicle in the world moves through my chest, right between my ribs, then slides back out.

I sigh, and grab my black glass to shoot video, but only a minute, because why spoil it. Krasinski always says that the photos and videos dampen the realness and that we should see things through our own eyes and not through so much screen. But he's like 44ish, so he has to say stuff like that. Dad says it all the time. In a moment like this one, though, I see what they're talking about. When I put the phone up to record it, I stop feeling anything, because *I'm* not watching anymore, the phone is.

Rockford slips suddenly and slams into Ellie, who yelps, and also slips, and they both go down in a thud, hysterically laughing. I place my phone down and leap into the pile, screaming, "HOOKA BLAAANG-YOTCH" (don't know what that means), I think I heard it in a Pokémon cartoon. We roll around in the dampened grass. It smells like soil and Ellie's skin and Rockford's hair pomade and that weird oyster-y smell of the little seedpods that Ori drops.

We spool, fake-wrestling, and when Ellie's hair wisps across my face and mouth and neck, a shudder runs through me, down to my lower stomach where it burrows in like a mole until I have to pull myself out of the pile and roll onto my belly to hide the front of my pants.

Ellie and Rockford lie on their backs with their hands behind their heads, looking at the sky. I listen as they catch their breath, how it gets slower until you can't hear it anymore.

"Wow," Ellie says quietly.

"Right?" Rockford says.

"What just happened?" she says.

"Right?" Rockford says again. Then he says, "Walshy, how do we do this?"

I push my face down into the wet grass, the blades of green tickling my eyelashes. "Pretty much like what you just did," I say into the earth.

"Yeah," Ellie says, "Okay. But what about the *rest* of it? All the stuff you wrote, Kirby. I mean...how are we going to *do* that?"

I can now roll over onto my back, whew, so that the three of us are in a cloud-watching line. Above us the sky looks glowy blue, like a Van Gogh, thick and globby. "Well," I say, "Think about who we know, or kinda know, that could build this stuff and make the effects work. I wouldn't have written it that way if I didn't think it could be done."

Ellie and Rockford look at each other and say, at the same exact time, "Santini twins."

THEE BARN

The Santini twins, Mel & Nic (Melissa & Nicholas) are 17ish. Last year, for *The Curious Incident of the Dog in the Night-Time,* they built the set and lit the show and did all the effects and music. They are extremely extremely extremely serious about theatre design. They wouldn't even call us by our real names. They called us by our character names. I remember when we were in our long days of tech—tech is when the show gets lit and the set gets loaded onto the stage and we wear our costumes and make-up for the first time and everything that we've rehearsed for the past six weeks gets shifted to fit the new design—Mel was working up in the booth high above the back of the auditorium and she and Nic argued over their walkie-talkies and we heard everything. Nic hung the big heavy black iron lights, perched at the top of his ladder, and Mel shifted through brightness levels and colors on the light-board in the booth.

"I'm thinking paler shades for Christopher," Mel said as the walkie-talkie squawked with static. "Based on the psychological narrative of the piece," she added. "Also, the actor playing Christopher looks better in paler shades. We might need to spotlight him through some scenes."

But *that's* how they are, that's *who* they are. They love lighting, and building, and tools. They love wires, and wood, and wheels. They love screws and nails. They may even eat glow-tape for breakfast.

So, the fact that they said yes, when I asked if we could come over to talk to them, is kind of shocking. A miracle. Not because they aren't interested in building a set, but because they don't let people enter their realm. Ever. Their infamous Theatre Barn is *thee* stuff of legend—no one gets to go in there. No one gets to see it. No one. I don't think we will today either, but who knows. I'm not expecting to. But, maybe?

The Santini compound butts against old land, before Weirville was built. Forests and fields spread as far as the eye can see. In their backyard, which is huge, a big red barn rises to the blue and white sky. It seems like an old-fashioned painting of a barn more than an actual barn, but it is, in fact, a real barn. I gaze at it from their kitchen window. Behind the barn, out in the fields, clouds gather in the distant sky. It will rain again. Mel and Nic hand us—me, Ellie, Rockford, and Lucius is here—shiny maroon cans of Dr. Pepper, and we all stand there sipping them. No one says anything. I think we're still a little shocked that we're here.

We just slurp our very fizzy sodas. So. Many. Bubbles.

Mel and Nic don't seem to like anyone, but they're not mean or bullies or anything like that. They know Lucius because they did his set for *The Seagull.* And they kinda know me. As total techie theatre-freak geniuses who know so much about set building and design, my feeling is they don't associate with a lot of people because they are not on the same level. Their futures shout Broadway and Hollywood, sure, but while in high school in weird ol' Weirville, they keep their distance in their wool hats, faded overalls, tool belts, and worn-in Doc Martens. Mel's are dark purple and Nic's are dark green.

"Um, thanks for having us over," I finally say, mouth full of bubbles.

Nicholas has hiccups and they're pretty bad. He's grown like nine inches over the summer. He jerks his head at his sister—so weird how they have the same exact face—and goes, "She's the boss."

"Anyone else and it would be a hard no," Mel says, "But the actor who played Christopher Boone is talented and I think he's cool, though I don't know that for a fact." She says this to her brother as if I am not standing right in front of her. "But," she continues, "I feel bad that his gay dad split and his little bro ended up in the hospital after the cheeseball funhouse ride gave him a nervous breakdown."

How does everyone know everything? I roll my eyes.

Ellie spits out her soda, slamming her hand to her mouth to cover the spray.

Lucius looks scared and asks where the bathroom is. Nicholas points, and Lucius flurries down the hallway in his long black coat, flapping behind him like a Marvel villain.

Mel shoots her arm out for the roll of paper towels across the counter, her hand brushing across Ellie's chest as she does. Her face flushes the same color of the can of Dr. Pepper. She quickly shoves the paper towels into Ellie's hands and then buries her own in the pocket of her baggy overalls. She's wearing her toolbelt today. I feel weird suddenly, because I can tell she has a crush on Ellie. Show of hands: who here is *not* crushing on Ellie?

So then my head starts moving around, looking for some mess somewhere that I can organize...ugh, but this is not my house. I take a deep breath. "First off," I say, placing my can of Dr. Pepper down on the counter. "I detest these. Tastes like medicine or butt. Secondly, Pop's not my 'gay dad' he's just my dad, even though he *is* gay, and he *is* my dad—one of them anyway, 'cause I have two—but it's like, don't say it in a derogatory way. We're not in Texas anymore, Toto."

Her eyeballs pop out of her head. "What? Holy crap. I *didn't.*"

Ellie goes, "Mmmyeahyoudid," and Mel fumes. "His brother was diagnosed with epilepsy and that's why he started having seizures. It's logical. It's science. It doesn't have anything to do with some stupid ride. He didn't have a nervous breakdown either."

Ellie might go full throttle here. She does that when she gets protective of me. It makes me feel safe somehow. Lighter in my head.

Mel's eyes widen. She looks mad.

Lucius comes back but stands off to the side, looking down, hands in his pockets.

Mel looks at Nic and says, "Wow, they're mouthy. They're bossy. I *like* them."

Nic hiccups.

No one speaks for a few minutes until Mel says, "Well now that we've broken the ice. We read the play, and we want to talk."

"Good," Lucius says. "That's why we're here. Now. Enlighten us with your *acumen.*"

Rockford goes, "Dawg, what? Accu-what? Accu-Weather forecast?"

Ellie spits out more soda.

Mel guzzles the last of her Dr. Pepper, craning her neck back to swallow it. She slams it on the counter afterwards, like a cowboy doing a shot of whiskey in a saloon. "Yeah. But first: Follow me."

Wait, what? We're shocked and can't say anything—what does this mean? We are going to The Barn? This is totes unprecedented. And I don't even know what that word really means.

As we walk down the hill from their house, the sky opens, and the rain gushes down, smacking against the roof of the barn. Lucius hangs back, I'm not sure why. He's walking several paces behind us. We see a giant Oak tree beside the barn with a big black rubber tire swing hanging from its lowest limb with old-fashioned rope, twisted into fraying braids. I want to hop on to it and swing like a kid, but Mel and Nic stalk to each side of the huge doors, each with a wide, bright white X painted across the front, and pull them open.

Mel turns to us. "No pictures. I mean it. I see one pic on Freak-Tok, Snapcrap or Litter, and I *will* come after you." She pulls a hammer out from the toolbelt and raises it. "With this. I will bludgeon thee."

She's joking, but I have this image of her scaling the side of my house, like a mountain climber, hammer in hand, headed for my bedroom.

We follow the twins. They hurry forward into the dark and veer to the left, where they switch on the lights. The whole barn lights up, buzzing, and dancing with dust. It is SO MASSIVE. Remember the scene in *Willy Wonka and the Chocolate Factory* when Charlie Bucket, Veruca Salt, Violet Beauregard, Mike Teavee, and Augustus Gloop first see the main chocolate room? Imagine it like that except better because theatre stuff is cooler than chocolate.

Ellie squeals and claps her hands excitedly. We are inside the legendary Santini Theatre Barn, originally created by their legendary dad who spent like 127 decades doing sets for theatre in New York, Chicago, London, San Francisco, Los Angeles, and Pittsburgh.

My heart fizzes mightily. Dust particles party in the stormy light. The rain beats against the roof like the apocalypse. Birds in the rafters burst up, an explosion of wing flaps. Vertical beams of wood stand from floor to ceiling, all in a row, on both sides of the barn from front to back. Horizontal beams up above connect them. So, it looks like giant H's, about eight of them. Holding the roof up, basically. But, it looks the way a barn is supposed to look. Flood lights hang on the H's. The whole place glows.

My brains are not foaming, thankfully. I might come upon a mess somewhere that will make me want to shift things around, but so far so good. This place is beyond amazeballs. The scents—I feel like a dog. Wood and mothballs and mint and metal and hay and powder and cattle. Shelves and bins and cubbies built out from the walls, stuffed with just about everything in the world you could ever imagine a theater could need or want. I have goosebumps looking at it all. It's almost not real. It's a sanctuary for inanimate theatre stuff that lives here like it's alive.

Ellie and Rockford head off together to explore. I feel the little needle slide into my belly. Are they a thing? Does she like him? Does she love him? Are they going to tell me anything? I sigh and kick a small black and blue button I see on the ground, and go the other way. Mel follows Ellie. Lucius gives me a weird look and goes off on his own probably to find Batman up in the rafters and execute him.

When the wind picks up, it makes the wood creak a little, like the barn itself is saying hello to us. Also, wind chimes sing in that tree outside, clinking a sparkly song that sounds spooky in the rain. Behind us, Nic's hiccups echo through the space. He's had those hiccups for a while, what's up with that?

I walk up and down the left side of the barn, listening to rain and wind and chimes and hiccups. Costume racks full of hanging party dresses, ball gowns and men's suits in every color line the wall. Black, blue, beige, brown, green, red, white... Every material—cotton, polyester, satin, silk, wool—every texture, every size, every style. One rack has only military gear with camouflage jumpsuits and army helmets, belts, boots, dozens of dog-tags hanging on a line of hooks. Then I find a rack that has suits of armor, whoa. Silver chain-link vests, and metal helmets, spiked gloves, boot covers, steel chest plates, all that stuff. I want to try one on. I want to clomp up to the others covered in armor and see what they say. But that image of Mel scaling the side of my house with a hammer in her hands comes back, so I keep walking. So cool though.

Rain spatters the roof.

It feels cozy in here, like I should have my hands around a mug of hot cider that smells like apples and caramel. I can't believe this place. I can't believe all we had to do to get us in here was mouth off to Mel. Good to know. I turn a corner and arrive at a wall of wooded shelves with endless books. Books with leather covers and gilded pages, new books with laminate covers and colorful spines, little books, big books, sets of encyclopedias. I take one down and open it, but it is not real. It's a prop. The other books, though, they are real, and I flip the pages across my nostrils to breathe in that woodsy-sweet smell, nutmeg and dust and the faded perfume of some beloved but deceased Librarian who wore cat-eye glasses.

Ellie yelps from somewhere across the barn, and Mel cackles. I wonder if she is following her around like a lost puppy, trying to impress her by sawing the head off a mannequin. Hiccups. I still hear them. Nic must be close, following behind me. Where's Lucius?

I walk into a large circular area where coils of thick black wires rise like king cobras. Gigantic metallic black stage lights sit beside the wires. There are white buckets full of silver wrenches and pliers, scattered tools—weird tools, big tools, bigger tools. And on the wall behind them hang hundreds of packets of plastic cable ties, the kind that make that awesome ZWIPP sound when you pull the long side through the little housing nubbin. Eight-foot-high drywall flats lean against the walls—some I recognize from plays I've seen at school. Wow. Will they be re-used? Painted over? Don't know. It feels like a lot of stuff is here more as a museum than a storage.

A gigantic armoire stands behind me, like something out of the Narnia books, and it's so stuffed with hats, bowlers and derbies and top hats and caps. They spill out onto the floor and create a messy little hat hill. I lean over to pick one up off the floor, a dusty green-velvet bowler, something The Hulk might wear to a pub in Dublin.

The corner of the barn, at the back, has plants, most of them fake but some are real. Plastic palm trees, cactus plants, a tall willow tree with cascading leaves clearly built for some big musical or something. Across from the plants, in the opposite corner, benches and chairs and couches and recliners in fabric, and leather, and wood, and metal. Wow, I've never realized just how many benches you should keep if you're going to turn an old barn into a theatre storage warehouse-museum...but come to think of it, plays and musicals really do use *a lot* of benches. I walk over and sit in one of them. It smells kinda skunky. I look across: every possible kind of chair you could ever imagine is stacked one on top of the other in several rows almost all the way to the ceiling. Whoa. Just, whoa.

I sit and stare at this majesty of chairs. I shake my head in awe.

Someone whistles loudly, as if herding us. The sound echoes through the roof of the barn and bounces back, so it's hard to tell where it's coming from exactly, but I imagine somewhere in between. I hop up and start darting in and out of tall aisles created by stacks of clear plastic bins filled with make-up, and wigs, and feather boas, and cans of hairspray, hair gel, hair mousse, body glitter, nail polish, powder. It smells like the 'pancake' make-up we dab onto our faces when we go on stage. The smell makes me think of playing Christopher in *Curious Incident...* and how I tried not to cry walking offstage the night that it finished, after we all bowed. Pop and Dad had tears in their eyes when they greeted me out in the lobby. That feels like a different life now. Well, that *was* a different life.

I stop—a rabbit! A big brown and white rabbit, fluffy white ball for a tail. It's hunched beside a box of Styrofoam heads. It looks at me, twitching its nose. Whoa, those whiskers. It's not afraid at all. It hops toward me, and I crouch down to greet it, holding out my hand. It sniffs at my fingers, hoping I have a carrot, some lettuce, maybe some seeds. What ears. It must hear everything, even people's thoughts. The rabbit nudges my hand and I pet its head. Hey, rabbit.

Its fur feels so soft, like a stuffed-animal version of a rabbit. Is this a wild rabbit? Or a pet rabbit? It seems so unafraid, so used to people petting it. Rabbits are the magic, aren't they? Its eyes are black as pitch, yet they see everything. It looks at me, looks into me, and...there's like a flood of thoughts, a rushing whoosh, and I travel far into my mind, and everything gets quiet. *Is it my fault? That we had to leave Texas, that Pop split, that Bax is transforming into something we are trying to understand and are pretty much afraid of? It's my fault, isn't it? It always is.*

Bunny spooks suddenly, as if it heard my complicated thoughts. It hops away, disappearing behind a crate full of batteries and body mics. I stand. I don't like the way the Styrofoam heads look in the box, so I take them out—there are 13 of them—and arrange them in a perfect circle on the ground. A Styrofoam circle of fake white heads.

"KIRBY COME TO THE DERBY," yells Nicholas, but it's cut off by a hiccup. I follow his voice out into the main area of the barn. Mel stands beside Ellie, her hands in her overalls. Rockford is leaning against an old wood-cutting table with a piece of straw sticking out of the corner of his mouth. I can't tell if the table is real or a set piece.

"We want to talk about your play," Nicholas hiccups.

"Hey, *Niccup*," Ellie says and we all laugh. "Maybe hold your breath? Maybe go get some water? Maybe just let Mel talk instead?"

Niccup takes a deep breath, his cheeks puffed out. After a bit, his face turns beet red.

"It'll never work," Mel says. "This happens every day. Nothing ever stops them."

Niccup gestures to Mel, like, 'okay then, you talk' and Mel takes off her tool belt and lays it on the table where Rockford is leaning.

"We have read the play," she says, clearing her throat like she's an important politician. "Bottom line: you were right to come to us. There's no one else who can do the stuff you've written into this. It's...some of it doesn't seem like it can be staged. I mean, that scene with the bed?"

Niccup goes, "The bed scene, whoa, yeah, wattup with that?"

"Well, I wrote it with you two in mind. And, the bed scene, yeah, that's how it feels. So."

"It's *complex*," Mel says. "The bed. It's really complex."

Niccup hiccups.

"So...what—you can't do it?" I ask.

"No, no, no," she says. "We *can*. I mean, it's easy. Like, it's..." She sighs. "We can do it. I'm just saying, it's complex. Simple, but, like, complex."

I nod. "So, you can do it?"

"Of course. I think. But here's our question: where do you want to do this? And when?"

"I need money for this seizure alert dog organization, so the sooner the better."

Niccup says, "Why don't you just do a Kickstarter?"

"We might, maybe. But, there's something bigger going on here," I say. "And it's not about asking kids from school and their parents to give us money online. If you read the play, you know what I mean."

Mel looks at me. "I'm not gonna argue with that. How much money you need to raise?"

"A lot."

She crosses away from the table. "Well, we can't do this at school, you know that, right? The Junior and Senior productions of *An Octoroon* and *Fences* and the Senior musical, *Hands on a Hardbody,* have the fall slots. There's no way."

"We're getting a real truck on that stage!" Niccup hiccups.

"In my backyard," I say. "Under the big tree. Its name is Quing Ori."

"Uh. What? A *backyard*? Wait—how big is your yard?"

"Big."

Niccup says, "But, two things: one, it's getting cold. We'd have to do it fast. And two, we're going to London to see my mom."

Mel scoffs. "*Nic's* going to see our mom, not me, but, yeah, there's a time crunch."

"Okay," I say. "Two more things: maybe you can build something that will keep everyone warm? And, maybe we can get started on it like right now?"

"Welp, we do have those heaters," Niccup hiccups to Mel.

"Yup," Mel agrees. "From the Mayor's inauguration ceremony." She looks at us expectantly.

"Right. That was awesome," Ellie blurts out.

"Mad as the hatter," Rockford agrees.

I applaud.

"Oh, so you all saw that? You were there?"

"Nope," Ellie says, "But I'm sure you slayed."

Mel rolls her eyes. "We'll have to come over and see the place, see what we're dealing with." She pats her hands like she's clapping dust off them.

Lucius pipes in, "I have seen the space, and it has great potential, but it will require your skills to transform it into a stage that I can actually direct on."

Everyone stares at him for a second. He blinks.

"Send the drone," Niccup says. "Map the space."

"A drone?" I ask.

"Good way to get the lay of the land, look at what we are dealing with," Mel says.

"Bird's-eye view," Niccup says, "Perspective!"

Rockford says, "You dawgs have a drone?"

"Four of them," Mel says. "Why."

"Can you show me how to use one?"

Mel shrugs. "Sure. If you like. Hey, where do you live, Kirby? St. Charles Estates?"

"No. That's the area with all the mansions and stuff."

"Oh. I thought all gay families were millionaires."

"Mel," Ellie says, and Mel looks at her. "Don't make me dog-walk you."

Mel blushes, her hands raised in defense. "Sorry!" she says. "I didn't mean anything!"

"We live at the end of Copse, down Grove," I say. "In a normal house. With normal grass and trees, and normal windows and doors. There's even normal food in the normal refrigerator and guess what? Normal cotton in the pillows."

Mel looks down at her feet and kicks something on the ground.

"Try getting a grip," I say, and it sucks all sound from the barn. Even the rain slows down. Lucius furrows his brow at me, shakes his head. Everyone stares at me for a second, then they look at Mel.

She says, "What? I'm fluid, okay? I'm demiboy, okay? I took online tests. And...other stuff. I don't define myself by the ancient systems."

"Then don't judge by them either," I snap back. I feel all the blood in my body rush into my head. The tips of my fingers fizz.

Mel sighs again.

I look over at Ellie and she winks at me. That makes the blood go somewhere else.

Outside, the sun slips through the clouds, and a shaft of pink-orange light floods the entranceway, making it look like a cathedral. We all look around as the golden light fills the barn. Nobody talks. Up in the sky, the clouds are puffy, and the air is wet. It's rainbow weather. In the distance, thunder rumbles. Loud, but far away. I can feel that Mel is mad at or upset with me. Ellie is being protective. Roc and Niccup are keeping quiet, and Lucius is confused and weird. It's a moody minute here.

Finally, I say, "This place is amazing. Where did you *get* all of this stuff?"

It snaps everyone back and you can feel the drama get slurped down the drain.

"Dad's old life, most of it. But now, he finds out when theaters are closing, 'cause they run out of money, or can't get funded, 'cause theater is so unappreciated in America, and he makes a deal, and he gets the stuff."

"Why?" Ellie asks. "Is he planning on doing anything with it?"

"Just giving it a home. A place to retire. And, you know, when new theaters pop up—*if* they do—they can come here maybe and get what they need. It's like a sanctuary."

"It's so organized," I say, dreamily. "Doesn't make me fizz."

"What?" Niccup asks.

"Nothing," I say, feeling my ears get hot.

"We take really good care of it," Mel says. "We're out here every morning and every night taking care of it. It's how we earn our allowance."

"Makes sense," I say, looking around.

"Nic comes out here and dresses up in the costumes and does weird accents," she says.

Nic says, "And Mel takes pictures of everything, labels it, catalogues it in the computer, so that we have a database."

"You have a *label maker*?" I ask. She looks over at me. "So jelly," I say.

I look around some more. I could never have imagined a place as cool as this. I wonder what it would have been like for me and Bax to have had this barn in our yard and played in it every day: the costumes, the props, the beams and books and bins and bales. The smells and the dust particles suspended in the rays of sunlight that laser through cracks in the walls. "Can I bring my brother here to see this?" I ask.

"We're particular about who gets to come in here," Mel adds.

"That's toe-stoops," Ellie says, hands on her hips.

Mel looks confused. Then she says, "Uh. Totally stupid?"

Ellie nods. "Don't you feel," she says, "Like at least every person in YOUTHEATRE should get to see this? Why are you, like, hiding it away? It's *stuff.*"

Mel's eyes go dark, like *How dare you call this 'stuff'?* She might take a sledgehammer to all of us, bludgeon us right here, stuff some wig bins with our body pieces, who would ever know? "I'll consider bartering," she says very seriously. She raises an eyebrow at Ellie. "For people to get in here and see this. *Bartering.*"

Ellie shrugs. "I mean if it were me, I'd charge a fee for people to come in and see it. It's like a museum. You could raise funds for these orphaned theaters. You could even raise funds for Baxter's seizure dog."

Mel looks at her brother and they raise eyebrows at one another, as if they'd consider it.

"No," I say, and everyone looks at me. "I mean, thanks, but we do it together by doing the play or we don't do it at all."

No one says anything. The rain falls harder.

Rockford suddenly hollers out, jumps up, does this perfect front walkover, FWHOOSH, a total ninja slice, right into a five-foot mountain of plush velvety black curtains that look like they were sent over from some Italian opera house that shuttered in the 1930s.

"Hey!" Mel yells at him. "Don't do that! Those are real velvet! They just got here!"

Lucius sneaks out the big double doors of the barn and hurries up the hill toward the house. We watch him go. I look at Ellie, who shrugs.

Rockford pops his head up from the black pile, a rising cloud of dust particles twirling in the light around his head. "Chill, polywog," he says, "Just wanted to see what that *felt* like."

"Hey!" Niccup says, echoing his twin sister. "Hey!" Then he tries to do what Rockford did, but lands on his head, limbs flying everywhere.

We all crack up. Mel shakes her head.

Niccup says to Rockford, "Yo, polywog, how'd you *do* that? Are you a Jedi knight?"

Rockford nods. Ellie and I nod. He is.

HALLWAY OF DOORS

I want to talk to Ellie. I want to ask her if she and Roc are a thing. Are they? I want to stop Mel from fawning all over her. Was she? I don't want to feel like the middle of my body is on fire, melting like wax. Is it? When can I talk to her? What am I gonna say?

I go upstairs, flick on the light, walk down the hall and open the linen closet. I rearrange the towels, napkins, washcloths, cleaning rags, spare sheets, and pillowcases. There is no linen. Why do they call them linen closets? First, I arrange by color, then size, then texture, then by what room they belong to.

I think the barn triggered something organizational in my brains.

I'm thinking about my play: what I wrote, why I wrote it, and what I want to do. I'm thinking about the plays I've read for Krasinski and maybe why some of those playwrights wrote their plays the way they did and for what reasons. There is a play called *The Normal Heart* written in the 1980s. The playwright, Larry Kramer, wrote the play because his friends were dying of a deadly disease called AIDS that was targeting gay men and slowly killing them. They couldn't get anyone to care enough to help them. He wrote it for his friends and to bring attention to what was happening. I know that Dad and Pop had friends who died of AIDS when they were younger. It was so sad for them at the time, and even to this day they feel bad about it.

There is a play called *for colored girls who have considered suicide / when the rainbow is enuf* by Ntozake Shange and it's a play of poetic monologues about black women who have been oppressed by racism and because they are women. It makes me feel so mad at the world. A new kid from Weirville High wrote a play last year called *The Windless Plains* about bullying because his younger brother died by suicide for being harassed so violently in their old school in Oklahoma. His family moved here afterwards. The play won a national award and is getting a professional production in New York.

I am not sure if my play is anything like these plays, but maybe someday I can write one that will be. My play is about a mystery called epilepsy that I still don't understand but I'm trying to figure out. Thinking about plays while arranging towels soothes the fizzbrainz for a little while.

Dad comes up the stairs, sees me, and stops. He decides not to say anything and starts back down the stairs. He pauses, comes back up, waits a minute, then finally says, "Champ?" He hasn't called me Champ since like 4th grade. I feel the same happiness I felt as a kid when he would say that, but also my eyes roll up into the back of my head.

I turn around holding some weird white round thing with holes in it. I ask him what it is, and he says it's a doily of Granbuela's. I don't know that word—doily—and because there is only one of these things, one doily, it doesn't fit in to the rest of the scheme here, so I have to decide to what to do with it.

"Is it messing with your magic?" Dad asks.

I nod.

"Try featuring it prominently, and it will feel better."

"What's prominently? Is that like the school prom?"

"No. Well, a little. It means make it stand out."

"Oh," I say. And he's right—making things stand out sometimes helps make the magic calm down. I always forget that.

Dad's watching me.

I turn to him: "What, Dad."

He buries his hands into his pockets. "Still won't talk to Pop?"

"Dad. I don't even know where my phone is."

"It's right here," he says, and I turn to see he is holding it.

After a long time, both of us standing in the hallway staring at one another, I finally say, "So what," at the same exact time he says: "We're still a family." I think that's what he says, but because we spoke over one another, I might have heard it wrong, but that's what it sounded like.

"You're never going to tell us what happened, are you?" I ask him.

Dad looks at my phone, turning it in his hands like a detective with a piece of evidence.

"You cheated on him, right?" I ask. I don't actually think this is true, but if he gets annoyed enough at me, maybe he'll tell me the truth.

He scoffs, nudges his glasses on his nose. "Please."

"Then what? Why did he abandon us and disappear?"

"I wish you would stop saying that."

"It was you, wasn't it? You made him leave. I know it."

He drops his head, disappointed. He goes back downstairs, saying, "I can always ground you again. Maybe until the end of the year this time."

"Dad!" I say, and after a second his head pops around the stairwell again.

"Yes," he says.

"I love you! Alright? I love you! Okay?"

Dad's eyes fill up. "Love you too, Champ."

We look at each other for a long moment.

"I still think it's your fault, though," I say.

He blinks. "What is this thing with you that it needs to be someone's fault?"

"Just tell me."

He sighs. "Do you need to talk to me about anything?"

"Huh?"

"Girls. Boys. Erections. Porn. Hair growing. Hormonal freak-outs. Pimples? Social media? Anything? I'm here for you, and I want you to know that."

"Oh my God," I say. "So cringe." I get a quick jolt of the shivers.

"Well, do you want to talk to someone other than me?"

"Who?"

"The school counselor, a therapist, or—"

"I have the towels. I can talk to them. I have this doipy, doiky, doi—"

"Doily."

I hold it up. "I have this doily."

He nods, shrugs, and disappears.

* * *

Later, I change, but my pajamas don't fit me anymore, nothing fits me anymore, so I wear sweatpants and an oversized *WICKED* T-shirt that went down to my knees when we bought it years ago. It's a close-up of Elphaba's green face. Now it fits me normally. I send a text to Lucius asking him why he left so suddenly and if everything is okay. He told me he was going to send a schedule for rehearsals that will work for his own crazy schedule. I never received anything. I ask him if he wants to meet and talk about design stuff, especially after having seen the Santini's barn. It's amazing that they're on board. I wait but I don't see the dots-balloon on my phone. He's not texting back.

Bax plops down onto his bed in his Captain America pajamas. He hasn't worn them in years, and they're too small for him. He looks uncomfortable. I can tell by the way he picks at them. He watches me for a little while, one eye sleepy, something in his face droopy, and younger somehow. He clears his throat and says, "Did you see the third symbol today?"

Chills spill. "I don't know...wait, was I supposed to see it?"

"I thought you'd see it today."

"Did *you*?" I ask.

He shakes his head.

"Oh, I saw a rabbit! Next to a giant bin of mannequin heads."

Bax tosses his head back, laughing. "That's not it, *dummy*."

I laugh. "HA HA, I see what you did there."

He grins.

We crawl into bed.

* * *

Later, I dream that I am walking down a long, dark hallway of doors, knocking on each one. The doors get heavier the further down the hallway I wander. The sound of the knocking changes with the weight of the door. The heavier the door, the harder I knock. The sound gets deeper, thunderous. Then it gets faster, the knocking. That's the dream. Knocking.

I wake up. It's 3:09am. The banging sound, the knocking from my dream, was real. It was Bax's head hitting the floor. He calls out his weird words, his un-words, yelps out: *MEE-WAAP, HEEOW-HEKKK, OPP-YEEUUUTT, FEELLLLP NARAY.*

I freeze in bed, stone cold terrified. My skull is an ice sculpture.

It feels like a demon is eating him in the dark right across from me, and the same demon has paralyzed me so I can't move, can't help him, can't even scream. I am afraid, but, it is beyond afraid. My teeth chatter. *Why can't I move?*

Kirby, get up and help him.

I stare at the glowing galaxy on the ceiling, the spill of neon green stars, the plastic tails of comets. It all blurs until I go really far away, until I am not anywhere anymore. It is quiet and tiny glowing dust particles fall all around me. Then, somehow, I blink and come back to the room. "My God," I whisper, and, finally free from the he-froze-me demon, tear off the covers and flick on the light. A fog has fallen to the earth during the night, but the moon still shines through, and the world outside is a big silver-gray fuzz.

Bax is thrashing.

I take his pillow and place it under his head, cradling it. If we had a seizure dog, it could be his living pillow. We have to get that dog. And Dad's friend, Brian—where I saw the second symbol, Dahlia's intersecting hourglasses—is building some kind of 'safety bed', but in the meantime, there's me. I crawl on top of my brother gently, softly pinning his arms down. I run my free hand through his hair, wiping away sweat.

I can't make this stop. It's a feeling like falling into a black hole. It feels cold in the bones, sad in the heart. All I can do is wait until it passes. Tears fall down my face in the dark and the light of the room. He finally slows down, comes through it, opens his eyes, blinks at me. "What are you doing?" he asks, sleepily.

"Making sure you're okay, you were having a seizure. C'mon, let me change you."

"No," he says, embarrassed. "Get off me." He shoves me off him. He peels off his pajamas, standing there naked as a baby. He hurries to his dresser and pulls out a pair of these old red overalls, from when he was a kid, and clambers into them.

He stands in the fog's haze, staring out the window, shivering.

I head toward the linen closet down the hall for fresh sheets. As I pass him, his hand juts out suddenly and grabs my arm. I startle.

"Give me a hug," he says.

I hug him so hard.

Outside, somewhere back in the trees, way out in our forest of a yard, an owl hoots.

"I'm scared," he says, though he sounds more annoyed than scared.

"Scared of what?"

"I'm not me," he says.

Chills. "I'm going to get you that dog." He buries his face in my chest. "I promise, Bax."

He sniffles into my pajamas. "I miss Pop," he mumbles. Again, he sounds annoyed.

"I know."

"Don't you miss him?"

Won't answer that.

CROP CIRCLE

We have been in school for like three and a half weeks already and the amount of homework. Why. Why this much? But, at least it's Geoscience. Do you know how much I love Geoscience? They organize everything. The lithosphere, hydrosphere, atmosphere, biosphere, each further broken down into specific fields. The opening spread of our textbook displays it like a gigantic tree, every branch off the trunk, every leaf off the branches, perfect and particular and precise. It makes me want to cry with joy. There is no way you could NOT understand it perfectly. Take the lithosphere: mineralogy and petrology, geomorphology, paleontology, stratigraphy, structural geology, engineering geology, and sedimentology. I'm in love.

Suddenly, I hear a high-pitched humming, like a robot-insect buzzing. I push my chair back and stand up, lean across my desk to look out the window and that's when I see two flying, four-armed, white and red machines with little rotors on the ends of each arm. Drones. They hover curiously outside my window for a few seconds until they burst upwards like tiny rockets and disappear over the top of the roof. I run downstairs and outside.

Mel and Niccup stand across the street from our house, holding drone controllers in their hands. I look up and see the little mechanical creatures floating toward the ground. Mel has hacked off her own hair, so now it's all spiky and asymmetrical and she has dyed it purple. Niccup wears a gray sweatsuit and gigantic neon purple high-tops.

"Hi?" I say.

"Sorry," Mel says. "We weren't sure which room was yours, so we flew by all of them."

"We have a front door. It even has a knocker on it. A *normal* knocker."

"Har har," Mel says.

"That's no fun," Niccup says. "Let Goldie and Kurt do the detective work!"

"Goldie and Kurt?"

Mel scoffs. "Didn't you ever see *Overboard*? It's the greatest movie ever made."

"Is that an old movie?"

"80s."

I roll my eyes.

"Take us to the yard!" Niccup yelps.

"Ay, ay, Captain," I say.

We walk around the house, and through the side-gate. Piles of brown, yellow, and maroon leaves gather along the walkway. We come into the yard.

Mel crosses her arms, taking it all in. "Whoa. I see why you want to do it back here."

I point to Quing Ori, and Mel nods again.

"Yup," she says. She points past Ori to the woods beyond the fence. "What's going on back there?"

"Trees. A lot of them."

"We will light those trees," she says. "That will make a sick-ass background. Like another dimension. A doorway."

A doorway? Like in Bax's drawings? Goosebumps race down my arms.

"Let's light them up so bright and perdy it'll look like magic fire," Niccup says with a southern drawl.

"Let me see what's going on back there." She fiddles with her little controller and her drone buzzes and flies, up toward the sky, across the yard, past Ori and into the trees beyond. "Nicholas," she says, "Get some shots of this area over by the tree. I think we need to build a stage or a platform coming out from the bottom of that trunk—and there has to be space *underneath.*"

"Right," Niccup says and sends his drone, but rather than lifting upwards, it jets on an angle toward Ori and the corner where I want us to do our little play. Then it rotates around that whole area from maybe about eight or ten feet above the ground. Niccup runs after it.

"Underneath?" I ask, looking at Mel.

"Hello? You *wrote* the play. Underneath? Get it?"

"Oh," I say, realizing what she means. "Right." The bed scene.

"Hey," she says, "I need to talk to you."

I look at her. Is she going to chop my head off? Profess her love for Ellie?

"I need you to know that the reason I'm saying yes to this thing is for my brother."

"Okay."

"See, he's not gonna get into any colleges with his grades. He's not book smart the way I am. He's super smart when it comes to all *this* stuff, but the only hope we have right now to get him in is to beef up his portfolio, like majorly, and this is how we're gonna do it."

"But don't you...share all of your projects, or whatever?"

"No, the ones we have for portfolio are mine. He helped. And...he needs his own thing."

"Okay."

"So, if I let him take the lead in a lot of places, you know why. Basically, that means I'll be bossing him around a lot and yelling at him to get stuff done."

"K."

"And I'll be taking a lot of pictures of it."

I nod.

"Sorry if it sounds weird. It's a...it's a twin thing."

"I think it's cool that you're doing that for your brother."

"Yeah," she says, "I guess we have something in common after all."

We both look over to where Niccup is. We can hear him hiccupping from over here.

"And we have to do it fast, because he's leaving."

"And because we need the money for the dog."

She takes me in for a second, and says, "Can I ask you a question?"

"Yup."

"Why did you pick Lawrence Meyers to direct the play?"

"Who?"

"Oh, sorry—Lucius Beetlemeyer."

I *knew* it.

"Krasinski said Lucius was the one to direct it and—"

"Dayum. That Krasinski is crafty."

"What do you mean by that?"

"Well why aren't *you* directing your play?"

I flash to the book Krasinski gave me, sitting unopened on my shelf. My brains jiggle like Jello. "I can't. I would explode. I can't do it."

"Okay, no clue what that means," she says, adjusting the straps on her overalls, "But I just need you to know that I've seen Lawrence—oh sorry, *Lucius*—be weird and kinda offensive and if we work together again, I might throw something. Like at his face. Like a hammer and nails. Maybe a power drill. Not that I condone violence."

I nod, chewing my bottom lip.

She and Niccup do their drone thing.

I sit down on the grass, check my phone. Still no response from Lucius. I'm worried. I *can't* direct the play. I don't know *how* to direct a play. I'm just gonna play me and be the writer. I can't do all three.

Wait—what does Mel mean about Krasinski being 'crafty'?

The grass is still damp, and I let them finish using their drones to take pictures of my yard and of the forest behind us. When they're done, they land the drones, and they sit down looking at videos and pictures they took, displayed on the small dark screens of the controllers. In the woods, birds sing. Except for one of them, yelping in a pinched cackle, which I think is a blue jay. They're so loud.

"Look at this," Niccup says and passes his controller to Mel. She leans in and looks at it.

"Looks like a miniature crop circle," she says. "What's that from? An animal?"

I stand and walk over. Niccup hands me the controller.

Icicles lance the back of my neck. "Oh my God," I whisper.

"What?" Mel asks, concerned. "Are you okay?"

It's a pattern in the grass, an imprint left behind from when Ellie and Rockford started experimenting with their roles in the play as 'the seizure' and 'the lightning people.' They were moving around, and because the grass and soil were a little damp, their movements left this...*pattern*: a tangle of snakes twisted and braided together, slithering in between one another's bodies, but they all end up back at their own heads. The way that the drone caught it, from above—like a crop circle, yes—you can see that it's the third symbol.

It's the third symbol. In our backyard.

I fly like a hornet to get Bax. He's playing ME & MY SHADOW and does not want to pause the game. He moves around the room in his headset, lost in another world. I hop over and yank it off his face. He yells at me, and I grab his hand and pull him outside.

"I told you they were close," he says, looking at the drone screen.

The twins say, "Who's close?" at the same time.

"The lightning people," Bax says, and walks to the spot on the grass.

My teeth feel like tiny blue ice cubes in my mouth.

"Close?" Niccup says, and hiccups. "Where? Like in the woods? Send up the drone!"

"No, you can't *see* them like that," Bax says. "They're magnets."

Magnets? What does that mean? I take a breath, looking around. What can that mean? Magnets, magnets. Like, refrigerator magnets?

"The lightning people. From the play, right?" Mel asks.

I nod.

"They're not *from* the play," Bax says. "They're *in* the play. Kirby included them."

I nod again, swallowing.

"They're helping us get Heddy."

"Who's Heddy?" the twins ask, at the same time, again.

"Our dog!"

"You *have* the dog already?" Niccup asks.

I had no idea the dog already had a name. I look at Bax like, *Why didn't you tell me?* And then I remember that he rarely tells me anything, that he's still pretty secretive. He lets out info whenever he feels like letting it out, and when he does, he makes it seem like we've all known it already for weeks.

"No," Bax says. "That's the dog the lightning people are getting for me. Well, Kirby is getting it for me, the lighting people are helping bring her here."

I blink, feeling the goosebumps prickle my wrist, raising the hair on my arms. I look into Bax's giant lighted eyes. "So, so, okay, they come down from the clouds, walk toward you, show you the symbols, then they go away?"

"As sillyheads. I can't see their faces." Bax looks away. "Can I go back, please?"

"Sillyheads?" the twins ask.

"Wait, Bax. How do they...*show* the symbols to you?" The hair on my arms stays standing, I can feel it like static cling when Dad forgets to put dryer sheets in the dryer and my clothes stick to everything and I get little shocks when I touch certain things.

"Glass...I think, but...um, I don't know if it's real glass."

"Glass?" Niccup asks.

Bax shrugs. "For them it's like their paper. For us it looks like big glass. I have to go!" He runs across the yard and up the steps to the back deck, disappearing into the house. My mouth feels raw, like I ate a bowl of Captain Crunch.

Nic goes, "Turns out we got glass, bruh. Can't tell you how much glass. So. Much. Gleeeees."

"In the barn?" I say. "I didn't see glass."

"WE GOTS D'GLEEEEESS."

Mel swats at him. "Stop it, doofus. It's there. It's covered. It's in the back." Then, proudly, "Our dad did a set for *The Glass Menagerie* that was made entirely out of glass."

"It won a hundred awards!" Nic adds. "GLEEEEES." Mel swats at him again.

I try to picture that. "Wasn't it reflective? Like, how did he do that?"

Mel says, "The magic of theatre. We'll show you pictures."

Nic adds, "Mostly glass, yeah, but mostly an illusion."

I chew my bottom lip, trying to picture this.

Grass. Magnets. Glass.

I plop onto the ground, right beside the symbol and run my fingers through the green blades where the symbol lives. You can't really see it from down here. I mean you can see that the grass looks folded, but the birds that fly over it, they see it, and I wonder what they think it is.

Mel says, "Hey. Where's Ellie today? She's not in your house?"

I dart my eyeballs up at her. "No. Why would she be in my house?"

Mel shrugs. "Thought you two were a thing."

She stares at me.

I stare back.

She blinks.

I blink.

INTERVENING JESUS

After school the next day, I'm doing endless amounts of homework in my room when I get a text from Lucius. He's outside my house and wants me to come down. I fling the window open. He's across the street, standing on the curb in a long beige overcoat, a beige sweater and a beige fedora. He looks like inspector Gadget. Maroon and mustard-colored leaves fall around him. It's one of our first cold days of fall, which worries me because I want to get the play up soon.

"Come up," I yell. "Just come in and go up the stairs."

He shakes his head and texts: 'Come down. Can't come in.'

I wonder if maybe he's sick. I can't catch anything, we can't let Bax get sick. I hurry downstairs, grabbing a gray hoodie from the hall closet as I pass by it. I flip the hood all the way up for some reason, thinking it makes me look tougher or cooler, or, I don't know why I do that, I'm not usually a hood person. It's Dad's hoodie, so it's big, and the sides of the hood flop all over the place, I can't even see and nearly trip off the porch. I hurry down the driveway and across the street. Lucius moves back when I get too close. "Are you sick or something?" I ask.

He looks down.

I say, "I've been texting. We need to cast the play, and make a rehearsal schedule, and start rehearsing, and get the Santini twins to start building. They don't have much time. And, I mean, there is so much to do."

He nods and looks up the street as if someone is waiting for him at the top of the hill. I look up there, but I don't see anyone.

"Have you just been busy?" I ask. "With school and stuff?"

He nods again, but then he shrugs and sighs very audibly. A big sigh. I close into myself and pull the hood back. It's almost four o'clock, the light is changing, the sky is dark-peach and eggplant purple, but for some reason I smell pancakes and bacon. One of my neighbors is cooking breakfast at four o'clock? Weirdoes of Weirville.

"I can't direct your play," Lucius says.

My stomach drops out of my body. "Why not?"

"It's against my religion."

I swallow, it's all phlegmy. It always gets phlegmy for some reason whenever *this stuff* comes up. I feel electricity buzzing through my veins. "'Cause of my fathers?"

He nods.

"You didn't know?" I ask.

"You never said anything."

"I mean, should I get branded? A symbol that lets certain religious people know to stay away?" For a brief second, I wonder what that symbol would look like, and where it would live on my body.

Lucius looks up the hill again.

After what happened in Texas so many times, I try my best to just feel the blood boiling over now like a spaghetti pot when the pasta gets too hot. My ears are so red, they burn the sides of my face. I breathe, looking at Weirville High School's most esteemed theatre director, for like a long time, trying to decide what I want to say. He slips the hat off his head and runs his hands through his dyed black hair.

I turn and look at my house. It's...it is so nice. I guess I never really realized how nice it was. A magical dark blue with many windows, white shutters, and all the best plants and trees everywhere. I see my bedroom up to the right. The light is on, and the room glows. The house is so quiet, even though Dad and Bax are in there right now. I turn to Lucius. He looks pale.

"Look, I can't get between you and your beliefs."

"They're my *parents'* beliefs, okay? It's not...it's not me."

"Well then your parents' beliefs. I mean, do what you have to do." I'd pulled the hood back, but now it feels like it's up, and smothering my head and face.

"I'm still living under their roof until I leave for Carnegie Mellon, otherwise I would sacrifice my beliefs for art, man. 'Cause that's what you do."

"Is it?"

"That's the calling of being an artist."

I clear my throat. "I need to get my brother a seizure dog. He could die if we don't figure this out. You don't know. You don't share a room with him. I'm with these seizures almost every night and it's freakin' terrifying."

He looks up the hill. "I'm sorry for you," he says. "I believe in what you're doing."

A slimy silence sets in, and it's as sucky as salt on a slug. I'm stuck here on a curb in a hoodie in sluggy suckyness with Inspector Gadget.

"Can you send me someone else?" I finally ask him. "I need someone else to direct it now. Now that Jesus or God or whoever has intervened." Jesus or God or whoever intervened a lot in Texas too. Pop said we could still expect this to happen anywhere we went in the world (if we weren't in the heart of a major city), but it was a matter of frequency and volume. I think that was what he said. I feel like I'm forgetting a lot of things Pop said to me lately.

"The more substantial question, as I see it," he says, sliding a pair of hipster sunglasses from his coat pocket and sliding them onto his face, "Is why *you're* not directing it. It's your show. You need to consider your future as an artist of the American theatre. All of your skills—acting, writing, directing, producing, designing, whatever they all are—can be rolled into one, so that you are an eclectic, versatile, multi-tasker. Think about a prism: a boring clear empty thing. You hold it up to the light and voila—all the colors bloom. Boom."

"You should see if there's an opening in the Guidance Counselor department," I say, but not in a mean way. He's a smart guy and a good director, and whatever he needs to do to deal with his beliefs—or his parents' beliefs—is not on me. I shake his hand and tell him thanks and good luck at Cardigan Lemon.

I leave him on the curb, run back across the street with the hood flapping against my upper back, and head inside. I dart back upstairs, slam my bedroom door so hard I nearly crack it, and I fume. I throw stuff around my room, slamming, kicking, punching, ripping, grabbing, doing it again, then again, finally calm myself down, catch my breath, and slowly float over all the mess I've made to my bookshelves.

I find the book Krasinski gave me*: A Director Prepares* by Anne Bogart. Shower curtain, foggy hand. I grab it, throw it against the wall as hard as I can, and pull my phone out. I want to text Pop: 'I am going to shove the rat pole up your butt hole.'

Instead, I throw my phone.

I walk over to the book, open it, see pages full of highlighted text and scribbled notes in the margins. Whoa, Krasinski must really love this book. I flop down onto my bed, punch my pillow, bury my face in it and scream as loud and long as I can. Then, out of breath and feeling like my face is on fire, and like I just tore my vocal cords to shreds, and so annoyed and so exhausted, I just start reading.

But I can't focus.

I slowly hurry back to my bookshelf, take everything down, and start to feel a little calmer when I re-arrange all the books by color: R O Y G B I V. There aren't enough orange or yellow books for this to work well, so I fill in the holes in my brains with other yellow and orange things in the room. It's okay. It doesn't need to be perfect, it just needs to calm me down.

It does.

Outside, the sun sets. The color streaming through my window doesn't fit on the shelves, it's too mixed. It's rust-gold-pink. It's 'Rusgolpin.' There. I've named a new color. I feel my heart rate slow down and as I back away from my bookshelf and see the arrangement of the colors, I sigh with relief. Maybe I can direct the play the same way I can direct the colors of my books? I don't know. Why does everything have to be a certain way for me? What does it mean? Why isn't everyone else like this, too?

I plop back down on the bed, sigh, and open the book.

This isn't a book for young people, like Krasinski said, but it's not hard to read. I make believe I'm a college student perched against a big oak tree, like Ori, on a university campus somewhere tucked away in the mountains. It's snowing, but the sun is out, and I'm reading this book and I'm 20-years-old. Maybe I have a beard. I have good boots on. I have a girlfriend, and a vintage convertible. I have muscles. Maybe an earing. Wait, what? What is happening right now.

I read.

The first thing in the book that gives me a jolt is that she says that every good play asks a question, and every *great* play asks a *big* question. I grab my notebook and write that down. I pace around the room asking my play what question it is asking. I mean, I'm asking myself that question because I wrote the play, but all I've really written—I think—is a recounting of what happened: we were sleeping, Bax had a bad seizure, I helped him come back to normal, and he told me the people from the lightning visit him and show him symbols...then the play 'shows' us the symbols.

What question am I asking?

Well, aren't I asking if we can make enough money from this to get a seizure dog? No, that's me asking, not the play.

What is my play asking?

It might be asking more than one thing, though. Is that okay? For example, it seems like the play is asking me to direct it. No, that's not it either. I sigh, feeling the blood rush back to my face. I look at the bookshelf again wondering if I can do this. A play, and actors, and technical stuff, and an audience...those things are not a collection of books that can be colorbetized. So, how am I going to do this? How *can* I do this? What's the freakin question I'm asking.

MARA GECCO

Ellie is playing John Proctor in *The Crucible.* She never dresses as a dude or deepens her voice or anything. She's just Ellie. She moves like water on stage. You cannot take your eyes off her. She makes my heart rabbity. I feel pressure and squirminess through the middle section of my body. It actually hurts.

She's performing a scene with a girl named Mara Gecco, who doesn't talk. Well, she talks, but not much and not in a regular way. A word or two here or there. But they are also sometimes made-up words; she has her own language. She loves theatre more than life itself. She finds her own way of playing scenes, and uses other ways to communicate. She is short, with dark hair cut to her chin, big dark eyes, a small mouth. She dresses kinda goth but it's her own goth. I think she said her father is from South Africa, he's black and Dutch, and her mother is Japanese and Australian.

Mara is playing John Proctor's wife, Elizabeth, who gets accused of witchcraft by the teen girl that John had an affair with. She has a monologue about the way women who are accused of witchcraft are brought into the court and if the girls claiming to be bewitched act out, twisting and screaming and crying, then the women accused are hanged as witches. No proof is needed. The Devil is all.

Mara performs with her hands and her eyes and her facial expressions and her body and little bird-like noises and stuff, but usually only says *one* word of the actual monologue, then waits for Ellie to say her lines.

Krasinski takes them through the scene two more times. Each time, Mara chooses a different word: the second time, in that same speech, she only says, 'bewitchin', points to the ceiling, walnuts her face, and silently screams. In the other speech, she decides to intone 'magistrate' and hangs her head down with the heaviness of it all. We never know what is going to happen with Mara Gecco, and that is both what makes it so cool and also makes me want to pull my face off. Some of the other kids in YOUTHEATRE think this is all an act. They call her a phony. They need theatre and acting to be sophisticated and important, which means there is no room for 'these weirdoes.' I heard Trista Lopez-Parsons say that in the hallway. Those are the kids I do not hang with, and they certainly don't want to hang with me.

I watch Krasinski directing. I watch like a hawk. I need to stay after today to talk to him, ask him some things. I envision myself directing, and it's all hands in the air, yelling at everyone, stomping my feet, pouting. Crap. How is he so calm? I feel like a piece of wood on the beach, the kind that looks heavy as a 16-wheeler truck, but when you pick it up, it's actually hollow and feels as light as a marshmallow and a million tiny sand fleas come jumping out and land in your hair. After this, I will leave the auditorium, go upstairs to the library, and re-arrange the Graphic Novels section by fonts. There are so many amazeballs fonts. I've done it a few times already.

I take a few breaths. I jot down some notes in my journal. I think about 'Ms. B from the Bogart book.' Something else she says in her book is that if theatre were thought of as a verb, the verb would be 'to remember'. We put on plays to represent memories. This is true—I think—because with my play I am trying to remember the experience of the seizures, right? Of being close to them, afraid of them, discovering something they are trying to tell me, to tell us. I remember the fear in my body, the smells, the sounds, the electricity in the air.

The urge to get this play up so people can see what I 'remember' is strong.

I still need to figure stuff out, though.

Like when Bax said, 'They're magnets.' What did that mean?

Krasinski is patient with actors. He jumps up on stage and moves around the space, always using his long arms and big hands to accentuate something, suggesting ways for the actors to find 'other ways through', something he says a lot. A sudden sense of calm comes over me, here in the auditorium. I look around at all of us in YOUTHEATRE and I feel...floaty. Like I am having an outer-body experience. I feel glad that I am here.

Next is a scene from a play called *Dog Sees God: Confessions of a Teenage Blockhead* with Shawna Neeley and Poe Patterson. The play imagines the characters of The Peanuts grown up, as, like, degenerate teenagers. Charlie Brown and Schroeder fall in love, and Lucy is in a mental hospital for setting someone's hair on fire. Krasinski claps his hands together and barks out at us in the auditorium, "Stay alert, people!" He doesn't allow phones in here. There's a phone box at the entrance of the auditorium where we put them when we come in. Someone drew a butt on it, so it looks like you are putting your phone into a butt. Still, sometimes we drift off, and he claps us back into the worlds of the plays, hanged witches and feuding families and visiting ghosts and Snoopy gone wild. Shawna and Poe are great, both of them, but they are big criers, so there's always lots of sniffling and wiping tears away in their scenes. It's not bad, but it's very distracting. Maybe just a single tear falling down a cheek would suffice?

Try that, kiddos.

Wait—is that directing? I'm not even directing yet and I'm already directing?

* * *

"Please," I say to him in his office afterwards.

Today, it smells like a Halloween candle in here. A snake of cold air slithers through the window beside us. We need to get this play up before it gets too cold. "Please come to the first rehearsal and just...get us going. Just start us off?" I slide off the wooly blue chair and land on my knees in front of the desk. I put my hands together in prayer. "I'm begging you, Taddy K."

Krasinski laughs. "Based on the fact no one has ever called me 'Taddy K' before, I'll consider it."

"Isn't that your nickname?"

"Thaddeus really only has 'Tad' as a nickname, but Taddy, that's new."

"Hey," I say, getting up from the floor. "Did you do it on purpose?"

"Do what on purpose?"

"Make me get Lucius Beet—I mean 'Lawrence Meyers'—on board because you knew he'd back out and then I'd have to do it?"

"What? Of course not. Why? What happened with him?"

"His religion. I'm essentially the spawn of Satan."

Krasinski looks at me, chewing his bottom lip. He throws his hands up and shakes his head, sighing. He says, "Not every God is a hurtful one, you know that, right?"

I nod. I feel bad for Lucius/Lawrence. It's not his fault. Is it?

"I'm not religious, per se, but I attend an Episcopal church and we don't believe that."

"Why attend if you're not religious?"

"I like the ritual. The staging. I like the vast space. I like the music, and I like the peace."

"It's like theatre," I say, and he nods, smiles.

"How are things at home?" he asks.

"They'll be better when I put on my play and raise the money for a seizure dog."

Krasinski gives me a high-five. "Good man. And how's my book report coming?"

I squirm in my seat. "Yeah. I'm reading it," I answer. "I mean I don't *get* a lot of the stuff—"

"What *do* you understand, Kirbenflakken?"

I tell him about the play asking a question, about the production embodying a memory, and he nods, proudly. He tells me to keep reading it.

Other kids wait outside his office, so he escorts me out, but before he does, he asks, "Who's playing you now that you are going to direct?"

I feel a strange fizz in my feet. "Jeez. I have a few ideas, but...any suggestions?"

"Cotter Wingham?"

"Oh. He's so...weird though? And he's too, like, funny?"

"And you don't think he's the perfect person to play you?"

"I saw myself as more...serious...in this play?"

"Don't," Krasinski says. "Don't shy away from humor. Ever."

I shrug. "I'll talk to him, I guess?"

Then: "Who's playing your little brother?"

I swallow. "I know it sounds crazy, but I was thinking of asking Mara Gecco."

"Good man. You'll need to be really patient with her," he says as he opens his office door. "But it will be worth it. You'll learn a lot. She's a wonder. She's going to bring something truly unique. Hop to it, Rentonfleister. Keep reading that book. I mean it."

The other kids from YOUTHEATRE sitting in the hallway give me stink-eye as I pass by. Word has gotten around that I am doing this play and the Santini twins are involved and now I guess they are jealous and hate me and want to stone me like the witches in *The Crucible* because they want to be a part of it, too.

COTTER WINGHAM

Cotter Wingham is a little dude with a big personality. He's brilliant at impersonations of people—he does voices and accents; he's so good it's almost creepy—and is at, like, *Who's Line Is It Anyway*-level genius when it comes to improvisation. We are in awe of him and also kinda can't stand him because he's way extra. I don't know him well, but, well, now's the time, I guess.

I know where he lives, so I go over after school to talk to him about my play.

He and his dad live in St. Charles Estates, the well-heeled hood of Weirville that everyone feels weird about because no one in Weirville ever thought there would need to be a well-heeled area, but as Pop always said, 'We're still in America.'

His dad, Cotter's told us, was a special effects and make-up guy in Los Angeles in the 80s and 90s. He worked on some famous horror movies, too. He tanked his life, though, because of drinking. I guess Cotter got stuck with him after his mom moved away? Cotter's dad takes care of one of the estates here, and they live in a carriage house at the back of the property.

Cotter answers the door wearing a backwards baseball cap, a loose-fitting black T-shirt that says *John Carpenter's THE THING*, with a guy in a snowsuit and bright light shooting out of his face, socks with red and green pizza slices on them, and purple high-tops.

He goes, "Whoa with this mint timing!" as if I am his best friend of all time. "Dad and I just got back from Grocer Ease and this place is Snack Shack Central! It's a Put-Your-Hunger-On-Ice Paradise! It's Stuff-Your-Face-Place! It's—"

"I think I got it," I say.

"Hub-for-the-Grub over here!" he says, pointing his thumb over his shoulder into his house. He steps outside and we sit on his stoop looking out at the big garden full of trees and plants and flowers. He tells me that he and his dad do all of it, the tilling and planting and pruning and landscaping.

"It looks really good," I say.

"Yeah," Cotter says. "It's good. I like to help him with it."

"That's cool."

"I mean, my dad should be on a movie set pumping gallons of fake blood through hidden tubes and wires to gush out some sad maniac's eye sockets, but that life is over and done with." Cotter shrugs and rolls an empty acorn shell back and forth along the stoop.

"So sorry. I mean, it's kind of a big switch." I finger the laces on my Vans, surprised that I actually feel bad for Cotter's dad whose questionable choices have led to the denial of fake blood pumps.

"Right? From prosthetics to plants." Cotter throws the acorn, dusts his hands. "So. Kirby Renton. The one and only Christopher Boone. What can I do ya for?" he says in a cowboy accent. "Thought you didn't lahk me, pardner."

I wince, and I feel my face make the wince, like a weird, twisty expression. "What? No. I mean, we don't know one another."

His phone dings and he flings it immediately up to his face, reads it, texts back in a fury.

"Who is it?"

"Aww, it's my girl, Tess."

"Oh. Tessa Sandoval? From school?"

"Yup."

I don't know her, but her mom died of breast cancer last year. Then a lot of wacko stuff happened, I heard. With her cat, a ghost, the goths, and also this guy Eddie Poffey. He's older than us, and kinda brain-damaged from a sports injury, and he disappeared after it all went down. No one really *knows* what had happened with Tess, and no one said anything about it either. I guess it's quietly legendary?

"Is Tess your girlfriend?" I ask.

"I don't know. Sort of. She's been on a road trip with her dad. They're in Mexico now. She sends me pictures she's been taking." He holds up the phone and shows us a selfie: Tess and her dad at the Grand Canyon. Her hair is longer than I remember, and her face seems brighter than it was in school. I'm not friends with her, but I feel bad for her. She's an only child, and I can't imagine what it must feel like for your parent to die. But I do feel like that, in my own way, because Pop abandoned us and disappeared.

"Um, I want to talk to you about a play I wrote that—"

"You want me to play the lead role," he says very seriously, placing his phone down.

"Oh. Uh, well, I mean, everyone in it has the same size—"

"Oh God," he groans, "Is it an *ensemble* piece?"

"Um."

He sighs dramatically. "I only consider projects where the story is one hundred percent about my character."

"What?"

"I have to be the guy the story is about. Or I don't do it."

"Oh. Uh. Well."

He starts cracking up. "I'm kidding! I'm imitating Leonardo DiCaprio. He said that to a director once. What a lunatic!"

I smile, wondering if maybe this was a bad idea....

Cotter says, "If you're doing a play with Ellie Abrams and Rockford Nakano-McKenna, I'm a thousand percent on board."

"Yeah. Do you love her, too?" Rats. I didn't mean to say that. My cheeks flush. I get fidgety. My foot starts going back and forth.

"Like *love* her? No, I have a girl (sort of). I think she's cool, that's all. She's so tall. And Rockford is like a lynx."

I nod. "Yeah. He is. She is. Yeah, they are." I suddenly feel this weird sense of pride that they're my besties.

"Tell me about the play," he says, then: "Wait! ChocoNutter?" he skitters inside and comes back with the whole box of them. "Love these things," he says, peeling away the noisy wrapper. While we eat our way-too chocolatey pucks, I tell him all about the play and why I wrote it. It's getting darker out by the minute, but the sky is so cool looking: it's purple, and black, and deep orange. Halloween colors. The garden back here gives off some rich smells and I can feel the millions of tiny hairs inside my nostrils come awake by a mixture of cucumber, orchids, apples, roses, something musky almost like a rotting animal, and the smell of Cotter's house, too.

I finish telling him everything.

He goes, "Whoa, so these lightning people are *real*?"

"I don't know because I can't see inside my brother's head, you know? When he's having a seizure? But…things have been happening, out in the world, that make me *feel* like it's real."

"Wow, really?"

"Anyway, the whole point is to raise money for a dog. Baxter needs a seizure alert dog."

"God," he says, very serious. "Seizure dogs. That is so…we are so lucky to be artists. We're truly the chosen ones, dude."

He stands up and shakes his head and walks around in a circle three times, his purple high-tops clopping against the deck. It's like he's in a daze, and then he lifts his hands and starts moving them around wildly. Like he's doing some alien sign language.

"Um. What are you—?"

"Auditioning to be one of the lightning people."

His 'audition' starts getting weirder and weirder, like he's starting to break dance or something. "Um. You can stop, Cotter. Rockford is playing the lightning people."

He stops and stares at me, then slowly pulls his hat off. "Huh," he says. "Rockford. I'm so jelly of that badass lynxdaddy."

"But you can be his understudy?"

He looks like I have just called him the worst name anyone could ever call another human being. "You want me to be an *understudy*?"

"No!" I say, "You're way too good for that."

"I thank you for acknowledging that as such."

I swallow. "Actually, um, I came here to ask you to play...well...*me.*"

His face drops. "*You?*"

My stomach twitches. I feel very little suddenly. "Yeah. Me. Kirby."

"But..."

"What?"

"You're so..."

"What."

"Basic."

I can feel my ears get hot and I hope it's not obvious. I hope he cannot see them all red and agitated. "That hurts, Cotter. Honest."

Cotter puts his hands up, as if to say, 'I'm innocent!' "I don't mean it as an insult, just as a fact."

I roll my eyes. "I'm not basic, you don't know me. I just blend in well. I kinda have to, you know?"

"Oh!" he jumps up. "Yes! Same here! The school counselor says it is a gift. A survival tactic. We're survivors."

"Good," I say. "We're warriors. We're theatre heroes."

"Kings, bruh."

I stand up. My stomach is twitching, my ears are on fire, my foot is fidgeting. I guess I didn't really know how weird and hard it would be to ask someone to be me in a play. It has me doubting this whole thing. It makes me feel like yelling at Lucius Beetlemeyer, Krasinski, Pop, and the lightning people, whoever they are. I sigh. "So, will you do it? I really need you."

"Can I make you a little more interesting?"

I tuck my chin down, 'cause it feels like my face is going to fall off my skull. "Um, sure," I say. "Make me more interesting."

"I already have some ideas—sit down and I'll tell you."

"Oh. No, not right now, but at our first rehearsal, okay? Can I email you the script in a little while?"

"Email? Are you twenty?"

"I can text it."

"Ugh, just e it. It's WinghamandBringem at me dot com."

"Got it. I'll email it. I'll text it, too, if you want."

"No, it's fine, Gramps. I *will* have thoughts," he says. "And I *will* tell you what they are."

I'm so tired suddenly. So tired. I nod, and he lifts his hand up for a high five. I can barely muster up the energy, but I do it, and then I trudge back home.

The sky is darkest blue, clouds to the west like lumpy blankets in your lap on movie night. Wow, movie night. We haven't had one of those for a while. Pop's the movie lover. He loves movies about musicians, singers, drummers, rock stars. Maybe that's because he always wanted to be one, deep down? He was in a rock band in Texas. Maybe he's in a new one now, who knows.

He loves *Sing Street*, and *The Runaways*, *Walk the Line*, and *The Doors*. Also, *Crazy Heart* and *Coal Miner's Daughter*. We watched all those movies with him. Well, I did anyway. Bax always fell asleep, and Dad would kinda wander away to his office because he would get inspired by the cool visuals.

I pull my phone from my pocket to check that he has been calling and texting regularly. He has. When I think about talking to him, I feel myself at the bottom of the rat pole, looking up, ready to climb to the top, where a crown of spikes has impaled a dozen rats, and their ratty blood drips down the pole, and I don't want anything to do with it.

I love Pop. I hate him. I love him and hate him. It never stops.

VIOLENT CHAIRS

Dad and Bax are eating some of Dad's famous Mac & Cheese, the kind with the breadcrumbs and bacon and Texas hot sauce. I could smell it as soon as I turned the corner onto our street. I scoop some into a bowl. The cheese is gooey and hot and stringy, and I sit down at the table and start eating. Bax yells at me for making gross noises but what can I do—I breathe when I eat, okay?

"You know it's your father's birthday Saturday, right?" Dad asks me.

I nod, eating. I feel completely annoyed with him. Not sure why.

"Do you plan on calling him or at least texting him?"

I shrug. A chunk of macaroni misses my mouth and plops onto the floor.

"Doofus," Bax yells. "Clean it up, slob-o."

I look at him. I have never heard the word 'slob-o' in my life.

"I was thinking of making a JibJab," Dad says. "They're funny. Want to do that?"

"I don't know," I say, "why—want to tell us what happened between you two?"

"No," he says. "I don't think you'll understand. I don't think you're mature enough."

I freeze, my body stiffened with anger. "You're a jerk. I'm fourteen. I'm mature. I have emotional intelligence. Ellie says so."

"Be that as it may," he says, pushing his glasses up on his face, "You're also not mature enough to not call your dad a jerk and not get grounded for it."

"You can't!" I say, standing up fast. The chair goes flying back and falls over.

Dad goes red. "If that chair, or the wall, are damaged, the cost to repair it comes out of your allowance."

I feel thunder booming in my stomach. "I have to do the play. I have to direct it now. You can't ground me—otherwise we can't do the play!"

Dad calmly places his fork down on the table beside his bowl. He raises his eyebrows at me, his face all pasty red. Then he says, "Do not yell at me. Calm down."

"I'm trying to *save* this family! Our other father abandoned us and disappeared—"

"Oh gosh golly, someone give this kid an Oscar," Dad says, leaning toward Bax.

I throw my hands up. "I can't stand you."

Bax looks at me, worried. "Stop it, Kirby." Then he looks at Dad. "Dad," he says quietly, "He has to do the play. Heddy's coming."

"Who's Heddy?" Dad asks, sounding very angry and annoyed.

"Our new dog," Bax says confidently, and goes back to eating.

Dad looks at me for a second. He throws his hands up, too. "We were having such a nice dinner!" He goes to the chair, picks it up, inspects it. He holds it up to me: I can see that I've left a bruise on one of the legs. Crap. He says, "I'll let you know the cost of that when I bring it to be repaired."

I leave the table and go upstairs. Jerk.

* * *

Ms. B from the Bogart book says that even shifting a chair on a stage is an act of violence. It is a violation against all other possibilities to decide where a piece of furniture is going to live, or even to set an actor's gesture or intention. Performers are heroes because they accept this violence and must bring fresh spontaneity to the art of repetition.

Wait, what?

My head starts to prickle when I think about all the 'violence' I have inflicted on the books on my shelves, the DVDs in the living room, the saucers, mugs, and glasses in the kitchen cabinets. The linen closet, the shed, the garage, the junk drawer, Krasinski's office. But, I wonder: is organizing things considered violent? I thought it was the opposite of violence. Okay, so, the performers are heroes for accepting this violence and working with it—does that make the directors the villains?

I hop over to my desk and email Cotter the play. I text Ellie and Rockford 'cause I miss them. I text Mel and Niccup to check on important stuff we need. I make a mental note: talk to Mara Gecco. I scroll through the texts Pop has sent, not reading them, just looking.

I do my seventeen hours of homework. Are these all acts of violence now? Wait—is *everything* a decision? See? I haven't even started directing yet and already my brains are totes explosion. They're gonna burst everywhere. All walls will be covered with big blotchy blood stains and dripping with little gooey chunks of brains. All walls everywhere. Walls and doors and all glass, too, bloodied and gooey'd with my brains.

Violence.

A DIRECTOR APPEARS

Krasinski is not here, at the house, for rehearsal. Rats. He had left me a 'packet' at school that has director-y things in it. I'm not freaking out so far. It's a nice Saturday, a perfect fall day for our first rehearsal, still a little warm, also a little cold. The leaves on the trees are changing colors but haven't fallen yet. The smell of pancakes and bacon drifts on the air because Dad made breakfast for everyone. Dad's breakfasts are fire. The man can make a pancake.

In the distance, we hear voices carried on the wind, from Weirville High's football game, the cheering, the hubbub. It sounds a little wobbly because of how it's riding the sound waves, and sometimes you can't tell what direction it's coming from, but the sound is comforting somehow. Bax is there, sitting somewhere in the bleachers with his friends. It is hard for us to let him go do normal things with his friends, because we are so scared that he is going to have a seizure, but how can we not let him go? We have a helmet that we want him to wear, especially when he is not with or around us. It's meant to keep him safe if he has a seizure and falls. He refuses. He thinks it looks dorky as hell. It does, but my plan is to find ME & MY SHADOW decals so he can stick them all over the helmet to make it cooler. The other thing we can do is make sure that whoever is with him knows what to do if he starts to seize. It makes my heart fizz thinking about it.

Speaking of fizz, Ellie's wearing her lime green Billie Eilish T-shirt, sitting in between Rockford and Mel. I look at her and my bones stretch. She smiles at me and gives me a thumbs up. We begin by sitting in a circle and introducing ourselves, even though we know one another already. It says to do this in Krasinski's packet, so I am going to follow it, even just to see what happens. Ellie, Rockford and Cotter all go first. Then Mel, and Niccup. Then someone named Bess, who Mel brought. She's a Stage Manager. A Senior. She's wearing maroon bell bottoms, black boots, an army jacket, a green wool skull cap, a lot of black eyeliner, and a deep scowl. I'm totes afraid of her.

She lifts a finger and whirls it around, saying, "Let's get this going, what is this—summer camp theatre for nine-year-olds?"

Oof. So I say, "Want marshmallows to toast with that attitude, Bess?"

Complete. Silence.

Oops.

Bess stands up and walks across the yard toward the house.

I stand, too: "Where are you going?"

"I don't have time for amateurs," she yells over her shoulder. "For little *marshmallows.*"

"Bess!" Mel yells after her. "Chill!" Mel looks at me. "You can't mouth off to her and get respect. She's not me."

"I thought I'd try," I shrug. I call after her, "Sorry!"

She stops, walks back to the circle, but refuses to sit.

We get to Mara Gecco. She's wearing a witchy-looking black dress that's too big for her, with bright red Vans. She stands and looks at everyone, but won't speak. Instead, she starts doing what looks like sign language, but is really her own language. We all look at her as her fingers and hands dance in the air. After a few minutes of this she embraces herself and says, "Full of such of the great," which I think means 'grateful'? She plops back down, drops her hands in her lap, and closes her eyes, joyous as a puppy.

Ellie looks at me, grins, shrugs.

I exhale.

The next item on Krasinski's list: a theatre game, uh, yikes. It is one we have played in class so it shouldn't be too weird, but I'm scared. I look at Rockford, whose hair is the longest I have ever seen it, a silky shard of it hanging in his face like a Manga character. He has that look on his face where I can never tell if he is absorbed or bored. I ask him to show us a few moves as a warmup. He cocks his head. I give him a scrunched-up face, eyebrows raised: 'Help me out, dawg, help me out!' tightening my grip on the paper in my hand so he can see I'm a little stuck.

He nods, hops up, whistles really loud (never heard him whistle) and starts gesturing with his hands, 'get up, get up.' The group hops up, everyone fixing and fussing and adjusting themselves like crazy and that's when I suddenly say, "Don't adjust yourselves," and everyone looks at me like I'm nuts. Did I just say that out loud? I clear my throat. "K. So. The platform is sacred," I say. "The stage is bigger than you, and when you step onto it, you need to rise to it and be like a warrior. When you fuss with your shirt, your hair, wring your hands, check your phone, look down at your feet, whatever, fuss fuss, then that means the focus is on *you,* on your insecurities, it's showing whoever is looking at you that you are concerned about your appearance or that you're scared to be in front of people. It shows fear. Don't do it."

I think the Bogart book and Krasinski's speeches have possessed me. Even though Krasinski never said this to me, and Ms B in the Bogart Book doesn't mention it either, it still makes sense. Maybe it was osmosis, like a mingling of their words of wisdom and my brains trying to process it all. And it's true. About the platform. But no one says a word. For, like, a minute. A really long minute. Ellie and Rockford give me encouraging nods. I see the rat pole peek out from behind the tree, like, 'Sup, you need me, bud?'

Cotter breaks the silence. "What if I have an itch? Like on my butt?"

"What if I have an urge?" I say, "To smack you upside the head?"

Everyone laughs. Whew. Cotter salutes me.

"What I mean is...can we start to think of this space as an elevated one?"

"Church," Mara chirps, and we look at her. She puts her hands together.

"Yeah," I say, "Like church."

Then I tell them everything: Dad and Pop, Bax's first seizures, the lightning people, the sketchbook and the symbols, the thistle, intersecting hourglasses, the pattern in the grass, and Heddy the dog. Afterwards, it's quiet.

Cotter blurts out, "Man, weirdness follows me everywhere!"

Everyone laughs again.

We continue then, with Roc showing us some moves.

I look up to see Krasinski on the deck. My heart thumps. How long has he been there? He said he wasn't coming. When he sees me spot him up there, he waves and comes down the steps and walks over to us on the taped-out section of the grass, an outline Mel and Nic made to show where the stage will be. He's wearing a thick maroon turtle-neck sweater and jeans with dark gray boat shoes. Pop used to call them the most heinous things on the planet, but Krasinski's are cool somehow. Everyone is in awe that our YOUTHEATRE god would stoop so low as to stop by my house on a Saturday. Mara stands up for him, then the others do, too.

Krasinski says, "Don't stand up for *me,* who am I, The King of Prussia? Sit down."

But everyone stays standing. Even Bess, who has her arms folded across her chest. She wears a big watch and looks at it and exhales like she's annoyed. *How dare this man come here and waste our time like this?*

Krasinski sits, and we all follow. Now he is in the circle with us. He smells like musky cinnamony powder, and it instantly relaxes me 'cause it smells like his office, and it smells like YOUTHEATRE. Pale orange leaves drift down from Ori's high branches, and we watch them as they settle on the grass all around us. Krasinski picks one up and turns it over in his hands, studying its veins and rivers. We watch this like he is a Marine Biologist caressing a starfish or something.

Rockford slides his script over and Krasinski shakes his head and gently slides it back. "No, Roc," he says, "Thanks, but I don't want to read it. I want to come see it when you get it up, I want to be completely surprised. Don't talk to me about it, don't tell me what it's about. Okay?" Everyone nods. "Don't tell anyone, in fact. Keep this to yourselves. When you talk about creative projects too much, you compromise their integrity. Does everyone know what I mean by that?"

"You give it away too early," Ellie says.

"Good, Ellie. Hold it close, like a secret. Let the anticipation of sharing it build and build in your hearts—except for Cotter Wingham, who has to hold it in his butt 'cause he doesn't have a heart." Everyone laughs.

Cotter says, "If I don't have a heart, it's because you stole it."

Everyone goes, "Awww."

Krasinski shakes his head, smiling. "I also just wanted to stop by and say that everyone who is volunteering their time to do this, to help Kirby and his brother, will receive extra credit from me, and that will bump your overall grade up."

Ellie and Roc high-five, Mara claps excitedly, Cotter stands and does the floss dance, and we all laugh.

"If you all write me a report, like a three-page report about your experience doing this, I will walk the reports down to Principal Washington's office herself and make sure her jaw drops, make sure she calls the local news station to interview you each on live television. Your parents will faint from pride."

"Not mine," Cotter says. "Dad's a ZOHMB."

Everyone laughs.

"No, but seriously," Krasinski says, placing the leaf down gently in the grass, "You mad little genius-freaks, I'm proud of you for taking this on. You want to know why?" He looks around the group, making eye contact with each of us: me, Ellie, Rockford, Cotter, Mara, Mel, Niccup, and Bess. "When you embody a play, and present it to a gathering, you are performing a service job. You are a citizen of the civil arena. You are, in your way, like a fireman, police officer, EMT worker, a schoolteacher, a nurse, a lawyer, a local politician." He looks at everyone. "Why is that?" He asks. "Why am I saying that?"

A fizz forms in my throat. "We're Storytellers," I say. "And people need stories."

"Right you are, Kirbackity Rentonfrackity. You young prodigies are Storytellers, and stories are deeply important. They inspire the brain to wake up and pay attention. They make the heart feel. They are responsible for our evolution as a species. Except for Mara here—no one knows where she's from or what she really wants."

Silence.

Cringe.

Mara stands up, looking hurt and angry. Then she drops the act and cracks up, makes a strange bleep-bloop noise and moves her arms like a robot. "Me Will Eat You Face," she says in a robot voice. Everyone laughs. Whew.

"I don't mean to scare anyone," he says. "I just want to convey that your choice to do art, to be an artist, even at a young age, even if you decide not to do this past high school, makes a difference, and it's precisely that difference that inspires change." Krasinski stands up and dusts himself off. "Does that make sense to everyone?" He looks around at us. "Yes? No?" Everyone kinda nods. "If it doesn't, say so. Ask questions. Always ask questions. It's how you learn." He looks into my eyes. "Kirby, let them ask you questions."

My knees feel shaky. I swallow, and nod. "Yeah," I say.

"Good."

I don't want him to go. Ever.

"One last thing," he says, "And this is more important than an Instagram influencer trying to sell you sunglasses that you don't need and that your parents can never afford."

Everyone chuckles.

"Have fun. If you stay present, stay in the moment, and breathe, you'll have fun. Nothing else matters. Enjoy this. That means you, too, Duchess Bess of the Scowls."

And she scowls. "Hey," she barks at him, "You started me on this crazy ass road when I was twelve. Look at me now—almost eighteen and an old hag. Stressed out because school is so hard and college next year and, like, now I'm stage managing a puppet play in someone's backyard?"

"Don't make me dogwalk you," Ellie says, and Bess goes red. Most people go red when Ellie pays them any kind of attention, good or bad. She looks over at me. My middle parts melt.

Krasinski cracks up. "Touché, Bess. I've made a monster out of ya, but I couldn't be prouder, kiddo. You're a wonder. But do me a favor: sail this ship here smoothly."

She swallows, looks down, like she might be feeling an actual emotion. She says, "Get lost, old man. I'll keep this ship of fools afloat."

As he's walking away across the grass, a shadow captures him, and he grows dark for a second. His form is a shadow, moving. Almost like one of Bax's 'sillyheads.' He looks back over his shoulder at me when the sunlight flashes through the leaves, when the light hits him again, and he winks at me. "How's my book report coming along?" I give a thumbs up, shake my head, grinning. Krasinski is one of the best things that has ever happened to us.

* * *

We warm up, playing a few rounds of some focus games we love: Pass the Clap, Splat Splat, Heads Shoulders Knees and Toes, Hop-to-the-Boop-Loop-Poop. Everyone is rowdy, which is good. I move us away from the fading pattern in the grass. I don't want it ruined.

We start rehearsing. I'm so nervous I can hardly breathe or get the words out. But, I do it. I do it. I *think* I'm doing it, anyway. I ask my actors (whoa, *my* actors) to play out the scenes the way they see them in their heads and in their bodies, and after I see them do it a few different ways, I just start to...mold it, I guess. Make it make more sense. The way I move colors to be in the order they need to be in, or should be in, or *want* to be in. Like that. But it's hard, 'cause my brains want everything a certain way, and so I try to focus on the leaves: they just fall where they fall and it's okay. Let leaves be leaves.

Mara and Ellie unravel the seizure scene, where Mara, as Baxter, moves with Ellie, the Seizure. They're figuring it out, it's a dance, and it's cool to see it interpreted, but it still forces parts of my body to feel frozen stuck in bed in the dark like when it really happens. I realize then how important it is to find some way to make other people feel that, too.

"Ellie," I say, and step toward her and Mara. "When you come out, from the bed, is there any way it can be, um, clearer that you're a part of Bax's brains, like...you are *him*, but also like you are something...else? Hmm. I don't...I mean, does that make sense?"

Ellie tilts her head, thinking, and she nods. She tucks her hair behind her ear, gently takes Mara by the shoulders, and ducks down behind her, then moves her body all up down around like she is coming out of Mara's head. She stops, shakes her head, laughs, tries something else.

"Ellie," I say, moving toward her again, "Can you change the position so that you're both in profile and we can...see you slide out from behind? Ha. Don't know what I'm asking...but I want to see it happen, if that makes sense." I'm just trying to be like Krasinski is with them in class, when they play John and Elizabeth Proctor.

Ellie and Mara shift their position and Ellie does this thing where she hides beside Mara. She shrinks down and nestles into her so that you can't see her at all. She slowly snakes out behind her, tries to make it look like she is coming out of her head, using her fingers, her hand, her arm, her whole body. Mara is a good sport, going with it and moving her body, but also looking at me like, What am I supposed to do here? I notice Mara's shoe is untied. PING.

"Mara," I say, "Tie your laces. Or, untie the other one, so they're the same, or take them off. Or...."

Everyone looks at me. Silence.

Bess suddenly hollers, "Three options, Robot Girl! Pick one and let's move it along!"

Mara ties the other one and nods emphatically.

I nod.

Ellie nods.

Everyone is nodding.

Ellie and Mara and the others continue working. I mouth 'Thank you' to Bess. She scowls and takes notes on her clipboard thingy. I exhale.

Whoa.

K, this is hard, but not having a seizure-alert dog will be harder.

* * *

We rehearse Saturday. We rehearse Sunday. I think it's working. I do everything I am supposed to be doing, like school, and homework. I think they want to kill us with homework, I'm not kidding. I'm reading The Bogart Book. Entire pages fly by in a blur, not sure what she is saying, sometimes it sounds bonks, but then she says she's discovered that theatre with no terror doesn't have any energy in it, and I am there. Terror is everywhere, especially in Bess's scowl.

Saturday was Pop's 45th.

Dad and Bax sang Happy Birthday to him on the phone. I shut the bedroom door and danced to "Kiwi" by Harry Styles, so I didn't have to hear. Bax misses him, so Dad brought us to WeirPie Pizza to make us feel better. Ellie joined us. I couldn't eat because her presence commands my attention and drives me up a rat pole, even in a pizza parlor. Bax ate his pizza like he did when he was five-years-old—peeling the cheese off in small pieces and putting it in his mouth—and it weirded me out. Why does it seem like he is growing younger?

I stared down at my slice of pizza, lost in thought. I ordered Sicilian. I like the thickness and the squareness. The bread and the cheese and the sauce and the pepperoni all work so well together. They belong together. It just works. Coffee and cream. Peanut butter and jelly. Melon and Tajin. But what if this play, what if all of it, doesn't work out the way we want it to?

STEVEN SANTINI

I go over to the Santini's place so I can talk to them about the set. Their driveway is long and muddy, and the giant pines have dropped their cones all over. Looking out the window down at the ground I see them scattered about like gnomes, little hard-scaled creatures felled but proud. Bax loves pinecones. "Bax, look," I say, but he's drawing ME & MY SHADOW characters in his sketchbook. He hides the thing in places he knows I will never find it now.

Today he is wearing orange pants and a purple Pokémon T-shirt with one of Pop's old green Carhartt baseball caps that smells sour 'cause he wore them when he lifted weights in the garage. Also, he smells like chemicals, as if the medicine he takes for his seizures is leaking through his pores. "I'll grab some pinecones for you," I say. Dad maneuvers the car to not run any of them over, but a few cones get caught under the wheels, and it makes a very intense crunching sound. Dad says he'll come pick me up later—he's gonna grab the special bed his friend Brian made for Bax.

"Is he your new boyfriend?" I say as I close the door to the Subaru.

"Kirby," Dad says, "Why on earth would you say something like that? Brian is my co-worker and married. Why would he be my new boyfriend?"

I shrug.

"Enough with the shrugging and rolling your eyes all the time." His face is redder than a Red Vine.

I shrug again and roll my eyes and close the door gently, and it's not enough to close it, and I know it, but I walk away. I hear him calling me through the glass, but I ignore him. As I walk up the lawn to the Santini house he gets out of the driver side, walks around the car to the passenger side, opens the door that I didn't close enough and slams it.

I look back at him standing in his dark green corduroys and faded caramel-brown Clark's that Pop used to say made him look like a Joshua Tree hippie, black turtleneck with the faded Cowboy Junkies T-shirt underneath, pushing his glasses up his nose as he glares at my back. His hair is long now, messy, his beard flecked with more gray each day.

I wish it were easier, the way it used to be, but this is how it is now with Dad. Good days where I love him so much, I want to just hug him and cry my eyes out and other days where I could go to jail for getting rid of him forever. Sometimes it switches back and forth, like in the same minute. This is the way it is now. It's Rat Pole City for me and Dad.

Mel and Niccup bring me down to their basement. The walls are wood paneled like a movie from the 1970s and a musty, sweet-sour smell fills the air, like apple pie and socks. Tables and chairs line the space, and on top of them stand dozens of tiny little models made from thick paper, some from foamboard, others from wood of amazing sets that their Dad built back in the day. Little worlds.

They have a pool table, too, covered with blueprints and sketches of how they want to design the play, and it intimidates me, like can't we staple some construction paper to a board or something?

"It's not *that* complicated," Mel says. Today she wears jeans and a pink and gray button-down shirt with a necklace and earrings. I think she has blush on her cheeks, but I can't picture her dusting her cheeks with colored powder. "We want the bed to move up and down and we can make that happen, and then we need hidden compartments in the beds, and under the stage, and that can happen, too. Also—"

"But how?" I ask. "How do we that?"

"Steven," Niccup says. "Steven!" he yells out.

"Who's Steven?" I ask.

The door to the basement creaks open and a man clomps down the stairs in brown furry slippers, jeans, a Led Zeppelin T-shirt, a beard down to his neck, an earring in one of his ears, his hair black and silver, and rings on almost every finger. He looks like one of the Hells Angels and Gandalf. He approaches me, thrusts his hand out, and smiles. "It's very nice to meet you, Kirby." He smells like shaving cream, which is weird 'cause he's so hairy, and cedar chips, the kind Dad puts in his plastic cases to keep moths out of his sweaters.

His voice is melting butter. No, hot maple syrup poured over melting butter. I immediately feel the same sensation that I felt when Baxter's teacher, Devika, the one who had the thistle in her bouquet, came near me. "I decided to come out of retirement and help my kids navigate this vessel."

"Wow. Thank you, sir," I say, "But—"

"You know I lost a friend to epilepsy when I was a teenager?"

No one speaks. My heart rabbits in my chest. I do not want that to happen to me, too.

"He had a seizure while he was driving. Went off the road and didn't survive it."

"I'm so sorry," I say. An ice-cold shudder rushes through my bones and veins thinking about all the ways Baxter could die or get hurt because of his seizures.

"The night I read your play, I had a weird dream about him. Showed up in the barn out there in this orb of purple light, and...well, here we are."

I swallow a lump in my throat. I feel dizzy. We walk over to the pool table and Steven runs his hand over one of the blueprints. He explains the way 'we're' going to do this. He keeps saying 'we' like we're all a family or something. I try to pay attention, but I'm distracted. I pretty much understand set construction and theatre effects, but this is complicated.

When we're done, we go upstairs for more cider and while Mel and Niccup heat it in the kitchen, I mosey down the hallway looking at all the framed pictures on the wall of all the shows that Steven designed and built back in the 80s and 90s. My favorite one is for *The Glass Menagerie* by

Tennessee Williams. This is the one Mel and Nic had told me about. The set he made for it is a gigantic piece of glass shaped like a unicorn, and the world of the play, the living room, is *inside* the glass unicorn. Wait, what?

Two framed pictures: one has the unicorn's horn jutting out, like a balcony. The other picture has no horn, because it has broken off and lies in a heap of shattered glass at the bottom of the stage beside the rest of the 'house.' The actors and crew sit on and stand around a couch on the set, all of them smiling, and they look so little, so you can tell how big the glass unicorn was. This play is so sad, it makes me feel so sad when kids from YOUTHEATRE do the scene where Laura meets The Gentleman Caller and the fight her brother Tom has with their mom afterward.

Mr. Santini comes down the hall, hands in his pockets. I point to the picture, and he chuckles.

"Won my first Jeff for that," he says.

"What?"

"Jeff Awards, Chicago. I won for that set there."

"Is it real glass?"

"Some of it. The rest is an illusion. Which is kinda the point. You know?"

I nod, all serious, like I'm some theatre set-design critic able to hand out Jeff Awards.

"We wanted it to be all glass," he says, "but it was cost prohibitive."

"Um," I say, "About *that*. This set and these things you—uh, we—want to do are—"

"Everything we need to put this up, I have out in that barn. And after that dream, I know it has to be done."

I feel a weight lift off my shoulders. I'm so light I could fly away. "Thanks."

"Theatre is bananas," he says. "The most extraordinary people come together to do the most ultraordinary things. Been in awe of it my whole life and not about to turn my back on it now."

I nod, feeling scared and grateful and excited.

"Listen," he says. "I can help, a little, but this is all on Mel and Nic. This is their thing. So, let them take the reins on this stuff, and I'll shadow from the sidelines. If they need me. Okay? This is on you, Kirby. Being a director, being in the theatre, it's a serious thing."

I feel the chills spill down my back, but at least they're warm chills, not cold ones. I nod, again. I mean I know *nodding* is definitely 'my thing' but I don't know about all this other stuff.

Mel and Niccup come down the hall and hand me a mug of cider. It has cinnamon sprinkled on top. That reminds me of Krasinski, and I grin. I take it in my hands and blow on it, looking at more of their pictures. One of them, near the end of the hallway, is of the twins when they were little. They're at a lake, in a canoe, wearing bright orange life-vests, smiling. Their dad sits beside them, his arms around them both. Behind them sits a pretty woman with long black hair and bright beautiful eyes. I can tell she is their mom because Mel and Nick have the same exact eyes. Steven is thinner, with only a mustache.

"Your mom?" I say.

"I don't know, is it?" Mel asks, all snarky.

"That's Mom!" Niccup says. "We haven't seen her in—"

"She's an important *actress*," Mel butts in.

"Oh," I say. "Wow. I didn't know that."

"She's so essential to the *craft*, she had to move all the way to *London.* Where *real* actors live, according to her."

"She has a new husband now. He was on that show!" Niccup says.

"What show?" I ask.

"About the angel detectives in the sky and the demon detectives in the ground."

"Don't know that one, I guess." I wonder what it feels like to have a mom who lives in London and who has a famous boyfriend. Does he sound like Daniel Craig when he speaks?

"So, you don't talk to her?" I think of Pop, and a spider runs across my heart.

Mel scoffs. "We *try.* But she's still mad at my dad for falling off a forklift twelve years ago and injuring his back. She's mad at him for how it ended his career, as if it was his fault that the forklift malfunctioned."

"Yikes," I say. I nod. Again.

"She's a turd," Mel says. "Like, imagine if a turd was pretty, important, and talented. A pretty important talented turd. That's mom. I call her 'Turd Streep.'"

"I love her a lot," Niccup says. "But yeah—she's kinda a turd, I guess."

Mel says, "She has this faux British accent now when she calls us. It helps her get roles."

We sip our cider for a minute, and Mel asks, "Where's *your* mom? You have one?"

"We came from a surrogate," I say. "But she didn't want to be in our lives like that." I've always felt like people expect me to be sad about this, but I never have been.

"Oh. Okay. Do you *wish* you had a mom?" she asks.

Not having a mom is the most normal thing in the world for me. I don't feel anything about it. I sometimes think about that drawing that Dustin Brisco did of my mom as a witch. But my brains and body don't fizz about this. "No. Why?" I ask, "Do you wish you had two dads?"

"That would be way too intense. Two dudes? Ugh."

"It's not. It's normal." Kinda relieved she didn't say something idiotic this time. "I know normal is a tough concept for you."

"Har har," she says, and sips her cider.

I hear Dad's horn honk outside. He's back. I blink, placing my mug down.

"Mel," I say, and her eyes dart over to me, strange in her pink-dusted cheeks. "Glad we're doing this. Glad we're becoming friends."

She frowns. She's too cool for that. But I see a gleam in her eyes. I think she's glad, too.

APPLICATION LETTER

After I get home, I snuggle into Dad's computer chair, and open the website for seizure dogs. There is so much information, it makes my brains itch. The page with 'Personal Seizure Dog Stories' is my favorite. Epileptics who have been living with seizure dogs talk about their experiences, and the pictures with the dogs are comforting. Also, scary. What if Heddy doesn't smell Baxter's seizures before he has them? What if she doesn't wiggle underneath him to create a pillow? What if we're not around or she can't find us to alert us? What if Pop comes back and we don't love him like we used to and then he feels sad and leaves again? What if Pop comes back and Heddy falls for him and then he leaves again because we love him less—will she be sad and not do her duties? What if once you lose love for someone you can't ever get it back?

Um. What am I thinking about? What is my brain doing? I am going to back away slowly from the bottom of the rat pole now. I see them up there, wriggling and dripping.

I open the page with the application. Holy Batman-slaps-Robin, so many questions. I'm going to fill out as much information as I possibly can: name, address, phone numbers, level of epilepsy severity (huh?), history of epileptic episodes, health insurance provider info, member info, group #, and an empty box that says, 'Please tell us why you are seeking a Service Animal.'

I blink. I feel a buzz in my fingertips. I scoot the chair in. I start to type.

Greetings, SeizurePeeps and DoggoTrainers. My name is Kirby Daniel Renton and my little brother Baxter (he'll be 11 soon) started having seizures after our Pop abandoned us and disappeared. His seizures are scary, and Doctor-of-Brains, our Neurologist, Joseph Seitz, told us they are tonic-clonic seizures, which are the wickedest kind. I help Baxter late at night when he has seizures. I make sure he doesn't fall out of bed and hurt his head, but sometimes I don't always get there in time if his seizure sounds don't wake me up. Baxter told me he sees The Lighting People during his seizures. They are mysterious beings that slither down from the clouds into a wide-open field and show him symbols. These symbols have made their way into our own world somehow, and now I am putting up a play in our backyard about all of this to raise money for your organization so we can have a seizure dog. We don't have $50,000 to buy one. By the way, that's boujee for a pooch. I'm in a theatre troupe at school that's totes-soops, so don't worry, the play is fire. I wrote it and will also direct it, too since my original director quit because his religion doesn't allow him to be around or accept people like me and my brother because we have two dads. I hope Seizure Dog organizations aren't like that, too. Baxter already knows the dog's name, it's Heddy, she's a girl. What breed? Don't know. I hope it's either a German Shepherd, a Golden Retriever, a Labrador Retriever, a Chocolate Lab, or a Dachshund. Are wiener dogs seizure dogs? That would rule. We live in Weirville. I think that's all you need to know. Thanks for reading this, now get back to training the magic seizure puppos. No matter what happens, I'm getting our family that dog. See you soon. From, KDR1.

I press 'Save Application' and it makes me create an account and saves my place. There is more to fill out, but I have nineteen hours of homework now. I drop my hands into my lap and look at Dad's desk. He has been doing a big job for a big client lately and his Pantone color sample books lie across his desk in a (somewhat organized) mess. The Pantone booklets have thousands of color swatches and are fanned out, showing almost all the colors. My brain fizzes and it's a thick burbly fizz. I rearrange everything colorbetically. If Dad had this set up in a way he needed it for work, he's not going to be happy when he comes in here. My face flushes hot with this realization, so I tip-toe out of his office and sneak up the stairs, avoiding the fourth step, which creaks when you put your weight on it.

I can't focus on my math homework.

I can't focus on my science homework.

I can't focus on my English homework.

I can't focus on any of this.

I grab the Bogart Book instead, and it feels like an old friend in my hands.

Ms. B says that directing is intuitive. It's about feelings and being in the room with actors, designers, and audiences. She says directing is not about control and making people bend to your ideas. I've never seen Krasinski be a bully, but I've seen him get frustrated with what he calls 'spoiled potential', but he says it mostly to the kids who don't try. Some of the kids in YOUTHEATRE are there because they don't know where else to go, or where they fit in.

They mostly want to watch stuff happening, scenes and theatre games and stuff, from a distance. They are too scared to participate because the thing is: it takes guts to go up on a stage. Sometimes I wonder what I would be like if I was one of them, sitting in the back and watching everything, feeling safe but scared. Would it make me feel better? I guess it's not worth thinking about it because I am not one of those kids. But, I guess I could be?

* * *

In the morning, I join Dad and Bax at the kitchen island. The house smells like breakfast, and the laundry tumbles in the dryer. The vent is on the side of the house, and the wind blows the dryer steam back in sometimes. Dad's eating sourdough toast with apricot jam and Bax has scrambled eggs with loads of ketchup. It looks like something died on his plate. I loathe eggs. I don't like their sliminess and their yellowness and their gooeyness. I don't like what happens to them after you crack the egg open. I like the egg, the outer part, the shell, the shape. But once you crack it open, I'll be scrambling very far away from them. Bax waves at me from his island stool, which is weird. He's not a waver. His sleepy eye looks droopier.

Dad asks how rehearsals are going.

We've decided to premiere the play the second weekend of October, which is about two and a half weeks away. The weather should still be okay. It's been warm. Our teachers say that the solstices and equinoxes are changing. But even if it gets colder, the Santinis have those heaters we can place in the aisles for the audience.

"I need to make the postcard, Dad," I say. "Will you show me how on the computer?"

We walk into his office and my face goes red when I see Dad has rearranged his Pantone booklets to how they were before I rearranged them colorbetically. Also, I can see on his computer screen that the window for the seizure dog application is still open. He has shifted it out of the way a bit for his graphic design software, but it's there. I swallow. I forgot to close it.

Dad sits down at the computer, sniffles, and swipes his robe across his face.

"Are you crying?" I ask him.

"It's nothing," he says, then sobs. "You've been so cruel to me lately and—

"Dad—"

"—I don't blame you, we're going through a rough time, but Jesus, you have a mean streak."

"Dad, I—"

"You're *way* more like me than I ever could've imagined," he says. He studies me, his eyes puffy and waxy, the green of them as bright as emeralds.

"You're not mean, Dad."

"Oh, you didn't know me before Pop came along. Pop, and then you two boys." He starts crying again. "And," he says, "I read what you wrote in your seizure dog application. It broke my heart. I mean, in a good way." He sniffles.

"Why?" I ask. "It wasn't sad. I mean, I was just...aww man, I don't know."

"I read it and I..." He drops his head into his hands.

"Dad, you know what, maybe don't read my stuff—"

"—It was truthful, Kirby. That's your gift. You're truthful. You're expressive. You're real. You're strong." He puts his hand on my cheek, tears streaming down his face. His hand is warm, kinda clammy. He smells like powder, coffee, and toast. He shows me what I need to do to make the postcard and directs me to a series of YouTube video tutorials where people show you how to do things. Sniffling and sighing, he gets up and leaves the room.

I watch him go.

I turn back to the screen and get to work.

I want the words to hover across the sky in a cool font, one of my Dad's fonts (they're patented, bruh) and beneath that, puffy cumulonimbus clouds full of lightning floating over a wide-open field at dusk. In the lower left corner, I want an outdoor stage with a big tree beside it. Quing Ori. I hop to it. Whoa. This Adobe software is not easy, at all, it's confusing, but the videos are helpful. I'll figure this out.

When I go back to the kitchen, Bax is staring out the window at the yard, hands in his lap, quiet. I walk to the window and look out. I see wind rustling through Ori's leaves. The Santini twins are hard at work on the world they're building back there. I turn and look at Bax. Is he growing younger rather than older? I see it. Is this what epilepsy really is? Each seizure jolts you back a few years, until you're a baby again, until you're whatever you were *before* you were a baby. Maybe that's who the lightning people are—here to take him home. To take all of us back to what we were before we were here.

I walk over and put my arm around Bax.

He snuggles into me.

EMBARRASSED

Mara and Cotter are not getting along the last few days, I don't know why, because since we started this whole thing, they've become super close. No one knew Mara could even laugh, let alone that she had a cackle. Now they're fighting? What happened? She likes him, maybe? And he said he has a girlfriend already, and she got mad because he told her that after he kissed her, maybe? I hope not, though.

In the upstage right area of the stage, Rockford is showing Ellie how to do a Dolphin Dive into a Rise Up because it's part of their dance as The Seizure and The Lighting People. He also helps her with her Death Drops and Dips, which they incorporated into their dances because they both love *Drag Race* so much. He keeps, like, adjusting her legs and thighs. Her CHVRCHES T-shirt keeps lifting when she's upside down, and when he touches her stomach to fix it, my middle parts fizz like Mentos in a bottle of Coke. Roc's hair is sky blue. He looks so BTS.

My insides snap and I fly up suddenly. "Let's take a break!"

Bess, who's upstage left with Niccup working out issues with the invisible wall (of glass) whips her head around, mashes her hands onto her hips as she stomps downstage, her very overloaded toolbelt jangling and clanking against her black jeans.

"Excuse me," she says, "But what did you just say."

I freeze. Uh-oh. This is gonna be bad.

"I call the breaks around here!" she snaps. "And we have another..." she whips her arm to her face to look at her watch, "...Twenty-five minutes. What's going on with you down there in the director pit that you suddenly need a *break*?" She says 'break' as if it's death by fire.

"Sorry," I say, and throw my hands up in a gesture of surrender. "Sorry, Bess. I meant me. Me. Just me. I need to pee. Sorry. I'll be back."

"That's what I thought," she says. As she turns and heads back upstage, she looks over her shoulder, "Try to keep it together, director boy. My aunt's a therapist if you need someone to talk to."

I...can only nod. I'm...very afraid.

Ellie intersects her as she's walking back upstage and says, "Someone toss me a leash. This canine needs some air."

"Shut up, Nicole," Bess says, and I scoff. What? Does she not know that Ellie's name is not Nicole? I die. Mara wriggles herself between them, gently nudging Ellie and Bess away.

I yell from the deck, "Don't kill one another! Back in a few minutes!"

The sun is descending behind me, out in front of the house, and the yard comes alive with shadows and golden light. When they all look over at me, they shield their eyes from the glare, and seeing them across the yard in the gilded light with their hands held up standing on the stage we made in my backyard is cool and weird. I fumble for my phone and snap a photo. It's otherworldly. You only see the light, and they are 'sillyheads.'

Down in the basement we have a closet full of old clothes, stuff to be donated, things Pop and Dad are storing. It's a mess, but on purpose—it's for my magic. I start by moving the objects around. Old shoes come first, so I arrange them by color, then type, then size, then by style. On the next shelf, kitchen stuff, mostly old utensils, and cooking tools. I arrange those by size and by which of them has a large protrusion at one end but a skinny one at the other. The fizziness starts to fade, Ellie's body fades, and something I read in the Bogart Book comes to mind.

Ms. B talks about embarrassment. She says that your work should embarrass you. You should feel afraid of what you're doing and how you're doing it because it exposes you and opens you and makes you and the process vulnerable. I don't think she means it in the same way as the kind of embarrassment I just felt from Bess yelling at me in front of my cast and crew and making me feel stupid, but maybe? Maybe there are all kinds of embarrassments, and we should feel them all? A spectrum of embarrassments?

When Baxter has a seizure in our room at night, I feel embarrassed for the noises he makes, the garbled drooly yelping and the moans. Doctor-of-Brains says it's his mind trying to put itself back together again after its inner explosion, so that's why the 'words' sound backwards and sideways and upside down. I feel embarrassed when he wets the bed and I clean it up and change the bed clothes. I feel embarrassed if he bites his tongue and bleeds, and dried blood stains appear on his lips and cheeks. I feel embarrassed, but I don't understand what *I* have to do with any of this.

When we lived in Texas the kids used to yell, "Aren't you *embarrassed* you have two fathers?" Was I supposed to have been? This is probably not the same kind of embarrassment that Ms. B is talking about...but this weird idea forms in my head. I finish arranging the bottom shelf, which has plant pots that smell like chemical fertilizer and soil. I've arranged them by size but out from the middle: biggest in the center, getting smaller as they spill toward the ends. My hands feel icky from the dust of the storage closet, so I hurry to the sink next to the washing machine and wash them off. The soap down here is a pump and it globs out all foamy.

I run back upstairs and head outside. It's darker now, and we need to finish soon so we can all go and do our nineteen thousand hours of homework. Roc and Ell are sitting close together on the edge of the stage looking at their phones. He touches her hair. I breathe through my teeth. Bess and Niccup are still working on the glass wall upstage, cleaning it with Windex and it squeaks as they rub paper towels across it. It needs to be crystal clear so that you can't see it from the audience. I walk up to Mara and Cotter, and I say, "Can we try something?" but neither of them responds. They look at me. "Are you two okay?" Mara does some weird hand gesture, like a karate chop that becomes a sewing needle pulling thread through yarn. Cotter nods as if he understands her completely. Huh?

"I need to put a new scene in the play," I say.

"Now?" Cotter says.

"Yeah. It's a pee scene. I want it in the play."

Cotter scrunches up his face. "A *pee* scene?"

"Yes."

Cotter throws his hands up, confused. "What's a *pee* scene?"

Everyone else looks over, curious. I start to actually feel embarrassed. "When Baxter has seizures in the night, he wets himself, and I want to show it." The others seem uncomfortable and confused, looking away, fiddling with things, wanting to understand.

Cotter scratches his head. "How? Like, Mara is gonna pee on me?"

Mara hops up, as if she's ready to try it right now.

"And you're going to clean it up."

"Whuut? Why me? Why pee?"

"Because it's embarrassing, and I want the audience to feel that."

"But what does *embarrassment* have to do with anything?"

"Ms. B says it has to do with everything," I say.

"Who's Ms. B?"

Everyone stares at me, waiting for me to explain. I sigh.

Bess barks, "Liquid! On this stage! We have to plan for that! It can't get near the effects! It'll short out the beds!"

"Someone should short you out," Ellie says.

"You're out of line, Anders!"

"Abrams. It's Ellie Abrams. Not Nicole Anders, but thanks."

"Whoever you are, you're still out of line!"

Mel is up inside Ori's branches hanging lights and I call her down. She scrambles down the tree's limbs to us and when she hops off the lowest bough onto the stage, leaves and twigs scatter everywhere. Her hair is messed up. She brushes off her overalls and adjusts her toolbelt. I ask her if there is a way for us to show pee, safely, and she scratches her chin and says, "We could use tubes, yeah. How much? Like a few?"

"No. A lot," I say. "I want it to gush."

Bess says, "I didn't sign up for pee!"

"I'm allowed to add things and take things away. It's my script. It's my play."

"Well, yeah, but—"

"Don't worry, Bess," I say. "You can talk to your aunt if you're too upset about it."

She stomps away.

Ellie is looking at me strangely. They all are. They don't know what this means or why I'm doing it. The truth is...maybe I'm not understanding Ms. B. But, I want this feeling—whatever it is, I don't know how to explain it—in the play, and that's all I know.

HEART YOLK

After I finish my forty days and forty nights of homework, I rummage through my bag to find my phone. I've been leaving it off lately, it's too much to deal with. Social media makes my brains hurt. I can't even open it anymore. There are voicemails from Pop, and a weird text from Baxter using Dad's phone: an eye emoji, a crescent moon, and a U. "I see you." Why would he text this?

I Google Ms. B.

Wait, what? She looks exactly like Mrs. Abbe, my old music teacher from Texas! She played piano and lived on a ranch with three horses that she loved so much. She was a champion rider, too. She wore oversized flannel shirts with long denim or wool skirts and other kids made fun of her for it, but I loved her because she said I had the voice of an angel. For every fall, Christmas, and spring concert, she always gave me a solo. I never really got to say goodbye to her. A slither of sadness snakes through my heart. Mrs. Abbe is responsible for me getting into theatre. And Ms. B looks just like her? Chills spill down my neck.

Suddenly, I'm texting Ellie: 'Do you love Rockford?' I don't send it. Then my thumb just jerks suddenly—TAP—and it's done. Aww, crap. See? I hate the phone!

A minute later it's ringing. She wants to Facetime? I dart into the bathroom for a second, shove my hand through my hair and rustle it, make sure my teeth don't have leftover bits of dinner in them. Then I smell my armpits which is dumb, 'cause she's not gonna be able to smell me. Anyway, they smell bad. Great.

I grab the black glass, and tap and flick.

"Sorry," she says, "I thought it'd be easier to Face."

She's wearing her purple hoodie, pulled up onto her head. Her auburn hair spills out the sides. She's in her room, on her bed, I can see her Duran Duran and CHVRCHES posters behind her on the wall. "You look cute," she says. "Your hair is all messy."

"Naw, I was just doing homework."

"Your voice sounds deeper."

"When the moon comes out, Imma wolf."

She laughs. "I can see it on your face. You might have to shave soon."

Silence. This was a bad idea, maybe. What am I doing? I want to hang up.

"So, um," she says, "I think we're just trying to figure stuff out."

"What stuff?" My heart is pounding, but why? Ellie is my best friend—why do I like her? I don't want this.

"Like, who we like and why and, um, *stuff.*"

"What 'stuff' though?"

"I might like girls, too, and he might like boys, and we're...supporting one another through it, you know? We don't exactly know. But that's okay."

I feel the little pointy-tipped pin slip into my belly. I clear my throat, I feel all phlegmy. I plop down onto Baxter's bed. I'm not sure why. "How come you didn't talk to me about this?"

She sighs. "I mean, Kirbz, your life is...I want you to be okay and I feel really protective of you and I'm just, like, by your side watching you go through all of this and—"

"But I want you by my side all the time. *All* the time. Do you know what I'm saying?"

She stands up, the screen image gets all jiggly and wobbly as she walks across her room and sits at her desk. Behind her, I can see out her bedroom window, where a willow tree's leaves flow like a green waterfall in the light of the streetlamp. The light dances between the leaves, it looks like some Insta filter, but it is real life. She says, "I know you do, Kirbz. But I don't...have feelings like that for you."

My stomach drops out of my body.

"I'm hanging with Mel, and—"

My intestines drop out of my butt. "Wait, what?"

"I know, I know," she says. "No one knows. But oh my God, Kirby. She came for me so hard after that day at the theatre barn, and you know what? She's cool and I kinda unexpectedly have weird feelings for her...but also I don't think we're soops compats 'cause she's really into, like, tool belts and stage lights and, um, different kinds of woods. And I'm into dance, and music, and clothes, and animals. But. I don't know. I don't know."

"Ellie."

"I wanted to talk to you, about all of this, but Kirbz, you're miles away from us."

"Huh?" My stomach and intestines that just dropped out of my butt start crawling across the floor away from me.

She doesn't say anything for the longest time. I can hear her breathing. Then: "Kirbz, you were already way ahead of the rest of us...I mean, c'mon. With your awesome dads and getting cast as Christopher and winning that big award last year. Now the separation, the seizures, the lightning people, the play, writing it, *directing* it. It's...like you exist in another dimension from us or something."

My heart cracks open like an egg. I feel the heart-yolk seeping out, warm and gooey, dripping down onto my ribs. I drop my head onto my chest. I feel so alone suddenly. A dark-gray ice-shadow of loneliness comes into the room and sits on the bed with me and wraps its hands around my throat, smiling while it squeezes.

"But you have stuff like that, too," I say. "Your dancing. The way everyone worships you. What does that have to do with *us*?"

"It's not a bad thing, Kirbz. It's not. It's just who you are. And when it comes to me? I mean, I hear you, yeah, but I'm a *girl.*"

"So?"

She sighs. "It's just different. It's different when you're a girl. Everything is...different."

"How?"

"It just is."

"Yeah but how?"

"'Cause we have to do, and be, and feel everything."

It's quiet for a minute.

"I love you," I say. My tongue turns to cement.

"I don't love you," Ellie says. Now the rest of my body falls out of me—heart, lungs, liver—and I am hollow, the crumpled shed skin of a reptile. "Like that, I mean. I love you as my forever best friend who I want to spend my life with, but not like as a future husband or anything."

My brain is just puzzle pieces. I rotate in space like an astronaut whose tether broke from the space station. I have this vision of her cuddling on a couch with Mel—who smells like WD40 and wood shavings and wears dirty baggy overalls. I see them laughing, and Mel touching her face, and a fizzy stream rushes up inside me, wanting to explode out the top of my head. Suddenly Mel turns into Rockford, and then Niccup, and then Cotter, too. Who's next—Mara? Yup, there she is, caressing Ellie's face. What the hell. Everyone gets to touch her except for me. What am I supposed to do with this?

The heart-yolk drips gooey and thick down onto my ribs, the only thing left in my body.

YOU CAN'T HAVE HIM

I wake up. In the darkness, I am hollow, with no heart or guts or anything else. I am miles away, just like Ellie said. I hear a weird noise. It's 4:04am. It's a rattling, a clanging. I toss the blankets off—it's freezing—I forgot to close the window in our bedroom because I pulled the shades down when I was doing my homework because the moon (Dad called it the Harvest Moon) was so big and so bright, it was distracting me as I sat at my desk. I go to the window and peer into the yard. The moon is still there, lower in the sky and still as bright. Clouds are passing over it, and it reminds me of a scene from a Halloween movie. I feel haunted by the conversation with Ellie from earlier. I place my hand on my chest. There is nothing there. It hurts so bad.

Clang, clang, clang. Is it coming from out there near Ori, near the stage? Maybe it's one of the lights Mel and Niccup hung in the trees clanging in the wind? I hear it again, and it is louder. It startles me and I gasp.

I turn around and walk over to Baxter's side of the room. The bed he sleeps in now, the special bed that Dad's friend Brian made us, keeps Baxter safe because it's like a crib but not for a baby. Bax calls it his 'bird prison'. I flick the overhead light on. He has rolled up against it and his body is shuddering, jerking against the wooden bars. That's the noise I hear, but it sounded like it was coming from out in the yard. Why? I can't tell if this is a seizure, or something else. I reach in and gently turn him onto his side, resting a hand on him to keep him still. His eyes are closed but his lids are fluttering. His eyeballs are pulsing, jumping, under his lids. I swallow. My heart begins thumping.

"Bax," I say quietly, trying to wake him, and for a second his eyes stop pulsating, but only for a moment before they start up again and his body starts to quiver. He is sweating, badly, I can see droplets of it all over his forehead. His Captain America PJs are soaked. I put my hand on his forehead—he is burning up, oh my God oh my God. I try to nudge him awake, but he won't wake up. Are they standing out in the field right now, hooded black shapes floating above the fog, shimmering in the purple light, showing my little brother their symbols? Why can't I go with him when he has seizures? Why can't I go? *Let me go there.*

I hear a thump from down the hall, from Dad's room. It startles me. I hear him shuffle across his room into his bathroom. He starts coughing, and wowza, that sounds bad. Really bad. Oh no. Is he sick? Is Bax sick, too? Bax seems to have calmed down a bit, I think he has fallen back into sleep. I watch him for a few minutes to make sure, then leave our room and go down the hallway and open Dad's door. I find him sitting on the toilet in his robe, head hung low, a thermometer sticking out of his mouth. He sees me and startles, then says, "Stay away," he mumbles, "I am sick as a dog."

I stand and stare at him in his green velvety robe that Pop bought him a few years back. Dad loves robes and pajama sets. He pulls the thermometer from his mouth, looks at it, and says, "Cheez-its Almighty, are you *kidding* me?" Then he has a coughing fit, deep and phlegmy and gross and so horrible. He's holding his hand up at me to keep me away. When the coughing stops, he says, "Are you okay? Are you sick, too?"

"Bax. He's burning up."

Dad bolts from the bathroom back down the hall to our room, his robe flapping behind him as he hurries down the hallway like a superhero with his cape not fully tied on. "Stay back from me, Kirby, I mean it."

I keep my distance from them both.

I keep my distance from a heart I don't have anymore, too.

* * *

Sam, Ellie's mom, picks me up from the hospital at 7:30am, and brings me back home. Dad is staying with Bax. Ellie is not with Sam; she's probably home, getting ready for school. I wonder if she's planning on hanging out with Mel later. I shake my head to dispel that. Sam makes pancakes and home fries when we get back to the house, but neither of us can really eat. We sit at the kitchen island, staring off into space. I run my fork through the syrup goop, watching the thick brown liquid drip off the prongs.

Baxter is in a 'coma' of some kind, or something. They can't wake him up, but he's not *technically* in a coma. I'm not too scared, though, because I feel like he's with them...somewhere. Are they going to bring him back? That's what worries me. "You can't have him," I say.

Sam looks at me. "Are you okay, Kirby?" she asks.

I stare at Dad's vase, the one he keeps on the island. He made it in a pottery class he took when we first moved here. He loves that vase so much, and he always puts wildflowers and fallen branches he finds in our yard in it. I reach forward and knock it over. It's heavier than I thought, and it crashes onto the table and breaks. Water spills everywhere, and the flowers and branches tumble free. It smells swampy.

Sam jumps up. "Kirby. What'd you do that for?"

The bottoms of my eyes fill up and when the tears finally spill out and fall down my face, they feel so hot, I wonder if they will leave scorch marks down my cheeks. My phone buzzes and buzzes and buzzes and I know it's Pop, I can tell from the buzz, I just know. I know Dad's buzz, I know Bax's buzz, Ellie's buzz, Roc's buzz, and I know Pop's. I know it seems weird to know a buzz, but I'm telling you, I know the buzzes. I glance at my phone: Pop. I turn the phone off right as it starts ringing. What does all of this mean? And what about our play?

THE MERMAID

Dad is sitting up in bed with his iPad. He's home for a little while to rest and to grab stuff he needs for the hospital. His eyes look baggy and dark, his nose red and puffy. Pills and packets cover his bedside table. Mugs, plates, spoons, and a pile of used tissues. A notebook, a pen, his glasses, his iPhone. I walk over to organize it. He jerks his head at me. "Out of this room. Now. I'm contagious." So instead, I knock everything on the nightstand over with one swoop. It crashes to the floor. He closes his eyes and shakes his head.

"Jesus Christ," he says under his breath.

"Tell me what happened," I say. My voice cracks. "And I'm not talking about Bax."

Dad shakes his head again, like he can't deal. He coughs, loud, deep, wet coughs, like his lungs are coming up through his neck. "Go stand on the other side of this room," he says. "Pull the window open and stay there. Do it now."

I walk over to the window that looks out on the backyard. It resembles a professional outdoor theater out there, and my body fizzes. Are we really doing this? Everything is happening. I open the window and slide down to the floor, hugging my knees to my chest.

Dad hacks up phlegm, great, and then clears his throat. "Pop's confused."

My stomach roils. The air snaking in over my head is cool and smells like leaves burning in the distance. "About what?"

My dad rubs his forehead with his hand, back and forth, back and forth, something he does sometimes when he is thinking really hard. "He's feeling confused about...his identity. His sexual identity, about his career, about me. He's lost."

"And? So. I don't—why did he *leave*?"

My dad looks at me for a minute, his eyes searching. "I said some things I should not have said. A chasm opened between us."

Dad's cough attacks him. It's so bad, he puts his hands on his head as if he's trying to keep it from exploding off his body. I see the tears roll down his cheeks, and he is shaking. I walk into his bathroom, fill a glass beside the sink with water, and bring it to him.

"I didn't want to lie to you both about what happened. I do not want to—and will not—lie to my children. I know that's arguably dumb, and practically impossible, but I swear it on my life. Your grandparents did nothing but lie to me and your Uncle Garrett, sometimes I think they made up lies *just* so they could lie to us. They were creepy pathological liars who made stuff up on the spot. That's not happening in this house ever." Sweat is pouring down Dad's face. I head back into the bathroom and grab a wash towel. I bring it to him and wipe up the sweat from his face. He motions with his hand to step back, step away.

"So," I say, feeling a slow rush of heat rise from my feet to my head, "I was right all along. What I thought—what I knew—the whole time: it's your fault he left."

"Don't be cruel to me—"

"Cruel? Try honest. It's your fault my little brother is lying, like, half dead in some *not-a-coma* thing right now."

"It's nobody's fault. Things happen."

"It started happening after Pop left and you know it. And you made Pop leave."

"No, he made his own decision to leave."

"After you said what you said to him!"

My dad coughs deep. "Lower. Your. Voice. Right now. Calm yourself down. I might be stuck in this bed, but I will ground you until Christmas, do you hear me?"

I scream, as loud as I can, and kick the stuff on the ground. It goes everywhere but I feel stupid kicking tissues and bottles around. My dad sighs, looking at the mess. He asks for the thermometer. I find it buried under a bag of Halls, clean it off, hand it to him, plop onto the floor. While it's sticking out of his mouth, he says, all garbled, "Look. I wasn't sure how to convey this to you. This is complicated. I mean, you can understand it, you're unique, and mature, but Baxter? What does he know about a middle-aged man's existential crisis, and the ups and downs of love, and of shifting preferences and ambitions? He just wants his Pop!" He pulls the thermometer out, looks at it, lifts his head up toward the ceiling and falls back onto the bed. "It's bad," he says. "Oh, God. I gotta get back to Bax. I have to go."

I grab my phone and call Sam, ask her if she can come over and help Dad.

"He's sick and losing his mind," I tell her.

Twenty minutes later, she's at the door, with Ellie, and she heads upstairs to play nurse while Ellie and I wander out into the yard, to our theater. It's so majestic on its own, just waiting for us. We sit on opposite 'stage' beds and watch the light fall on the yard, which glows October gold while red and yellow leaves fall everywhere. The air smells like a campfire.

The outdoor heaters Mel had been talking about stand like robot sentinels in the corner, near the house. Ellie looks at me and I tell her everything Dad just told me. She listens, nodding, chewing a fingernail, curling her hair around her fingers. She has her hoodie pulled up so I can't see her face, only her profile behind the lip of the hood. Being near her isn't helping. At all.

She says, "God. I guess it's even more complicated than we already knew it was."

"What?" I ask.

She shakes her head. "Everything."

The yard grows darker, and a light pops on up at Dad's window. It glows amber in the falling light. The sky above the house is purple and blue, wispy pink clouds streaked across it like confused thoughts. Ellie reaches her hand out for me to take. I do. Her hand feels warm and soft. She says, "Try not to worry, Kirbz. Let's just...God, let's just put on the most goddam amazing play we can and get the dog for Bax. He's gonna be okay. I know it." She shifts her body over so that she's pressing up against me, and she tucks her head into my chest and stays there, breathing. She smells like cinnamon, vanilla, mints, fruity shampoo, dryer sheets. She smells like home. Tears fall down my cheeks, but I stop them before they fall off my face and land on her. I feel a million miles away from Dad, Pop, and Bax. I feel like it's just me, stopping tears from falling onto the person I love.

* * *

That night, in the dark, deep down in the deepest sleep, I step into the backyard and there's nothing there except a giant black pond. No theater, no Ori, no trees, grass, nothing but a glimmering black pond. Its surface is so clear and tranquil, the sky is reflected in it, which looks like the famous painting of the man in the bowler hat with an apple for a face. I melt into the pond, and it feels warm and clean and safe. I swim around. I can't touch the bottom. It's too deep and I am afraid of the depth. When I try to swim to shore, the shore gets farther away. I rest near the center of the pond, kicking my feet to stay afloat. I'm stuck here in the still black water that grows.

Suddenly, Ellie is there. But she is a mermaid. I see her fishtail below the surface of the water and its scales glow green and purple. She goes under and swims around, leaving a trail of light that marks the pattern she is swimming, like bioluminescent plankton that glow when they are disturbed. When she is finished, I see she has swam the shapes of the symbols. They glow brightly just under the water, then slowly fade. Ellie swims underneath me somewhere, deep down, I can *feel* how deep the pond goes, a black hole in space made of water here in my yard.

She then races up, up, up through the water, swimming straight at me like a missile. The pressure is *intense.* She lands right between my legs and suddenly something explodes below my belly. I cry out. All the water turns white, like milk, and I can't see through it anymore. It gets thicker and I can't swim in it. It pulls me down like quicksand, and I go under, unable to breathe. Everything is white. My heart explodes and red, red blood mixes with the milky white and everything turns a streaky pink.

I startle awake, just past 3:00am.

I turn on the light. Baxter is not sleeping in his bird-cage bed. He's in the hospital, and Dad's with him, coughing his brains out. Sam and Ellie are sleeping in the guest room down the hall. I can hear Sam snoring. I take off my pajamas, remove all the sheets, ball them up and throw it all in the hamper. I clean myself off and crawl back into bed and pull the blanket up to my chin.

I feel hollow, little, cold, and old.

THE PLAY

I want you to know we are all having a good time. Krasinski said to have fun. And, we are. But I think about Bax and Dad, both still at the hospital. Baxter is still stuck in his mystery sleep. Pop is calling and texting. I want to find a dark corner to curl up in, close my eyes, make the world leave me alone.

But more than that, I need you to know what our play is—how it will go, what we will do, what it will look like—before we actually do it. 'Cause we are going to do it. I don't know what to say about everything else, but I will say that we're doing the play.

And, it's almost time.

So here is what it will be:

Lights will rise on the stage....

Two beds sit opposite one another downstage. Two boys, me and Bax, (played by Mara and Cotter) get ready for bed. The stage is slightly raked, which means it's on an angle, so you can see the beds better than if they were flat on the stage. The bed on the audience's left is Baxter's, covered with a colorful, swirly pattern blanket. There is no headboard. On the audience's right, my bed. It has a big headboard, but the blanket is plain green. Kirby/Cotter turns down the covers and climbs into bed. Baxter/Mara kneels at his bedside and prays. That's not what happens in our room, ever, but Mara insisted we put it in. She makes gargling noises as she prays. Like gargling mouthwash. We don't know why. It's actually a cool sound.

Suddenly, Bax/Mara screams (Mara kinda squeaks but opens her mouth like she is screaming) and then pulls a giant rubber snake out and throws it across the room at Kirby/Cotter. That never happened either, but I felt like putting it in the play. Something Ms. B said in the Bogart Book about surprises. Just something to throw them off the scent. The snake looks real, and it's attached to a piece of fishing wire that you can't see from the audience. So, it lands center stage, and they laugh about it—stupid rubber snake ha ha ha—but then it gets pulled from off stage, and slithers away, and the boys scream, and hopefully everyone will gasp and think it's real. It looks real.

After prayers and slither-snakes, Bax/Mara sits on the end of the bed:

Bax: "I miss Pop, Kirby. Do you?"

Kirby: "No."

Bax: "Why not?"

Kirby: "He abandoned us and disappeared."

Bax: "No. They separated to work some stuff out and that's all."

Kirby: (pulls Battleship game out): "Battleship?"

Bax: "I have a bad headache."

Kirby: "Like how *adults* get headaches?"

Bax: "My head feels numb."

Kirby: "Too much thinking."

Bax: "I can't help it. I'm smart." Bax turns out his light.

Kirby: "By saying that, are you inferring that I am *not* smart?"

Bax doesn't say anything.

Kirby: "Bax?"

Bax: "You arrange things. You're a freaky fixer-upper."

Kirby: "It's not my fault. I'm organized." Kirby turns his light off.

It gets very dark on stage. After a minute, from the darkness:

Kirby: "Bax, it has nothing to do with us."

Bax: "Huh?"

Kirby: "The Pop stuff."

Bax: "Just go to sleep and pray the snake doesn't come back and get you."

Kirby: "It was fake."

Bax: "But then it became real."

Silence. Darkness. The sound of a clock ticking.

A big round clock hangs on the wall above the beds, and warm blue light shines onto its face until the hands strike 3:03am. Music begins. The music is...well, I played Niccup a few songs from one of my Dad's favorite albums, called, "The Blue Notebooks" by a composer named Max Richter. He loves to listen to that album when he is working. It's cinematic but not in a cheesy way. It sounds like something is coming on top of something that's already happening. And this band called Cranes that he loved when he was younger. He still listens to them. I like them. The music is dreamy and strange and the singer's voice sounds like a little girl stuck at the bottom of a well—but not in a bad way. She's happy down there in the dark and the damp.

Baxter begins to rustle around in the bed. Because of the blanket's pattern, it looks like the whole bed is moving, like a web of snakes. Then the sound of the *un-words* begins, which echoes through the audience because of how Mel and Niccup arranged speakers out there. Surround sound. They put subwoofers underneath the seats. So everyone will feel the noises Baxter makes, the way I feel them when I am lying in the dark across from him when it happens in real life.

Kirby turns on the light. He looks over at the other bed and sees his brother moving around weirdly and making strange noises. An icy blue spotlight shines down on Kirby suddenly, to show that he is frozen in place with fear. Everything stops still as he remains stuck like a statue. It stays that way for about thirty seconds. It's suspenseful. The music swells. It's one of the moments where I get the chills. The spotlight goes out suddenly. The room floods with purple light as Baxter's bed slowly rises from the stage—yes, it really rises—moving up, then outward toward the audience, as if it is being lifted by a giant hand from underneath the floor.

So, Ellie is inside the bed. She is hidden underneath Mara. When the bed reaches the angle where it is almost straight up, and looks like a door, Mara lets go, slides down, the blankets all slide down with her, and she lands at the bottom as Ellie slithers through, wearing the same exact pajamas as Mara.

Ellie clambers out, looking like disturbed water. She lifts Mara from the heap of blankets at the bottom of the bed, floating with her to the center of the stage. They stand together so you can see that they're wearing the same thing; they're the same person.

The seizure dance: step down, step back, step down, step to the side, arms out, arms up, arms to the side, and a series of turns. Ellie lifts Mara up and whirls and flips her onto her back so that Mara is lying across her like she is levitating or floating in the sea. Ellie starts to writhe and shudder and spin and thrust while Mara holds on and makes the noises/un-noises that Bax makes when he has a seizure. It's beautiful as a dance but also very scary because it's showing the audience what a seizure looks like in a weird kind of way. It makes me feel full of electric jelly, 'cause it's so awesome what they do here.

Ellie separates from Mara and kicks and twists and back flips three times to Niccup's amazing music. She does four Death Drops. We hope the audience will gasp. I think they will. Sounds of very loud electricity come blaring on. Ellie flips up onto the bed, then makes her way backwards to the floor where Mara waits for her, still calling out. She lowers herself as Mara rises so that they are shoulder to shoulder, Ellie a little behind Mara, to look like a shadow, and then they do the 'frimmy'—Mara named it the 'freak shimmy'—together: Forward, back, around in a circle over and over, and it makes you dizzy to watch it, but that's the point.

Then the audience sees the purple lights rise on the trees in the forest behind the stage.

That's the signal that the lightning people are arriving. Mel designed it so you'll see the first lights appear from the furthest trees, the ones at the rise of the hill and then move forward, downwards, like a wave of purple light approaching. When they first did it, we all felt goosebumps. It's so bonkers-ass awesomesauce. It looks like the aurora borealis. When the lights reach Ori, her leaves and branches light up from the innermost part of the tree. You can't see the hung lights or wires, only the glowing. Rockford is hiding up in the tree. He slithers down the trunk in the magic light and hovers upstage waiting to begin his Lightning-ninja Symbols-dance.

While he is upstage waiting in the dark, Rockford attaches a 'Puppet-thingy' to each arm. We made them out of old Halloween decorations, witches mostly, each about three-feet high, that we covered up with dark fabric to match what Rockford wears, which looks like a wetsuit. The puppets hang from his arms and when he does minty ninja moves all over the stage—ducking, flipping, diving, kicking—they follow along, and in the magical lighting, they look like two other people on stage dancing *with* him. It's an illusion, like Steve Santini's set made of glass, but it's also real.

Then the best part of all: while the upstage area is lit for Rockford to be the lightning people, the downstage area goes dark. Unseen, Mara and Ellie move the three glass panels in place. When more light comes up on the stage, the audience cannot see the glass yet. You see the glass panels once Rockford heads downstage and takes his place in front of the first one, where he reveals the first symbol: the thistle. We painted the symbols on the glass using invisible glow-paint that only lights up when the blacklights come on.

Behind the panels of glass, Rockford looks shadowy as he 'paints' the symbols in the air but then they appear on the glass when the blacklights come up, so it looks like he's...depositing them there. The symbols hang in the air, glowing for a while, and music builds, and light gets bright and when you think it's all going to explode, FWOP, everything goes black.

The lights rise on Kirby/Cotter center stage, cradling Bax/Mara in his lap, a spreading large puddle of dark yellow liquid beneath them that flows downward (because, remember, the stage is raked). We colored the water using food coloring. Mara wanted the pose to look like The Pieta. She showed us images on her phone of the artist Michelangelo's famous sculpture, but I was like, "Um, Jesus is dead here," and she said, "No, is to be of the holding, in a holding, his holding." She wouldn't budge, so we put it in. Ms. B from The Bogart Book says theatre is a collaborative thing. So does Krasinski. My vision did not include, like, religious iconography, yet it made its way in there, so pray for us, I guess? Pieta fiesta!

Behind them, upstage, close to the trunk of the tree, Rockford and Ellie can be seen in dim light, just slowly swaying, The Seizure and The Lighting People. I told them I wanted it to look like smoke after you blow a candle out. Like when you wake up from a weird dream in the darkest part of the night, and it's alive and real, but only for a few minutes because it fades, and you don't even remember it in the morning. Like that.

Kirby: "Bax, wake up! What happened?"

Bax: "I don't know. Get off me, fart-eater." We're hoping for some laughs here.

Kirby: "You were yelling out noises and having convulsions."

Bax: "No no no."

Kirby: "I'm scared. What's happening to you?"

Bax: "It was only a dream."

Mara runs downstage, looks around, then turns and looks upstage, seeing The Seizure and The Lightning People swaying like candle smoke in the corner. They float toward her, reaching out, but they fade before they reach her. The lights on the trees in the woods move *backwards*, away from the audience, in reverse, as if The Lightning People are retreating, going back to wherever they came from. It resembles a storm rolling away, like heat lightning in the distance.

Bax: "They're real."

Kirby: "Who's real?"

Bax: "The People from the Lightning."

Kirby: "Who from the what?"

Bax: "I saw them in my dream."

Kirby: "Who are they and what do they want?"

Bax: "They show me their...things."

Kirby: "Their *things?* What things? Like, their willies?" (Cotter wanted that line, claiming it adds character to Kirby.)

Bax: "No, their *symbols.*"

Kirby: "Cymbals? Like on a drum set?" (He wanted that line, too. Imagine me rolling my eyes as far as I can roll them up into my head. It's important to Cotter that he's funny and people laugh at him. This means the play feels, in some places, like a five-year-old wrote it.)

Bax: "S-y-m-b-o-l-s, not c-y-m-b-a-l-s!"

Kirby: "Wait, what." (He added that on his own because he says I say that all the time and I was like, 'I do?' Because I thought I only said that in my head, but I guess I say it out loud sometimes.)

Kirby: "What are these symbols, Baxter?"

Then the symbols appear again, glowing. They see them and stare at them. They get brighter. All the awe of the world lives in them. Then, the lights fade.

That's the end of the first section. It takes about twenty minutes.

In the second section, Bax/Mara and Kirby/Cotter go on a journey to see the Doctor-of-Brains. We made it seem like they had to cross treacherous landscapes and dodge death at every turn by having them 'walk in place' while Ellie and Rockford move things around them. There are mountains painted on a piece of paper and glued to a stick, dragons flying overhead, and we spray water at them for rain, tossing chunks of white confetti for a blizzard, holding up a small Vornado fan behind another painting of a tornado to make it look like they are caught in an F5. But then they make it to *The Lahnd of Braynz*.

Dad is played by a sock puppet on Kirby/Cotter's left hand. We dressed him up just like Dad, his hair and beard and glasses and sweater. He is a small sock-version of Dad. Dad doesn't know he is in the play as a sock puppet. I have not let him see any rehearsals or read the play because I want him to experience it as raw as can be. Cotter voices Dad perfectly. He sounds exactly like him. I hope Dad doesn't get mad, but he needs to be in the play, obvi.

Ellie climbs on top of Rockford so that she is standing on his shoulders to create one very tall being. I told them I wanted the character to look like No-Face from *Spirited Away*, an animated Japanese movie I've seen like twenty times. It is Dad's favorite movie and one of the reasons he became a graphic designer. They stay close to Ori for balance. Ellie has a hand resting on the tree, so she doesn't topple off. Not that she would topple off or that Roc would drop her, but just in case. A very long large doctor's white coat with black stripes on it covers them both. It's supposed to look like a giant creature puppet monster thingy.

It looks like No-Face, but instead of being a spirit, I imagined it as a 'Wizard of Oz' floating head, where the heroes of the story go to talk to the head that is supposed to make everything better. But doctors don't fix things, they just suggest to you how *you* might fix things.

The Doctor-of-Brains tells Dad-puppet, (and Kirby and Baxter) about seizures and epilepsy. Ellie pulls out a long pointer. A diagram of a huge glowing brain drops down from Ori, and Ellie and Rockford move together so that the doctor can 'teach' them. This is the part of the play where I added all the stuff I learned on my own about epilepsy, thanks to Google and Doctor-of-Brains, Dr. Joseph Seitz.

Doctor-of-Brains (floating, 10-feet high in the sky): "In the olden days, epileptics were believed to be Mystics and Healers and Messengers of the Gods, or, in some tribes, a conduit, like for a pagan."

Kirby: "A conduit for bacon?" (Cotter again.)

Doctor-of-Brains: "Pagan. Not bacon. Pagan."

Kirby: "What's a pagan? Do you eat it?"

Baxter: "It's a magical person who worships trees and eats mud and talks to crystals."

Kirby: "I see. Go on."

Doctor-of-Brains: "Shamans of the Villages would learn the way of the seizure and teach the villagers the moves so that they could perform it as a dance for the Gods, thereby opening the channel of communication."

Kirby: "So, epileptics were like early books, or TVs, or radios that brought messages?"

Doctor-of-Brains: "Sort of, young man."

Baxter: "Cool—I'm kinda like a TV!"

Doctor-of-Brains: "But some early humans thought epileptics were demon channels and that their bodies were used by devils to come through to our world and bring evil to the planet."

Baxter: "I'm a demon channel?"

Doctor-of-Brains begins to 'float' away upstage, but Kirby/Cotter stops it—

Kirby: "Wait, Big Bird." (Cotter again.) "So, what do we do? How do we solve this? I mean, my little brother is a TV-Demon and Lightning People want to eat his brains."

Doctor-of-Brains: "I recommend a seizure-alert dog."

The music swells very dramatically here.

Baxter: "Whoa. I've wanted a dog forever."

Kirby: "We were maybe gonna get one before Pop abandoned us and disappeared."

Doctor-of-Brains: "This dog is intensely trained to alert you when a seizure is about to happen."

Kirby: "How do they *know*? Are they psychic dogs?"

Doctor-of-Brains: "They can smell it."

Baxter: "Whoa, that's the magic."

Doctor-of-Brains: "We scientists and doctors have come to understand that a chemical is released in the body before a seizure takes place. Seizure-alert dogs, who have amazing olfactory sense, are trained to catch the scent, and warn the epileptic—or a parent, spouse, or friend—"

Kirby: "Or *brother*."

Doctor-of-Brains: "Or brother, yes, of the *imminent* seizure."

Kirby: "By playing an Eminem song?" (Mine, actually, not Cotter's. I'm funny, too.)

Doctor-of-Brains: "Precisely. I prefer Slim Shady, how about you?"

Kirby: "Hello? Do you not see this vomit on my sweater already?"

Baxter: "It's Dad's spaghetti."

The Doctor-of-Brains jiggles up and down, side to side, and up and down, laughing.

Kirby: "So how do we get one of these seizure dogs?"

Doctor-of-Brains (the big beast moves to face the audience) "Well, that's where *these* nice people come in..."

Kirby: (looking around) "What nice people?"

Baxter: (will spot the audience, then run downstage) "People! See them out there?"

Kirby: (will join him downstage) "Have they been there the whole time?"

Baxter: (shrugs)

Kirby: "Did the lightning people bring them?"

Baxter and Kirby, and the Doctor-of-Brains floating upstage, stare out at the people sitting in the seats in the yard for a minute. Baxter pulls Kirby down to him and whispers in his ear for a minute. Kirby nods. They will step to the foot of the stage.

Kirby: "Listen up, you dead people!"

Baxter: "Kirby!"

Kirby: "What? That's a line from *Beetlejuice*."

Baxter: "Oh, kk."

Kirby: "We are going to dance for you now, to show you what life will be like with our seizure dog, to thank you for coming and paying for a ticket because your money will help us get the dog—"

Baxter: "Heddy. Her name is Heddy."

Baxter and Kirby do the BOYDOG DANCE, which Rockford and Ellie choreographed.

Kirby/Cotter gets down on all fours and plays Heddy. The Dad Puppet is also in it. He feeds Heddy and trains her and takes her for walks. They all dance. While they do, the stage lights dim, and the black lights flicker on, so the glowing symbols appear on the glass. They get glowier and glowier until it looks like they might burn up.

When the lights are at their brightest, the lights suddenly FWOOSH to all black—but you can still see the symbols for a beat; they become imprinted on your iris, like when you look at the sun and then shut your eyes tight and still see it floating bright behind your eyelids for a few seconds.

That was my idea. To imprint the symbols. To make them stay there.

Ms. B from the Bogart Book says directors can't hide. She says the relationship between the audience and the director is the most visible thing, even though it cannot be seen. It can be felt, though, so even though you never see a director on a stage, you see more than your eyes show you. I felt like I wanted to show the relationship Ms. B talks about by imprinting the symbols on everyone's eyeballs.

I don't know. Maybe it's dorky. Maybe this whole thing is dorky and dumb.

Welp, that's how it will end. That's the play. That's our play.

I asked Ellie, Roc, Cotter, Mara, Mel, Niccup, and Bess to write down a possible title and place it into a hat, and this is what we pulled out:

SEIZURE'S CREATURES
WHO ARE YOU WHAT DO YOU WANT!
SYMBOLS NOT CYMBALS
JOLTS FROM BOLTS
THE RISING OF THE BED
P U R P L E P E O P L E
THE LIGHTNING PEOPLE PLAY
THE THISTLE, THE I-H & THE 8 HUGGING SNAKES

We voted, and there was a tie between THE LIGHTNING PEOPLE PLAY and THE THISTLE, THE I-H & THE 8 HUGGING SNAKES. That one was mine, but I didn't tell them that. I-H stands for 'intersecting hourglasses.' I knew from the handwriting on the little pieces of paper that Mara wrote down the other one. She writes like a kid, careful and intentional and a little messy. I decided to go with that one. Mara plays Bax, and she chose that title. It spoke to me in a way that's hard to explain. I didn't tell the others whose was whose. She knew that I knew, though. When I looked over at her, she nodded, hugged herself, looked at the sky. Up where the lightning people live.

Cotter wanted mine. He kept saying it with a lisp: "The Thithle, The I-H, and The Ayth Hugging Thnaykth. C'mon! Ith perfect!" And we all cracked up.

But I feel bad when I laugh.

So, whenever something makes me feel happy, I feel sad. I feel sad about feeling happy. I know if I told Krasinski, he would say it was okay, that this is a part of every play—'a maelstrom of emotion,' I think he has called it. For me, it basically means that if complicated feelings are a major part of a good play, then it means they are a major part of a good life, too.

HELLO YOU ARE HERE TO SEE

It's the day of the show, y'all. That's from a movie about a community theatre group that is expecting a Broadway producer to attend one of their productions and it makes them all go crazy. It's called *Waiting For Guffman* and Cotter quotes it almost every single rehearsal. He quotes it and acts out scenes. It's one of his favorites. He made us all promise we would say it out loud sometime today. I'm at the hospital, but I'm saying it, anyway: "It's the day of the show, y'all."

They no longer have Bax hooked up to machines with tubes and cables sprouting from every part of him and disappearing into humming, beeping contraptions standing beside his bed like metal night-demons. He's now hooked up to heart monitors and an IV drip for fluids and they are regulating his brain activity, but Joseph Seitz says he is strong, all of him: his heart, his mind, his body. I place my hand on his face. I know he is having an adventure with the lightning people.

My phone is full of messages. It feels twenty pounds heavier in my pocket. Dad sits in a chair by the window, looking out at a red and white helicopter landing on the roof of another building of the hospital. We are over in the children's ward. He's wearing his dark green corduroys and a plaid shirt and there is a mask over his nose and mouth, for germs. He is still working through this flu. Bax has the flu, too. But because he is...sleeping?...he can't feel it, though he has a fever. I'm busted up that Bax won't be at the play tonight. I'm so sad.

And Dad, well, Dad won't leave his side. Joseph Seitz says it's okay to go, that if anything happens, anything at all, he'll call. And even if he came home to see the play and then went right back to the hospital, that wouldn't be a very long stretch of time. Dad is planning on coming—in his mask, sitting in the back, out of the way.

My face is itchy. Nerves, maybe. Can't believe it's all happening tonight. Can't believe it's happening at all. How many people will come? Krasinski will be there, and some other teachers. All the YOUTHEATRE peeps, we know that. Parents of the cast. I don't know who else. Guess we'll see. I pull at my face.

"Kirby," Dad says, and coughs. "What are you doing?"

"Clawing at my face, what does it look like?"

"Are you having an allergic reaction to something?"

"It's just the play, Nate. It's happening and I'm scared."

"You're calling me Nate now? Is that where we're at?"

"Yup. I've changed." Maybe it's the nerves, but today I just see and feel things differently. My feet feel bigger. Those things that connect us all to the ground. They feel wider. I'm wider.

"Speaking of changing," he says, "When you get back to the house, take a long hot shower, wash your hair, and put on your nice blue suit and a nice matching tie with the brown shoes that you will polish first. You hear me, young man?"

"No, Dad. I can't tie a tie."

"Pop showed you twenty times."

"Exactly. And where is he now."

"Kirby Daniel, this is your night, and you are not wearing jeans, a V-neck T-shirt, worn away Vans, and a smelly baseball cap. No, no, no, no—"

"Okay, okay, don't have a cow!"

He collapses into a coughing fit. "I'll have as many cows as I want. I'm your father and I have the cows."

I put my hand on Bax's face again. Nothing. Nothing at all. His little body moves up and down as he breathes. I feel so scared. "Baxter," I whisper. "Tell them to come to the play tonight." I want to leave the hospital but keep my hand on his face, as if my arm could stretch all the way across town.

On my way out, a frail, old lady with white hair like spider silk and the brightest eyes I have ever seen, pushes herself along in a wheelchair in front of me. I try to go around her but she thrusts her hand out and grasps my arm. She looks into my eyes. Her pupils are purple. She cries and says, "Papá, vuelve a casa," over and over, and she won't let go of me until a nurse comes and wheels her away while she weeps alone.

I hurry out of the hospital, arms fizzing with goosebumps.

HELLO YOU ARE HERE TO SEE

THE LIGHTNING PEOPLE PLAY

WRITTEN AND DIRECTED BY

KIRBY DANIEL RENTON the 1ST

IT IS ACTED BY THESE LUMINOSITIES:

MARA JANE GECCO AS BAXTER RAYMOND RENTON

COTTER WINGHAM AS KIRBY DANIEL RENTON

ELEANOR LIZBETH ABRAMS AS THE SEIZURE

ROCKFORD NAKANO-McKENNA AS THE LIGHTNING PEOPLE

&

PUPPETS WE MADE OURSELVES THAT DO NOT HAVE NAMES

EXCEPT FOR:

THE SOCK PUPPET AS 'DAD' (NATHANIEL GRINNELL RENTON)

THE SETS, LIGHTS, MUSIC & SPECIAL EFFECTS WERE ALL DONE BY

THE AMAZING SPIDER MAN. KIDDING, IT WAS

MELISSA 'MEL' & NICHOLAS 'NICCUP' SANTINI

THE SHOW WAS STAGE MANAGED BY

'BOSSY' BESS JACKSI AKA 'BEST' JACKSI

THANK YOU THADDEUS KRASINSKI FOR BEING OUR THEATRE

TEACHER AND A GOOD DUDE WITH A DARK BEARD AND

MAROON SWEATERS

THANK YOU STEVEN SANTINI, FOR HAVING

THE BEST THEATRE BARN

THANK YOU DAD FOR LETTING US TAKE OVER THE BACKYARD

THANK YOU, AUDIENCE, FOR COMING TONIGHT

TO HELP US GET HEDDY

WE R REDDY FOR HEDDY

The pages in the program have the play written out for the audience, because we don't know if Mara will say the words. Somehow it works, because she is playing Baxter, to not know what's going to happen. What will she say? What will she do? We never have any idea. My brains have been fizzing for weeks worrying about this, but I have gotten used to it.

When I get back to the house with the box of programs, the air smells like Halloween, which is nearly two weeks away. Leaves, pies, costume plastics. Those smells. Candy waiting in bags. Pumpkins freshly carved. They're appearing on stoops everywhere. It only takes a few days for them to begin to soften into sad lumps and grow green-white fuzz all over their hollowed-out insides. The sun is talking to the horizon, so the sky is colored rust, apricot, and the blue of Bax's pajamas, the ones he is wearing in the hospital.

I step into the yard holding the box of programs. I breathe. It's happening. I'm so nervous, I could hurl chunks. But something else is bothering me, and I can't put my finger on it. It's like the rat pole is *behind* me. Can't see it but I know it's there, a shadow that moves with every step I take. The way the moon follows you. I look out across the yard from up on the back deck: it's epic. It reminds me of a film set or something.

All the chairs are set up on the back lawn and the overhead lines of outdoor lights zig zag from our roof all the way across to Ori, and back again. I feel a spitty froth in my head because of how the seats are arranged—I want to fix them. They should line up at the edges. There needs be the same amount of space between each seat. I want to move them around so badly, it makes my face itch again.

Instead, I close my eyes. I see dark swirls of light behind my lids. I breathe. I hear this weird voice in my head that says, *The chairs are okay the way they are and that moving them is not going to change the way the evening plays out, or anything else.*

Wait, what?

Was that my voice? My inside-my-head voice?

I open my eyes and shake my head like a dog after getting out of a pool.

A dog.

Cotter and Mara come onto the stage to work something out. They seem happy again. Mara keeps pointing at something on the stage, then she moves a few steps, points down, takes another few steps, points again, moves some more, points some more. A strange dance. Cotter nods, like he totally understands what's happening. Mara reaches for his hand, takes it, and smiles.

When they see me, Mara claps, runs backstage, comes back on holding something, flies off the stage, trips and falls—yikes! Then she's upright again and hurling up the aisle toward me. She stops short when she reaches me, raises her eyebrows like she's asking me something—no idea what, but I nod—and she moves in and hugs me hard, her arms around my neck. She smells like salted peanuts and seashore-scented shampoo. "I'm the say," she says, out of breath, "That all we are legs must to break," and her eyes get watery. Tears fall down her face as she thrusts something out to me. It's covered with a dark velvety cloth.

"For me?" I ask, and she nods. I place the programs down and take her gift. She wipes away her tears. I place it down on the grass and pull away the cloth. It is a miniature version of our stage, created inside a box, like a big shoe box. It has Ori in the upstage left corner, the two beds on opposite sides, the panels of glass downstage center with the symbols visible. Oh my freekin God—how did she even do this? A tiny little figurine lies on Bax's bed. It's Bax! Or Mara as Bax, anyway.

She kneels to me on the grass and shows me a tiny, hidden piece of fishing wire attached to the figurine on the bed that leads up and out the top of the box. She nods to me, like 'pull the wire' and when I do the little figurine rises, up, up and disappears behind a small slip of dark fabric she has hung at the top that I didn't see 'cause it is so well concealed. After the figurine disappears up behind the cloth, three bolts of purple lighting with faces painted on them come down, as if the whole thing is rigged to be some mini counterweight system.

"Mara," I say, "This is incredible. How did you do this?"

"My idea," she says. "'Diorama for Kirby!' and Santini twins," she clasps her hands together like she is praying, "and whole cast help in the reality." She reaches forward and gently touches my face. "For you, because ask me the Baxter to be and change the everything of me."

"Wow." We gaze at the diorama together quietly for a minute while a breeze rustles Ori's leaves above us, as if the tree is warming up for its performance. It's really one of the best gifts anyone has ever given me.

Cotter walks up to us, and I ask him if I can talk to him in private. Mara covers the diorama with the cloth and says, "I take to the room of beds," and heads inside.

Cotter raises his hand for a high-five. "Wattup, K-Ren?"

"Cotter, thanks for being so cool with Mara, never knowing what's gonna happen."

"It's called riffing. We do it in improv. It's like a big improv thing."

"Okay. Well. You're really good at it."

"Well, thanks for letting me make you more interesting."

I shrug.

"Not that you weren't interesting, it's just...playing you felt easy."

I want to say that playing me is one thing but being me is another, but I don't.

"Oh. Here," I say, and grab a program for him.

"Ah! Here it is!"

"We put the actual play in the program so that people would, you know, know what the play is about if Mara doesn't end up saying any of the words."

"Good idea. She might say all of them. She knows them, she just...."

"She has her own way. I like that."

"Yeah, 'cause you're weird. But I like that."

"I guess being weird is better than being not interesting?"

"Yossss, freak."

Mel and Bess start yelling about something. Bess is on the stage, looking up into the tree. Mel is in Ori, probably adjusting a light that lives in the branches and leaves. Mel adjusts lights that don't even need to be adjusted just to have a light to adjust. I'm confused about Mel. We have a complicated thing. I think she knows how I feel about Ellie. I never said anything, but maybe Ellie did. At first I wasn't sure about her. She's salty, and she's said offensive things about my dads, but not in, like, an aggressive way. And yet, I can see why Ellie likes her. And that makes me like her, too. She's wise, and she cares about what she does.

I can hear her toolbelt from here. She wears it around her waist 24/7, like a Kangaroo with a Joey in its pouch. Between her, Bess, Niccup, and Steven's toolbelts, the sounds of clanking, swishing, swinging, jangling, and the sound of pants being yanked up, are a major component of my world.

"This thing might not go off the way we want it to," I say to Cotter. My mouth feels dry.

"That's theatre," Cotter says.

"As Krasinski would say," I echo.

"'And what is theatre but life itself in pancake and pantaloons,'" we say.

We watch Niccup, Mel, and Bess adjust things on the stage. The sun light starts to change. The rust, apricot, and blue of earlier melts to a hefty navy with wisps of blood-pink clouds over the yard.

"Ms. B from the Bogart Book talks about 'leaps'," I say. "A door opens, and you go through it with no thoughts about the consequences but also you accept that the leap doesn't guarantee anything."

"Um, who's this Ms. B you keep talking about?" Cotter asks. "Is it Beyonce?"

I crack up, promising to lend him the book after I finish it (and write a book report).

I turn and go inside. I need to shower and change into my blue suit and brown shoes. I promised Nate. And the cows he's having.

FLOWERS, STARS

I smell it, I know it.

Citrus-y, sandalwood-y, vanilla-y, clove-y. Why? What does it mean? I follow the smell down the hallway to the bedrooms. I walk into Dad's room and over to the window onto the backyard. The sky is a marbled dark blue, and the zig-zag lights strung from the house to Ori look magical. The stage is empty, quiet, everything is set, and people are arriving. I see Krasinski and a beautiful woman. Is that his friend? Girlfriend? Sister? I can see the people down there, looking around at everything. The heaters have been turned on and they stand at intervals down the aisles, glowing orange. It isn't that cold tonight, but they're on, anyway. My nose lifts, sniffing the air like a blood hound, really breathing it in.

I take a very quick shower. I walk into our bedroom, pull my nice blue suit from the hanger, tear away the plastic it's in from when it got dry-cleaned, wriggle out of my clothes, hop into the suit. It's too small down at the ankles, my legs have grown longer, and it is snug in the thighs and crotch. I haven't worn it since last Christmas. Great. I run to the bathroom and goop the fruity hair gunk into my hands, slap it onto my head, and move it around until my hair hopefully looks like Daniel Craig's in *Quantum of Solace.* It doesn't. At all.

The shoes are dusty, I wipe them clean and slip them on. My feet are too big for them, and my toenails are jutting up against the front part. I run across the hall to Dad's room and slide his closet door open. I find a pair I like, slip them on, they're a little big, but it feels better than the tightness of mine. They make me walk a little slower than normal because my feet slide around in them.

I go back down, walk through the house, flick a few lights on, keeping them dimmed. I head out back and find Krasinski in the yard, near the back row of seats, talking to Steven Santini. I walk up to them and stand there. Steven turns to me and shakes my hand, then heads to his seat up toward the front. I look around. It's...um, pretty empty. I hope more people come.

Heddy.

A spider dashes across my heart; I don't think we will make the money we need. I'm relieved Bax isn't here—he'd be sad about this. But I can't think about it now. I can't.

Krasinski introduces me to Helena Cleary, 'the most celebrated thespian on the east coast.' She swats his arm. He knows her from Carnegie Mellon and their professional theatre company in Pittsburgh. She looks like Neytiri from *Avatar,* Gamora from *Guardians of the Galaxy,* except not the blue skin, or the green skin, and not ten feet tall. When she smiles at me, my insides slide away.

Krasinski pulls me over to the side of the deck, away from everyone. "Kirbacon Rentonsausage, look at you in your slick blue suit, hair all done up, you dreamy little dude."

"Nate made me do it."

"You're shaking. Heh. Welcome to directing." He does the Bwah-hah-hah Evil Scientist laugh. He places his hand on my shoulder. "I'm proud of you all. I'm looking forward to what you came up with back here." He looks out at the yard, at the stage. Mel has switched on the fog machine, so now the haze is filling the stage and the yard and the lights, and the seats. All of it. All of it is here, and it is happening. Haze is happening, people.

Haze. "This is pretty major, Kirbsnakes Rentonslither. Those Santinis—they know theatre. This looks so epic. Look, you have *haze.*"

I smile.

"But, I'd expect nothing less. From you, Ellie and Rockford, Cotter and Mara, Bess and Mel and Nicky. I haven't come across this level of dedication in a long time. I can't say what it is with this group, exactly. But young Gen Z gives me hope."

I grin.

He holds up the program: "You put the play in it. Wise. Does she say the lines?"

"Sometimes?"

He shrugs. "Did you go backstage and say *merde* and give them all flowers?"

"Huh?"

"It's a director's responsibility. Go back there and greet them, circle up like we do in class, play a theatre game, get them warmed up, and give them flowers."

"Flowers? I don't have...where am I supposed to get flowers?"

"I have them."

I look over and see Dad standing in the shadows, watching all this.

The outdoor lights hanging overhead give off a warm, amber glow and a breeze moves the black wires that hold the lights, so the shadow shifts back and forth across his face. He's changed into a suit, he looks nice, like...*Dad*, and I get sad because he's still sick, and Bax isn't here. I still smell that scent from earlier but can't deal with it, and I...can't deal.

He walks over. "Hey, Thaddeus." He's so calm.

"Good to see you, Nate," Krasinski says.

"I'm sick, so don't shake my hand, but hi."

Dad stares at me. I start to feel all squirmy, so I say, "Okay, Nate, stop," and he nods and walks away, pointing up into the house, where I guess he left the flowers and wants me to go get them. Looking around, oh, more people have arrived now, okay. Maybe we'll be almost half full?

Bess is out front in the driveway collecting money and handing out the programs.

I can hear her walkie-talkie squawking every few minutes. I think she's talking to Mel and Niccup, who are backstage. I don't think they need to talk about anything, I think they just like using the walkie-talkies.

I head into the kitchen.

Dad picked up several big bouquets of flowers and Sam, Ellie's mom, is styling smaller bunches from them. She wraps roses, carnations, lilies, irises, and tulips in colored paper, handing them to me to bring backstage. Dad is so tuned in to the visual part of life that he actually chose flowers whose colors match the play. Even though he hasn't even seen it yet. That is *so* weird. I gather the bouquets and head out back.

It's a quiet but throbby energy behind the stage. Ellie and Rockford are stretching over in the corner, practicing their choreography. Mara is sitting cross-legged in the grass staring down at the script, her hair hanging over her face. She doesn't see me. Cotter is gesturing in front of the mirror. Mel and Niccup are under the stage checking and double-checking and triple-checking Baxter's bed that levitates above the stage, and the glass panels for the symbols that come up from under the floor. I can hear them whispering but they don't sound panicked. I call everyone together and we gather in a circle.

"My arms are full of bouquets for each of you."

"Oh, I only accept expensive chocolates," Ellie says in a posh British accent.

"Precious jewels for me," Rockford says. "Emeralds, preferably."

"Gimme d'moneys," Cotter squawks in a Mobster accent. "Got shtuff I needy to poi-chuss." Everyone laughs.

Mara clasps her hands together and holds them up high and looks up at the stars: "The prayers," she says. "For Baxter and all the us and all the Baxters."

Everything, and all of us, here, and the stars. This play, this set, this cast, this night. And the rat pole, too. I'm nervous. I nod for the cast to join hands, and we do.

We stand there a while, together, holding hands.

We don't need to say anything. So we don't.

FAR AWAYNESS

So, I cannot watch the show from down on the grass, down in the seats, from where I usually watch. Tonight, it feels too close. I need to see it from farther away. Also, I still can't believe I didn't rearrange the chairs earlier. That feels like an itch inside my ear canal I cannot scratch. Instead, I watch it all from above, from Dad's bedroom window. It's like a mezzanine view, like when we saw *Hamilton* in Philadelphia and sat front row first level.

I feel lonely, though, as if nothing is real, none of this is real. This is a dream. I gaze down at the yard, the seats, the people sitting in them, the stage, Quing Ori, the trees behind the fence.

Chills spill when the spooky lights travel down from the trees in the forest beyond our yard. It gives the impression that a storm is rolling in. I hear them all go 'Oooooh' when they see it and that makes me smile so hard.

Ori lights up: bright purple, a little scary. Rockford slides down the branches and ninjasaults in slow motion onto the stage to begin his Lighting People dance behind Ellie and Mara, who have finished the Seizure section.

Wait, what? That's where we're at?

I'm catching it in flashes, jump cuts. It's going by too fast. It's hard to pay attention to it.

After the symbols emerge onto the glass panels—glowing and floating in their eerie majesty—I take in a deep breath. They are so striking, and mysterious, especially seeing them from up here, at a distance...but, the thing is, I still don't understand what they are, what they want or are trying to say, and it confuses me. Actually, it angers me a little. Why can't we just *know?* And when people ask about them later, what are we supposed to say?

After the symbols sequence, I sigh.

Then, I see something else.

Then, I remember nothing more.

* * *

I snap back from some Far-Awayness when I hear applause and see, down in the yard, that all the people who came tonight are standing up and clapping. My heart starts pounding, I can feel the bones of my ribs vibrating. I must've gone to The Far-Awayness after what I saw, in the fourth row. My brains shut down, and the rats wobbled lower than they've ever dared to wobble. I don't even know what happened. Did the play go okay? Did they mess up? Did Mara say the words? I exhale and go downstairs. The people are still clapping like crazy.

I step outside onto the deck, and I see Ellie and Rockford and Mara and Cotter standing downstage in the purple lights and the floaty haze, holding hands and smiling while everyone stands and claps for them. Ellie sees me way across the yard and gestures for me to come over, but I shake my head very vigorously. Then—aww crapsnacks—she hops off the stage, runs up the aisle, darts up the stairs to the deck, grabs my hand and pulls me all the way back to the stage. When we step back up onto it...I smell Ellie's sweat and shampoo and Rockford's pomade and makeup, the tangy odor of the dry ice fog. I see the people—all standing—in my yard, but it only kinda half-computes. It feels like a dream, hazy and warped and illogical.

Ellie says, "Thank you for coming to our play. I wanted to...um...so this is Kirby Renton. I know most of you know that already, but he directed this play and—" A roar of applause, and my face goes so hot, I think the flesh might be melting off my skull like the dude in *Raiders of the Lost Ark.* Ellie continues, "So we're doing this for his little brother Baxter's seizure alert dog, so if anyone wants to make an extra donation, we'd appreciate it. And, um, Oh—we have a gift for you, Kirby."

My ears rush with blood. My cheeks feel hot.

Mara skittles over and whispers in Ellie's ear.

"Oh," Ellie says, "You gave it to him already? When?" Mara whispers some more, then shrugs. "Never mind, he has his cast gift!" The people in the audience chuckle. "Do you want to say anything?" Ellie asks and puts her warm hand on my lower back and moves it around, encouraging me, which makes my groins fizz (please not now) and I cross my hands down below my belly as nonchalantly as I can.

I step forward and say, "Thank you for coming," and my voice cracks a little, great. I clear my throat. "Thank you to Mr. Krasinski, and to Mr. Santini, and to Nate, and everyone's parents, because we worked hard on this. Thanks Mel and Nic and Bess." I exhale, looking into the hanging lights above the seats and the way the haze makes them look like tiny lanterns floating in the air above people's heads. "This whole thing is for my little brother. He couldn't be here tonight. He's in the hospital, but, it only cements the reason we're doing this."

I have never used the word 'cements' in my life. What the hell is happening. *Cements?*

I feel hot puddles of sweat in my armpits. Awesome. I wave—without lifting my arm up—and step back, step away, letting the cast take more bows and receive flowers from their parents who have gathered at the foot of the stage to hand over their bouquets.

Backstage, I step off the platform; it's dark back here, and higher than I think, so my foot hits the grass too fast and too hard and at the wrong angle. My ankle snaps and I go down hard.

* * *

Krasinski pulls me away behind Ori where no one can see us. I'm totes limping. I think I sprained it, maybe worse. It throbs down on the outside part of my left ankle. It feels puffy and full of fluid. Krasinski swallows, clasps his hands together, shakes his head, leans against the trunk of the tree, then slides down so that he's crouching with his knees against his chest. Is he having a breakdown? What is happening?

"What in the hell did I just watch?" he asks.

My heart plunges into my belly, then rolls off the cliff of my stomach and falls lower, down my legs and into my feet, where it meets my twisted ankle and makes it throb harder.

"It was bad. I knew it. I told you I didn't want to direct."

I turn and limp away, feeling smaller than I have ever felt in my life. I can't believe this. He thought it sucked.

Krasinski grabs me by the shoulders and turns me around and pulls me in close. "It is one of those most impactful things I have ever seen, and I don't.... Kirby, how did this even happen? How is this possible that you did this thing? Here—in your backyard?"

"Wait, you liked it?" Little sweat beads pop out on my forehead.

"How did you do this?"

"What do you mean? We did the play, it's our little play. *You* made it happen."

"But it's NOT a little play. It's mind-blowing. Those *symbols.* I can't believe this—those symbols will haunt me for the rest of my life."

I swallow, not sure how to respond. I look down at Dad's nice brown shoes that I have slid around in all night. Then I realize that they're not Dad's. They're Pop's. Is that what I've been smelling? Oh. I feel dizzy. My heart makes its way slowly back up into my chest, like a record in a jukebox after it's done playing its song. The 1950s Diner in DoWe, The Malted, was Pop's fave place to bring us. A giant old-fashioned jukebox stood inside the door and Pop would give us money to play songs on it. He would wear his leather jacket and do his hair in a pompadour. He loves the 1950s.

A spider skuttles across my heart thinking of how much things have changed since the beginning of the summer.

"I'm gobsmacked here," Krasinski says, dipping his head down and putting his face in his hands. He sniffles. Is he *crying*? "I really thought I'd lost the younger generations to goddam iPads and iPhones and iCrap and social media diarrhea and virtual reality where dudes just shoot each other's heads off for bitcoin...a generation lost to the sad black glass that's utterly deteriorating society."

"What?"

"But...holy hellions, maybe it's not true?" He's talking to himself now. He's looking up at the sky, rambling, sniffling, his fingers dancing in his beard. "Maybe what I'm doing is getting through...I don't know, I don't know, I don't know...I'm so lost—and so found!—here tonight."

It's quiet for a minute. Out front, I can hear people talking, laughing, a lot of energy—you can feel the buzz. I'm sure they're wondering where I am, and Dad probably wants to see me before he rushes back to the hospital. I need to go with him to see Bax, but also 'cause my ankle is killing me. I feel like I just got the arm cast off, and now this?

"Talk to me," Krasinski says quietly. "Tell me how you did this."

"Uh. Well, I mean—"

"God, you know, I knew it. I knew I needed to make you direct. I felt it, the same feeling those symbols gave me when they appeared. Jeez, if I shut my eyes, I still *see* them there."

"I don't—"

"I mean, the sock puppet! That sock puppet! And that giant Doctor-of-Brains floating monster ghost-beast thing! What the hell was that—I was dying!"

"I just wanted to find a way to raise money for the seizure dog organization, but...."

"When I was your age, we did car washes to raise money to do theatre."

"...but barely anyone came," I say, "and now we won't have the money. The whole point of this didn't even happen."

Then, an idea strikes me. Like lightning.

Krasinski looks at me, eyes wide and glowing.

"Can *you* bring us some people?" I ask him quietly. I can almost *hear* my ankle throbbing.

He furrows his brow, paces, fingers in his beard, pondering.

"Kirby?" It's Ellie.

"Walshy, where you at?" It's Roc.

Krasinski darts out the other side of Ori and hisses to them: "You two. Get back here now." Ellie and Rockford come around Ori, worried looks on their faces. They have changed out of their costumes. Ellie wears her Florence and the Machine T-shirt and Rockford wears his black hoodie with the neon glowing faces on it that says The Head on the Door.

"What's going on?" Ellie asks.

"Everything okay?" Rockford asks.

"Sit down, both of you," Krasinski says, and Ellie and Rockford plop onto the grass. They look concerned, like we are about to get in trouble for something.

"Are you crying?" Ellie asks Krasinski.

He leans down, close to our faces. "Can you get this up again next weekend? Just like you did tonight? Can you give me an encore?"

I look at Ellie and Rockford. "I think so. I have to ask everyone."

"I can."

"Me, too."

"Ask them now. And let me know. This is important."

"Okay," I say. "Okay, I will."

Krasinski paces more, scratching his beard. "I'm gonna have dreams about those symbols. What do they mean?" He takes me in, his eyes so alive. "Kirby, what do they mean, what are they saying?"

I shake my head, remembering them from earlier, watching through Dad's window. They looked like magic purple-blue jellyfish bobbing in nighttime waters, moonlit, doing their own thing. I look at him and he places a hand up as if to stop me.

"Nope—say nothing," he says. "It's up to us. They're for *us*. You were wise to not be pedantic about it. That would be hubris. Leave it the way it is."

"Puh-what?" Rockford says.

"Hu-what?" Ellie says.

"Pedantic, pedantic. It means to thrust your own opinion on someone you think doesn't understand something. You know, like half your teachers at Weirville Junior High."

Ellie scoffs.

"And hubris—excessive pride. The mark of an empty soul. Usually a dude." Krasinski looks right into my eyes, "You know what? I *knew* you had to direct this. I knew it." He claps and claps, whooping.

I've never seen him like this. He's, like, one of us. He's acting like Cotter. It's like he has transformed into a fourteen-year-old again but is still stuck in the body of a furry big guy with huge feet and a beard.

Krasinski points to Roc and Ellie. "You two are a duo. A vibe. You're a...futuristic-Gen-Z-Fred-and-Ginger."

Ellie and Rockford look at one another and then at me.

"A who?" Ellie asks.

Roc says, "A what?"

"HA!" With that, he disappears, darting around the thick trunk of Ori. We don't see him for the rest of the night.

"I need to find Nate," I say. I start walking, well, limping, around the tree when Ellie stops me. I turn around. She and Rockford are standing there, their faces pale, worried, like they really need to tell me something very important.

But I know what it is. "I gotta go."

Ellie looks at me, then touches my face. My heart is a spider.

I limp away.

DOCKS, BOATS, CAPTAINS

I see Cotter and Mara talking to some kids from YOUTHEATRE. I hug them both. Cotter goes, "Went great, right? Wanted to riff more, but Mara said almost all the lines."

Did I know this? I got lost in some other dimension while watching the show. Mara shrugs and says, "I was so the sacred of the scared. I had to have words to help me feel not the afraid. So I speak the all!" She shrugs and gives me a big hug. "Please," she says, "This hug I am, give to Baxter. From me, forever and ever. We fly the play. The symbols are now the free."

I ask them to do the show again, next week, if they can, and they jump up and down.

Some kids from YOUTHEATRE, younger members, a few older, seem in awe. They mostly stand back and look at us, and when I start up the aisle toward the house, they watch me go, and two of them applaud. That makes me feel like such a weirdo. I raise my hand and wave like I'm the President of the United States walking across the lawn to hop onto his plane to go golfing. I don't know. My ears burn. My ankle throbs. My heart's a spider.

Baxter's teacher, Devika, approaches. Whoa, she's here? I feel the same warm tingly relaxed feeling I did when I first met her in her classroom and discovered the thistle that looks like the first symbol. The feeling slows me down, and I stop. It's like getting a massage without anyone touching your body. She is wearing a dark blue and green sari that reminds me of the ocean at night, and her wavy hair spills down her back. She reaches her hand out to me, and I take it. It's like sinking into a warm bath. She smiles.

"Many messages," she sighs. Her eyes are black spheres flooded with honey and syrup. "I've always believed people who do theatre are shamans. Storytellers of the stage. Like church, you must be there, in the pew, to be in church, to be in the service. Shamans enter trance states during rituals, to communicate with the healers in the ether. Theatre does this, too." She is really holding my hand. What I mean is: it feels like my hand is being held. I look at our hands intertwined and my face feels like jelly, like it is globbing off my skull.

"How come when you are near me, I feel like I'm melting into a warm bath?" I ask.

She lets go of my hand and touches my face for a second. "Your brother is doing such good work these past few days."

An icy spill fizzes down my spine. "He's...in the hospital."

"He's been visiting. He told me to come tonight. To tell you the people from the lightning are here now."

The hairs on my neck stand up—how could she know that? That's what he would say to *me.* Did he also say that to her, maybe, in school? No. Why would he? I start to sweat a little, even though the air is getting colder. I feel dizzy. When Devika pulls me in for a hug and I feel her body against mine, I loosen again, melting, and feel like a cat probably feels when it starts to purr because its ears are being scratched. She says, again, "Many messages," in her soothing way. When she looks me in the eye, I feel seen.

Who is she?

Shamans, messages, rat poles.

Limping up the aisle, I am stopped by Brian, Dad's friend who made the birdcage bed for Bax. He is with his partner, the glassblower, Dahlia, where we found the second symbol, the intersecting hourglasses. Dahlia is wearing a chunky gold necklace that makes her look like a rapper. It's an Egyptian eye and when she comes closer, it feels like the eye is looking into me.

Brian comes over and shakes my hand. He pushes his glasses up his nose, thrusts his hands down in his pockets, and shakes his head. "That was beautiful," he says, pointing to the stage, very matter-of-factly. "Not surprised at all. At *all.* Not from what little I know of you personally, but like what your dad has told me about you and your brother. Your friends from your theatre troupe. I wish more people were here to see this. That more kids would take a cue and do this, too." He thrusts his chin at the stage. "I think you should keep this back here. This stage. Forever."

Amazing idea. "Thanks, Brian, for making Baxter the bird-bed," I say.

Dahlia touches my arm—another jolt of meltiness, whoa—and I instantly relax. "I knew I was going to see that hourglass tonight," she says. "After I gave it to you, I started to have dreams that I had made it intentionally. Which was not the case—it was a mistake. But after those dreams started, where I would be making intersecting hourglasses on purpose, I started making them in life."

"Wait, what?" I say.

"Come over and see them. I think you need to see all of them together."

I have a blurry vision of her shelf, completely covered with intersecting hourglasses, of what that might look like, what picture it makes.

I make it a few more rows toward the house before someone nearly knocks me down by hopping in front of me. "Hey!" the person shouts, and I step back: it's Lucius Beetlemeyer, dressed like The Babadook in a long black overcoat and creepy top hat.

"Oh," I say, "Lawrence Meyers."

He smirks and thrusts his hand out at me. I take it, for like a split second. It's not the same feeling as taking Devika and Dahlia's hands. This feels more normal, or something. "It's weird," he says, "Because after you sent your play and I read it and I started to imagine what I would do with it...it wasn't *this.* And this is exactly what it was supposed to be. So, I'm glad I didn't do it. It wasn't supposed to be me."

I look down.

"And I have to tell you something, Kirby. I don't, uh, share my parents' beliefs, okay? But I was scared. I'm scared of them. My dad's a litigator, and my mom teaches French for God's sake—but after seeing this play tonight, something surfaced for me: Those symbols...they tell you things about yourself." He wipes tears away with the sleeve of his coat. "Can we go to lunch soon so I can talk to you about, like, how you did this?" he asks. "I care so much about directing but I feel like I'm a jerk and I want to be a better person because I don't think jerks should direct theatre. I just want to do something important like this."

I blink.

Ms. B in the Bogart book talks about this experience where she was auditioning actors for a project, but she had no money to pay them, and no hope for any kind of success. But the phone rang and rang and so many actors showed up. One of them boasted about his impressive resume filled with Broadway credits, films, television, the works. She could smell the alcohol seeping out his pores, and then he wept. "Please," he sobbed, "I want to do something that has *meaning*."

I accept his invitation to lunch and shake his hand again. Now it feels fizzier.

I limp further up the aisle. I feel like after every time someone stops me, I become somebody different. Is this what it's like being a director? Being in theatre when you grow up? You just morph every few minutes. I make it to the deck, walk up the steps carefully, and look back out over the yard. The haze has faded a little, but it still looks misty in the lights. The stage, out against the back fence, beside Ori, looks like it is floating off the ground. I think it's happy. I think the stage itself—the wood, the curtains, set pieces, the lights—is proud.

Audience members linger in the aisles, talking. Devika and Dahlia stand beside one another like sisters, see me up on the deck, and wave simultaneously. I get goosebumps. I wave back, thinking, *Who are they?* I see some more kids from school, but none of them said anything to me about the play. Maybe they didn't like it. Oh well.

I limp into the house calling for Dad, but I don't find him. Overhead, the lights are flickering. In the living room, in the kitchen. That's weird. I go to the switch and raise the dimmer so it's at full, and that seems to stop it. The scent haunts me, to the point where I don't know whether it's real or not. Maybe I am imagining the whole thing. "NATE!" I yell out, thinking he's in his office or maybe upstairs grabbing more things for Bax before heading back to the hospital. "I have to come with you. I think I broke my ankle. I know, I know, don't get mad, okay? It was an accident. Don't have a dozen cows, okay? Wait for me. I'm gonna change." My voice sounds different.

I hear clomping on the stairs, someone coming down, but it's not Dad. I can tell from the clomps. I know those clomps. I know. I stand in the kitchen, a statue, immobile. My ankle throbs. I see the freezer and want to move there to grab an icepack, but I'm frozen in place.

My hand moves away from my body suddenly, yet slowly, like a little curious snake. It slides open the junk drawer in the kitchen island. It's a mess in there—intentionally—because after I organize it, I come back and mess it up again, so I can organize it when I need to. I start putting everything onto the island: pens, pencils, Sharpies, rubber bands, paper clips, chip-clips, hair clips (whose are these?), batteries, thumbtacks, pennies, dimes, receipts, coupons, small round bottles of essential oils for Dad's diffuser, keys, a cologne sample, a little chewed Teenage Mutant Ninja Turtle keychain, Scotch tape that smells like Christmas morning, an envelope opener, a purple tape measure, scissors, post-it notes, two blue eyeglass cases, an octopus LED keychain, an iPhone charger, a monkey bully blinder, an iPad charger, thumbnail drives, Dad's old business cards, Halloween spider rings, a filter for the refrigerator, matches, lighters, and a silver necklace chain with no charm.

I rummage through the stuff and begin to arrange it loosely.

Out the corner of my eye, I see him walk into the kitchen: leather jacket, black jeans, black boots, belt, hair, mustache, dark eyes. The next thing I know, I am flying, through the air, in slow motion, and I land in his chest. I feel his arms go around me tightly. I cry so hard, I can't breathe.

When I pull back from his chest, it's only because I need to catch my breath.

"Kirby," he says quietly.

But his voice causes something to snap, I don't know, and in the same way my hand slithered away from my body on its own to slide the junk drawer open, my fingers curl into a fist and my arm juts out and clocks him as hard as possible in the jaw. I also lift my leg, the good one, and kick him. But that makes me put too much weight on my bruised ankle, and it screeches with pain. I holler out and go down.

Pop's down, too, against the refrigerator, looking at me sprawled against the kitchen island, looking at him. He's here, at our house, sprawled on the floor. I hurt him and I'm glad I did. The lights overhead start flickering again, even though I put the dimmer up to max. Why are they flickering? More than before now—they're going nuts. We both look up at them, the frosted orbs of light recessed in the ceiling throughout the kitchen and living room, flashing.

"Where's Nate?" I say, out of breath. "I broke my ankle, I think."

"Dad got a call from the doctor that Bax woke up."

I try to scramble up. "When? Oh my God."

"During the play, so, he snuck out."

I swallow. My mouth feels so spitty. I wipe tears away. "What part of the play?"

"Um. When Rockford slid down from the tree. Right in there. I think."

That's the arrival of the lightning people. That's when Bax woke up. My blood runs icy in my veins, but a warm kind of icy.

Pop pulls himself up, opens the freezer, pulls out two icepacks and places them on the island. He comes over to me, kneels, takes me in his arms and helps me up. He sits me down on one of the stools and gently pulls off my shoe and sock, then wraps the ice pack in a kitchen towel and places it on my ankle. He holds it there for a minute, patting my leg.

I shove him off. "What are you doing here."

He places the other ice pack on his jaw and sits on another stool, the way he always sat on it: one leg bent up on the rung, the other straight down, like posing for a photo shoot or something. No. He can't just come home and sit on stools the way he sits on stools. No.

"I came soon as I got the call about Bax," he says calmly.

"What call? Who called you?"

"Dad called me."

"Well, I don't know, he didn't tell me."

"Because of the play. We didn't want to throw you off."

Another thing Dad withheld from me. I feel clouds of steam materializing in between my ribs. I roll my eyes so hard.

"That was amazing, Champ. I can't believe how amazing that was."

"It wasn't amazing—it was real. It happened because you left. Don't call me Champ."

"Every single day over the past few months. Right? So, if you're not going to—"

"I don't respond to people who abandon me and disappear. It's one of my rules."

He nods. "Cool."

I throw the ice pack and it lands on the floor behind him with a plop. The bag splits open and the blue goo globs out, a gloopy neon blob. "After you abandoned us, Bax started having seizures." I start flinging the items from the junk drawer off the island one by one. They clatter onto the floor. "Lightning people showed up." Fling. "Rat pole's been after me." Fling. "Nate and I fight like crazy." Fling. "My magic is crapsnacks." Fling. "And,"—I swoop the rest of it at once— "Guess who had to direct my goddam play."

My face is fire, the veins in my neck are pulsing, my fingers fizz in flames.

The back door, off the deck, opens and a second later, Ellie and Rockford are standing in the doorway to the kitchen, kind of hanging back, as if they don't want to be seen. They both look pale. I think it's because they haven't wiped off the Seizure and Lightning People make-up yet. They don't enter. They don't say hi. They stand back in the shadows, unsure of what to do.

"I did not abandon you," Pop says. His mustache is thick and moves along with his lips, but the scruff on his cheeks is speckled with gray. It wasn't like that a few months ago. But back then, I didn't have hair growing on my body, either. "Dad and I came to an agreement about the best way to move forward, so we did that, and you and your brother were included in that the whole entire time. You know it."

I look for more things to fling.

"I can't make you talk to me, Kirby. I'm okay with you needing space from me, and being mad, it's part of the deal, and I get it, but do me a favor, Champ—don't tell the world I abandoned you. Okay? That's hurtful."

"Oh. Because what you did wasn't hurtful or anything, right?"

"All of this is hurtful. And guess what—I got hurt, too. So can we call it even?"

I look over my shoulder at Ellie and Roc, still half-hidden in the doorframe to the back hallway. I can smell them. Powdery, cinnamon, musky, sweet. I can smell their deodorant, the make-up and hairspray. I blink and turn back to Pop. He's moving his hand over his lower jaw like it hurts. I've never punched anyone or anything in my life. My hand hurts from hitting him. The bones ache.

Outside in the back yard, people are laughing. I don't know who. I'm not sure why people are still here. Isn't anyone going home? Who's still back there? Are they waiting for me?

"So what now?" I ask. "You're a Texan again? Did you find a girlfriend down there? Now that you're not gay anymore?"

Pop drops his face heavily into his hands and shakes his head, breathing hard. "Is that what Dad told you?" Pop groans, a very deep, heavy, sad groan with every single feeling imaginable inside it. It's the Groan of all Groans. It's very loud and very scary and it gives me goosebumps. Even Ellie and Roc feel it in their hidey-hole behind us. I feel them shifting like maybe they want to leave.

Pop pulls his head from his hands. His eyes are wet, marbled clove-brown and emerald-green, glowing like vampire eyes. He takes my face in his hands and says, "I love your dad more than anyone or anything I have ever loved, or thought I could love, in my entire life. The only thing I love more than Dad is you and your brother."

Tears fly out of my face, with speed, like Katniss's bow shooting arrows to kill some plump woodland bird. Snot, too. Like lava flow but snot. Snotflow.

"All I wanted was exactly what I got—your dad, and you, and Bax. But..." he says.

I feel scared. I start shaking. I'm afraid he's going to say: 'Things have changed and I'm out for good'.

Instead, he says, "No matter how much love is there, and how much love you feel, and are surrounded with—and that's me, and I know it—it doesn't point the way forward when things fall apart. Love takes you to the dock. It doesn't get on the boat with you. Love is not the ship's captain. No one was more pissed to discover this than me."

I peel his hands off my face. "What are you talking about? Docks and boats and captains. Shut it, poet. I don't want to hear it."

Pop tears a paper towel off the thingy that holds the roll. "If snot could be harnessed to stop global warming," Pop says, "Kirby, you'd be the planet's best resource."

"I'm like Charlie and the Chocolate Factory except it's Kirby and the Snot Factory."

Pop laughs. His laugh travels through my chest, where it meets a thousand memories of the sound of that laugh and how much I have always loved it. But then, like a person jumping out of a plane whose parachute doesn't open, my feelings fall too fast and go SPLAT against the ground.

Pop sits on the stool next to me. His jean cuffs lift over the top of his boots, and I see his socks: black with little purple chili peppers on them. The peppers have arms and they are holding up tiny lime green stars. He's always loved cool socks. He picks the icepack up and places it on his lower jaw.

"Think of it this way," he says. "You rehearse a play for like a month, right? You learn the words, the staging, everything. You're 100% ready. The night the play begins, you step on stage and there are other people out there doing a different play on a different set wearing different costumes. And you're up there, on the stage, in front of an audience trying to figure out what to do. What do I say? Where do I stand? What happened? That's what it feels like."

"What *what* feels like?"

"Life."

"Nice one," Roc says from behind us.

"SHUT IT, ROC!" I yell out.

"Sorry," he mumbles.

Pop gestures for them to come into the kitchen. They do, looking very worried.

Pop says, "Know how amazing you two are? The way you move. You're like Olympians. Everyone was great. That whole thing was mind-blowing. I'm sitting there in my own backyard watching this in complete awe."

When he says, 'my own backyard', the icy tip of a sharp pin slides in and back out of my chest, near my heart. Is it still his? Still his yard? It feels weird to hear him say that.

Ellie hugs me from behind. When she touches me, my heart, guts, and lower parts all melt like butter on toast. Rockford stands next to me like a guard dog. Just his presence calms me down, but the calmer I feel, the sadder I feel, too.

"So," I say, sniffling, "You going to leave again?"

"Bax woke up. That's the most important thing. Granbuela's not well. Uncle Vic's a child, there's no help from him, and she needs me. I gotta be there. That's all I know right now."

"So, you're leaving," I say.

"Kirby," he says, and groans again, but much less. "Your dad and I separated. That's the deal. But we also have to figure out you, your little brother, and my mother, and where we go from here. I don't know yet."

"Yeah, but—"

"—I don't have the answers. I'm scared, too. Just because I'm a middle-aged man now doesn't mean I know anything. Okay? I'm scared as hell. What else do you want?"

Can't help it—fists. I slam them onto the island and start beating as hard as I can.

Ellie gasps and tries to stop me. Rockford tries, too, but I elbow him. Pop comes up from behind and bear hugs me. He whispers in my ear, "Stop, stop, stop. It's okay, Champ. Stop, stop, stop. I'm here. I'm not going anywhere. Stop."

I can feel him breathing against me. He's here and not here, mine and not mine. I love him and I hate him in the same second. Can't feel my hands.

Pop brings me over to the sink and runs my fingers under ice-cold water for a few minutes. "We have to get to the hospital," I say. "Bax is awake. Let's go. All of us."

"I'm on my bike," Pop says. "I can take you, but where's your helmet?"

I sniffle, "Downstairs. Ellie, Roc, can you two take an Uber? Is your mom still here?"

"We'll meet you there," Ellie says and heads for the back door. "Roc, c'mon!"

Rockford turns to Pop, "You rode your motorcycle here all the way from Texas?"

Pop says, "I live on that thing."

"Dawg," Rock says, "Can I get a ride sometime?"

Pop grins. "Sure."

Seeing his grin that way, as if everything is normal, makes my stomach drop out, and I almost puke in the sink.

CHANGE IS A TAKER

Bax won't let go of me, so I just keep hugging him. Ellie is holding my free hand, and also holding Rockford's. The hospital lighting is a zombie movie, everyone looks blue and dead. Bax keeps saying he missed me. He feels a little boney and smells like unwashed hair, Downey softener, and chocolate pudding.

Pop's in one corner of the room, near the window, looking out at a helicopter taking off from the roof of the neighboring building. Bax didn't seem surprised to see him. He laughed, like he always did with Pop, as if he never even left. Dad is on the opposite side, arms crossed, a little tense, wearing the same surgical mask, exhausted.

Baxter pulls back from the hug and checks out my outfit. "What are you *wearing*?"

"Nate made me do it," I say to Bax.

"You look very handsome," Nate says from his corner. "Grown up."

"Who's Nate?" Bax asks. "You mean Dad?"

"Kirby has decided I'm not his dad anymore, or something, so now I'm 'Nate' instead."

I roll my eyes.

"That's stupid," Bax says. "You're Dad, and you're Pop, and Kirby is crazy. Okay, I want to hug Ellie now." Ellie steps in and takes Bax in her arms. He says, "You smell good."

"I missed you so much," she says.

"How come?" Bax asks. "I was only gone for a week."

Silence.

"Gone?" she says.

"Yeah," he says. "With the lighting people."

I sigh with relief. I suspected this. It doesn't make me feel any closer to knowing any more about them, but I feel reassured.

"Where'd you go?" Ellie asks, looking at me.

"To Lightning World," he says, like he's talking about a Wal Mart or something.

"Kirby," he says. "You did it."

Everyone looks at me. I swallow. Dad and Pop look alarmed.

"What do you mean, Bax?" I say.

"The play."

"Yeah, I mean, we all did it, we just did it tonight."

"I know. I was watching."

My fingers fizz and I am lightheaded. I look at Roc and Ellie, who look back at me as well. I feel solid but hollow, like an egg with nothing inside it. I nod at Bax, grinning. *Lightning World.* I don't know what that is, or where, or what it means, but on this night, somehow it makes sense.

"K," Bax says, "Now you, Roc."

"Aww, yeah!" he says, and lifts his arm and walks around the room like a boxing champion. Bax cracks up. We applaud. He bows to us all, straightens up, steps up to the bed for his big bad Bax hug.

***

Sunday night, Bax comes home. Dad and Pop get him to sleep in his birdcage bed, which is easy 'cause he's so tired, and so are they, and I am, too. But I can't sleep. Pop's sleeping downstairs, I can hear him snoring. I'm sitting on the floor with my ankle taped up. It's an eversion sprain with the deltoid ligaments badly torn. Great. My 'taplop' is open (that's what Ellie calls it) and I am working on stuff, trying to make myself tired. But with Bax being home, Pop sleeping in the house, and Dad hacking up his lungs, it feels like I will never sleep again. I prop my leg up on a pillow, but my taplop keeps sliding off my knees. MacBooks are too slippery. Why did they make them like this?

The lights are off, but the moon is full, and shining bright. It spills through the window onto the floor beside me, a square of milky silver that reminds me of the glass panels we used in the play for the symbols. I stare at it a while, the frame of moonlight on my bedroom floor, thinking about how everyone is here: my family is here, we are all here, and everything feels normal again. But sometimes a feeling isn't true. Feelings can lie, too, even though we are always told to trust them.

Why am I thinking this?

Later, I wake when I hear a weird noise; I have fallen asleep on the floor. The square of moonlight has moved to my other side. It must have crossed over my actual body for a little while as I lay here sleeping. I didn't even know I had fallen asleep. I pull myself off the floor, because the noise I am hearing...it's Bax. He is having a seizure, and it's a bad one. His hands are curling and uncurling into fists and his feet are flexing and pointing in turn. He yelps his backwards words, and his mouth and jaw jerk and jolt. I slide the panel on his bed down and sit beside him, gently moving my fingers around his face to make sure he doesn't bite or swallow his tongue. I place my hand firmly on his chest, and he relaxes a little, like he knows I am here, even though he might be far away inside his seizure.

I am calm because I have to be. This is my life now.

Earlier, when I saw the chairs in the audience and wanted to rearrange them—I felt it so deep in my bones to patch up their position. I didn't do it, I listened to that weird voice in my head. Even though it felt like my internal organs were leaking creepy liquids into the in between places of my body, nothing bad happened.

But when I realized Pop was at the house, I went ballistic on the kitchen drawer. Wait, that's not true. I wanted to fix the drawer, to arrange, but I didn't. I pulled everything out but flung it away. And later, when we cleaned up, I didn't arrange it back in the drawer—I just put the stuff back in there.

Why? Is it from directing the play? Will it happen again or was it a one-off? How can I be me if I don't feel the things that have always made me *me*? This is why change is so weird—you're supposed to still be you even though you're not, not really. Change takes our old selves, our bodies and faces, and gives us weird new outfits and masks to wear instead. Change takes the us-ness of us and carries it off somewhere. Maybe to the Land of Rat Poles, where it smirks, proud of its collection, its gallery of former selves.

I caress Bax's face, wiping sweat away. His eyes are moving beneath the lids. I wonder what he is seeing, what he is doing. What is the Lightning World? Where is it? What does it look like and who lives there? Why did they take him there? What do they want?

I do not want to be afraid of his seizures anymore. Even when we get a seizure dog, this might still happen. Me, in the night, keeping my little brother safe. Heddy might wake me up when she feels the seizure coming on, so we'll have a heads-up, but if he has them in the darkness, during the night, all the time like this, it's still going to be me who needs to help him, isn't it? Out in the world when I can't always be with him, well, that's something else. That's why we need Heddy.

Epilepsy is so much.

This seizure isn't stopping or slowing down, and my heart starts pounding, I feel it thumping in my upper back. I exhale. Do I need to wake up Dad and Pop? I lay myself across his body like a heavy blanket. "Let him go, right now," I whisper. "Please," I add, and he calms down. I hug him tighter, trying to squeeze all my love into him. He stirs awake, looks around, groans, and says, "I was on a train in the stars and the train tracks were made of lighting."

BAXTER THE MYSTERY

I sit with Krasinski in his office, my crutches leaning against the wall beside me. "Before we put it up again, does anything need to be changed? We can work on it this week."

"Well, tell me what *you* think first. What needs a little finagling?"

I pull out my list.

"You have a *list*?"

I hand it over. Five pages. "Oh," I say, "That's the wrong one—but that's for you, too."

Krasinski looks at it. "A Report on *A Director Prepares* by a Director Who Did Not Know How to Prepare." He licks his finger and flips through, shaking his head. He raises his eyebrow at a sentence near the bottom of page one. He places it down. "Excellent, I'll read this later."

I pull out my notes for the show. This one has two pages. But he doesn't take it.

"Let me talk to you about something." He stands and crosses his office so that he's standing in front of his bookshelf, which he leans against and crosses his arms. He is wearing maroon corduroys, brown boots, a snug gray sweater. His office smells like cinnamon toast crunch mixed with minty church incense. He says, "Under normal circumstances, like if this was a professional piece about to open in a professional theater, you'd have previews, where you'd get the opportunity to see the show on its feet for either several nights, or several weeks, depending on the situation. Broadway can get up to two months of previews, and smaller theatre companies and black-box productions can get, I don't know, anywhere from two weeks to two nights. During that time, you fix things, make changes, you listen to what preview audiences are saying. If the play is a world premiere, the playwright will poke and prod about almost every scene and stuff will get cut and the actors will have temper tantrums and the drama escalates to the umpteenth degree. If you decide to follow this path for the rest of your life—and I hope you will—you're in for a plethora of delectable nightmarish treats and incomparable rushes of glory and pride.

"Once the show opens officially, you typically cannot go in and make picky little pokey adjustments through the run. Sometimes, yes, sometimes things happen but for the most part, you let it live and grow and morph and the Stage Manager keeps the train on the tracks."

I immediately think of Bax's dream of a train in the stars with lightning tracks.

Then I have this image of Bossy Bess hollering at everyone for accidentally moving an unseen pencil during a performance and Ellie going up to her like, 'Step off, dragon. Don't make me MEME you.'

Krasinski continues, "Technically speaking, though, because you're going to show this again this weekend, you could theoretically consider last Saturday's performance a preview...but this list," he darts back to his desk to pick it up, "is too much. You want to leave it alone as much as you can right now."

I feel squirmy, a little fizzy. "I'll leave it. I'm nervous with all these people coming."

"Hopefully," he says. "*Hopefully* coming. If I can work some magic. Fingers crossed."

"Do you think Cotter is, like, too funny? Is it too much?"

"It works because it balances out something about this play that is...off-putting."

"Welcome to my world," I say, and he chuckles.

He gets quiet, gazing at the floor. Then he looks up and says, "Those symbols."

I think about the first time I heard of them, through Baxter, even though he wouldn't tell me what they were. Then, discovering them in his sketch pad. Later, seeing them fold into our world from Devika's classroom, Dahlia's glassblowing studio, to Roc and Ellie's 'crop circle'. But now I mostly see them glowing on the glass, appearing during the play, and the audience drawing breath at them.

"It's not like a movie, where the answer comes in the end," I say. "Maybe they just want to be experienced instead of, um, what's the word?"

"Interpreted."

"But it sounds different, like something 'fur'"

"Deciphered," he says, fingers in his beard.

"Deciphered."

I wonder what the symbols really want. Maybe it's different for every person? They were always meant to glow, though. The way we made them glow in the show. I know that. I know because when they glowed, it felt like they started talking to us, even though we don't know what they are saying.

* * *

A hurricane is spinning up the coast.

By the time it reaches us, it might swing out to sea, but the prediction is three days of torrential rain. Tuesday morning, the Santini twins and Steven pull up in front of the house in a big dark green pickup truck filled with tall poles and wide tarps. They immediately get to work out back, ramming the poles into the ground around the corners of the outdoor stage to create posts. They pull the tarps over the posts and secure them. After that, they work on the lights in Ori and the ones in the trees in the forest behind the backyard. The lights themselves can stay hung, they're outdoor lights, the Gobos and Ellipsoidals and Follow-Spots, and most LEDs are waterproof, anyway, but they need to disconnect the circuitry. Lastly, they fold up all the chairs and lean them against the back fence in a row. They work like a team. They *are* a team. I watch from the middle of the yard, standing with my crutches, awed by them. How Mel helps Niccup.

Wednesday and Thursday, it rains so hard, they cancel school. The buses and cars can't drive through the flooded streets. That leaves only Friday night and Saturday afternoon before the show to rehearse. I hobble through the house feeling anxious and holding off, as much as I can, the fizz in my chest that wants to rearrange drawers, closets, and cabinets.

Baxter and I stand at our bedroom window looking out on the yard. The rain beats down in watery sheets. It makes a thunderous sound against the tarps, but they capture it and siphon it to the ground like a gutter. The sky is purple-gray and hovers low, almost right over the treetops. The wind is a dragon. Branches break off the older trees and twist and turn as they bolt toward the house, smacking against the wood and glass with scary-sounding thumps. I'm scared for our stage. The yard is a mess.

"Don't be worried, Kirby," Baxter says from beside me.

"Trying, but it's hard."

He slips his hand in mine. A gust of wind shrieks, pulls at the air. The window rattles like something wants to get in. Something heavy lands on the roof, THWOMP, and we both gasp and step back and look at the ceiling.

"It's okay," he says. "They're on their way."

Chills spill. "I thought you said they were already here."

"*Some* of them are, not *all* of them."

"How many of them are there?"

"This one is a family. Now they'll be together. That's why I had to go to the Lightning World—to give them our address."

My head suddenly feels loose. "Um. Our home address?"

"Also our planet's address."

My eyes go wide.

"Now they're almost all here. To see the play. And drop off Heddy."

The top of my head tingles, a buzzing, like electricity snaking through an invisible wire that sizzles down my neck, then fans out through the rest of my body. We stare out at the rain. I exhale, not realizing I have been holding my breath. "What does Lightning World look like, Baxter?"

"What do you think? Lightning."

"I know but, *how?* Is it like...another planet?"

He doesn't say anything for a minute. He scratches an itch on his foot. "Roots," he says.

Roots.

"Like you are underneath the ground, underneath the trees where the roots spread everywhere. It is like lightning bolts everywhere there, but they don't just appear for a second and disappear. They stay that way all the time. Like a picture of lightning."

I guess that makes sense—sometimes lightning bolts look like bright white tree roots in the dark sky. But why would there be a lightning world in the first place? "What does it feel like?" I ask, trying to be nonchalant. Who knows what might make him get annoyed at me and then kick me in the wiener?

"Magnets," he finally says. "It feels like you are being pulled toward some things, but shoved away from others. You have to move all the time out of the shove places and into the pull places, otherwise you'll just get shoved further and further back."

I am so glad he is talking to me about this. "And the lightning people live there?"

"Duh."

I nod, like 'okay, no big deal.'

He says, "They're really good at the moving around thing, but I'm not."

"What do the lightning people do there?"

"Make the lightning and mail it out across the universe."

Wait, what?

"Really? Why?"

"Because we *need* it. Lightning is like a massage for the earth."

I will ask my science teacher at school, Mr. Wirkus, about that. "What do they want with *you*, though? What about the symbols?"

"The symbols are their stamps," he says. "For the mailing."

Chills.

Bax scratches his butt. "My butt hurts."

I stare out at the rain cascading from the sky.

"They like you, Kirby," Bax says, then yawns big and wide. "They said they are glad you are my brother. They said you and your friends have work to do, and they're here to help."

I look at him, exhale.

"I told them you were a hairy fart-butt who likes plays and counts out paper clips." He grins and bolts from the room. A minute later, I hear the eerie electronic music from ME & MY SHADOW start playing from the basement.

Baxter the mystery. I guess he always has been. Before this, he wore suits and combed his hair and loved school, learning, playing sports and video games with his friends. Now he is full of color, snark, and wildness. He is this seizing and convulsing thing who communicates with beings from another dimension who mail light across the universe. What will happen when things change again? Like, let's say Pop comes back for good. What then? Or what if Dad and Pop split for good instead? Wait—what's with the expression 'for good' when there would not be any good at all? I can't stand that expression.

CHAIRS. AGAIN.

Friday after school—after one hundred and seventeen hours of homework—we all rehearse again. It's fine, it's good, it's sloppy. I think the days of rain and wind and no school have made everyone restless. Mara doesn't say any of the lines. Roc seems depressed, cut-off. The air feels charged, and open. Cold, too. Leaves and branches and pieces of roofs and sheds and toys and lawn furniture lay strewn in the streets and on lawns.

Afterwards, we sit on the stage in a circle and talk, the way we do in YOUTHEATRE when working on scenes or discussing an assignment. Some placement issues need to be adjusted. Placement is like 'blocking', which is the place things happen and where people move from and to on the stage. I feel nervous because I want the show to be as good as it was last weekend and right now, it doesn't seem like it will be.

I feel a heaviness all around me, a sinking feeling. It makes me sad.

From up in Ori's canopy, we hear a walkie-talkie squawk. Mel is up there readjusting the main light, which got all funky in the storm. She climbs out of the tree, wet with leaves and twigs, her hair dark purple and a silver ring hanging out of her nostrils. She stands with her hands on her hips. Bess comes over and they have a few words.

Bess says, "Everyone out front now."

"Hey, Boss," I say, "I'm giving notes here."

"Just get out front now, master hobbler," she barks. "This is uh-SEN-chul."

We walk/hobble across the yard and out to the front. We see Steven Santini pull up again in his big green pickup truck. The back of it is loaded with folding chairs, the same kind we already have for the audience. Loaded with them. Spilling over the sides of the truck's bed.

Bess hollers, "Grab as many as you can, carry them out back and arrange them."

Steven hops out of the truck and closes the door, hitches his tool belt up his waist and waves to me. He walks over. "Hey," he says in his velvety voice, watching the cast bring the chairs up the lawn and into the back, "I had a dream about my friend."

"Matt," I say.

"Matt, right. We were playing cards in the dream, and he said something about chairs. I don't remember, 'cause I'm old as the clay from the dinosaur age. But sure enough I get a call from Krasinski. He says to me, he goes, 'Can you double the chairs in that yard?' Seems you got a lot of people showing up."

I feel the blood leave my face.

"He's arranged for a few buses to bring folks from Pittsburgh. Subscribers to his theatre. So, chairs. Also, I think we need to bring the heaters back out, 'cause the temperature has dropped after this storm. So, I'll swing around later or tomorrow with those bad-boys."

My knees are jelly, my ears are red beets. I am jelly-beets, purple-red and drain-faced. I sigh, and turn to look at our house: Dad and Pop are standing on the lawn outside the front door, curious about what is happening. I wave to them, and they both smile. They are here, together, at our house, but even standing beside one another, there is distance. You can feel it, or *I* can anyway. It makes my heart crackle like the crispy, milky sheets of ice along the curbs in winter, the kind you step on and it sounds like eating potato chips. I feel happy they are both here to smile at me when I wave at them. Then I feel stupid that I waved like a little kid and I kick a rock hard with my good foot. They look at me all weird. Okay so they're here and I'm happy about it, but those two crapsnacks over there keep ruining my life. I nearly flip them the bird as, like, a follow-up to the wave, but, then I might get grounded.

* * *

Two large buses arrive at 6:30pm, idling across the street. They gleam in the rusty glow of the streetlamps, which reflect off the buses' dark windows. About two hundred passengers step off and cross the street, walk along the side of our house into the backyard and mill about for a little while, talking and looking around. Teens, adults, older folks, a few kids. If these are some of the subscribers to Krasinski's theatre company in Pittsburgh, I want to meet them all.

Dad's gone into major superhero mode: he pulled a fold-out table from the garage, covered it with a nice cloth, decorated it with little twinkly lights, and made several gigantic pots of hot cider for the audience members to drink. Pop, and Ellie's mom, stand behind the table offering the warm drink, which smells like Halloween, Thanksgiving, and Christmas all-in-one. You can smell it all over the yard.

Dad also booked it into DoWe earlier to make copies of the program, which get handed out to everyone as they wander around, admiring our yard, our stage, our lights, the seats, and regal Ori, who stands proudly in the corner, a wooded sentry full of leafy pride and stage lights.

Dad also put on a flannel—uh, that means business. That means, 'I'm the boss here, get out of my way and do what I say.' He looks like the guy on the paper towels. He tousled his fingers through his hair with fruity gunk that makes his hair look like a Hollywood dude. But the biggest thing—wait for it—he put in his contact lenses. His green eyes are glowing all over the place like he's some kind of Super-Dad-Program-Copier-Cider-Maker-Vampire-Eyes. When he sees me, he smirks and says, 'Chillax, spawn, I got this.'

Um. Okaaaaay.

I watch the play from up above again.

I wear the same blue suit.

The show is even better than last time. It's just more confident or something. I notice things I didn't catch last time. For instance, Cotter knows how to move like me. It's weird to see but is no match for Cotter's strange brilliance. He's like an octopus—he becomes whatever color and pattern is required. And Mara doesn't say as many of the lines this time, but what she does with her hands and her face and her body, how she expresses the lines in her own way, is even better somehow.

The people in the seats below stand and applaud when the show ends.

I breathe a sigh of relief so intense, I feel it in my toes.

Ellie, Rockford, Mara & Cotter leave the stage, but the audience keeps clapping. I hobble-clop downstairs as fast as I can, hobble-fly down the side aisle where I can't be seen, hobble-hop behind the stage: "Go out for another bow. Go, go, go!" They look at me like I am nuts, but this happened when we did *Curious Incident*—if they keep clapping, you go back out. Then Bossy Bess shows up, literally like pushing them back out onto the stage.

"Bow, freaks, bow!" she howls.

They go out and the audience roars. It fills up every part of me like a tub that has a bath bomb in it, when the neon fizz fills the water and makes a million colorful bubbles, and you settle into it and it smells like salt and candy. Bess walks over and stands beside me. She pats me on the back. I look at her and she smiles at me, her eyes glassy, and her bottom lip trembling. Lord's gourds, Bess *feels* things. I'm agog. She nods and nods, like a proud soccer mom.

Baxter bounds backstage. He's in his colorful pajamas, with his favorite sneakers on, and a Steelers hat. He hugs me from behind, holds on tight, and won't let go.

"Hey, Bax," I say. "Hey, buddy."

"Hi," he says. "Hi hi hi."

"What did you think?" I ask him.

"I didn't watch, but it was so great," he says. He lets go of me, high-fives Bess, and runs off.

Bess takes a tissue out of her pocket and dabs at her eyes, then blows her nose.

She pats me on the head like a four-year-old, or a dog, then walks off squawking into her walkie-talkie to Mel and Niccup. "That was so amazing," she says.

The cast comes backstage again and we come together all at once in a group hug and stay that way for the longest time. We just hang on to one another, listening to all the people out there. Ellie, Rockford, Mara, and Cotter each feel like they are charged with particles, a living electric glow, like a cuttlefish flashing in the sea, but no one can see it but me.

"Many the people," Mara whispers. "I had insane the nervouses. I did unsay the every single word oy oy oy."

"I riffed like the Mad Hatter," Cotter adds.

We laugh.

"I never felt anything like that in my life," Ellie says. "Like I was dancing *above* the stage. Like...like we were doing the play in space with no gravity."

"Yes! Me the too!" Mara says. "The nothings in the feets!"

Interesting that they both had that feeling. I wonder if that had anything to do with the lightning people. *They move like magnets.*

"Walshy, you think we made the money?" Roc asks, hair sweaty on his forehead.

"More of it," I say. "I don't know about *all* of it."

"So we do again, and again?" Mara says, "Until the Heddy money all and she come?"

I shrug. "I don't know. Maybe."

Rockford says, "Maybe like a lemonade stand instead? I'm way too tired to do this again. Also, my costume smells bad. And my parents are about ready to kill me. What ever happened to that Kickstarter thing?"

Everyone laughs.

After we separate, the others change into their regular clothes and I walk to the corner and place my hand on the big Doctor-of-Brains costume, the lightning people figures that dance with Rockford, and the sock puppet who plays Dad. I just touch them, I don't know why, maybe to make sure they don't feel left out of the group hug? Seems like they are glowing and buzzing, too. "Hello," I say to them. I say, "Thanks."

I step out into the yard.

The stage haze hangs above the lights again, a fog, a cloud blanket. The guests are back on the buses. I can hear the engines roar as they pull away. Plenty of audience members hang around, though. I look up at the deck and see Devika and Dahlia talking to one another. They came to see it again? How did they know we were doing it again? I stop and watch them for a minute, wondering what they are talking about. They turn their heads and look out across the yard at me, at the same time. They raise their hands and wave, in synch. Whoa. I raise my hand to them.

Krasinski comes up from behind me. "Sir Mr. Renton." I startle and turn around. He is there with four people, all looking at me. An Asian woman wearing all black, and cool thick glasses, a tall black guy with blue-gray eyes and awesome dreadlocks under a bowler hat, a hefty guy who looks like a priest in all black with a red beard and blue eyes, and a much older woman in a dark dress, with a cane, who looks kinda like Selena Gomez if she was 100-years-old.

"Hey," he says, "These are my friends and associates: Izumi Ito, Holt Kennedy, Phillip Glenning, and Juana Delgadillo. We used to run a theatre company together. Severed in the recession, so we had to split up. We're at different organizations now, but we're still family. Juana and Phillip are the ADs of Steelworld Rep and Izumi and Holt run Playwrights' Bridge and teach at Carnegie."

"Hi," I say. "Kirby. Thanks for bringing all these people." They look at me for a minute. I feel like one of those hairy orange and pink tarantulas at the pet store that people gawk at.

Izumi adjusts her funky square black glasses and says, "I am in awe. Bravo, young maestro."

I swallow, look down at the grass. My ears get hot.

Phillip says, "I must confess that when the symbols appeared, my heart started beating, and I took my phone out because I had to capture them...but...look." He hands me his phone.

I can see the dark picture of the stage, the glass panels, but the symbols do not show up in the photo.

Chills spill down my back. I take a breath. I nod. "They kind of have a life of their own," I say, as if I know the symbols intimately or something. *Do I?* The others nod, too, studying me. "Also," I add, "That photo will cost you double the ticket price—this is a fundraiser, sir."

They all laugh. Phillip's cheeks turn jolly rancher red and he smiles.

Juana steps forward, takes my hand. Her skin is paper, delicate and birdlike, but she's solid and strong. She smells like lavender. She says, "On *that* note, we would like to talk to you about transferring this piece to our theater in the city."

I gasp, feeling my cheeks fill with hot blood.

Wait, what?

I look over at Krasinski.

He steps forward and places his hand on my shoulder. That makes me feel good.

Juana looks around the yard. "I fear it may lose some of its impact by not thriving in this here environment. Obviously, we can't bring the trees, the grass, the sky...but perhaps we can find a way to replicate these elements."

My heart squirrel leaps in my chest. The haze seems thicker, like it's dropping down, as if we are at the sea, little lighthouses standing in the fog on a cliff. Devika and Dahlia stand on the deck, looking at me through the haze. Dad and Pop are talking to our neighbors down by the stage. Every few seconds, Pop looks over his shoulder at me and grins like he's the proudest man on the planet.

I blink, looking at Juana and her deep brown bird eyes.

Holt says, "Turns out, we have a two-week slot available over Thanksgiving." He has a thick British accent! "It's usually reserved for a popular music revue, but that isn't happening this year. Their tour bus overturned a few days ago."

"Oh gosh," I say.

"In a freak lightning storm."

Goosebumps. On my face. A freak *lightning* storm? I exhale. "Wow."

"They're okay," he says, "but they've canceled the rest of their dates."

Juana says, "That's where you come in. You and your friends."

"And the lightning people," Izumi says. "Bring them, too, yes?"

Oh I think they'll be there.

PURPLE GUTS

I'm sick. Stomach flu. Feels like something is living inside my guts, like an eel slithering around. I empty myself out about every hour and am running a fever. Ellie, Rockford, Mara, Cotter, Mel, Niccup, and Bess all have the same exact thing. We've spent a lot of time together, yeah, yet none of us were sick, so we don't know where we got it. Dad was sick, but he stopped being contagious way before, and besides, what he had was different from this.

I keep picturing each of them in their houses, scattered around Weirville, lying under blankets shivering while we each watch TV or a movie or read a book. I see us throwing off the blankets and bolting for the bathroom. I wonder if we are all doing it together. Clockwork vomit.

I doze off and dream that I travel down into my insides, which are filled with purple light and mysterious beings building cocoons in my intestines. I can see them, and they can see me, but they will not communicate. Dad says fever dreams are the worst, basically hallucinations, and he's right.

Bax comes in wearing an old cowboy hat of Pop's from Texas. It's huge, and his head and face look so little underneath. He's wearing red overalls over his pajamas and my tap shoes from when I took lessons as a kid. They're too big for him, so he's clomping around and tap tap tapping. What. Is. Happening. He comes over to me and points the infrared thermometer gun at my forehead and presses it. BLEEP BLEEP after a few seconds.

"Still really high," he sighs. "They really got ya."

He turns to leave the room—I grab his arm.

"Bax. How many more came? The family, I mean. How many?"

He places the thermometer down and counts on his fingers: one, two, three, four, five, six, seven, and stops. "Eight."

Eight. Kirby, Ellie, Rockford, Mara, Cotter, Mel, Niccup, Bess: *Eight.*

Driblets of sweat pop out on my forehead. "Why are they inside us like this?"

He leaves the room, tap tap tapping as he goes. I think he says, "It's just their way, fever-wiener," but I'm not sure. I doze off into vivid dreams of glowing entrails. My intestines flash and jolt as if electricity is coursing through them. Purple. All purple. I keep meaning to text the others, but the phone is on the dresser, I left it up there accidentally when I came back from puking and now, I can't get up to get it. I feel too weak. This is crazy.

Look, if I die, I'm probably coming back as one of the rats on the rat pole.

IT'S YOU

Three days later, we're all weak and cranky, but no more fever and vomiting, and no more dreams of purple-alien eel-people coursing electricity through my intestines. I didn't say anything to the others about that, the whole 'eight' thing, because I can't even remember now whether that conversation really happened. I think it did. I think I know it did. Here is what I know is happening, though: reading and eating. Cannot stop reading—like *speed* reading, like a half a book a day—and eating eggplant, blueberries, blue corn tortilla chips, plums, purple carrots.

Purple food. All purple.

I am sitting on a stool at the island in the kitchen reading a book of Collected American Plays from the 1990s that I found at the Weirville Public Library, eating blueberries by the spoonful. This one play, about physicists, is called *Copenhagen* by Michael Frayn, and I love it because it's very strange, and not direct, and exists in a kind of nebulous space. It feels like what is happening to us lately, and I wonder how Ms. B from the Bogart Book would approach this. I feel like she would know exactly what to do. The language is *sciency*, but I somehow understand.

Pop comes in wearing his leather jacket, holding his duffel bag in one hand and his helmet in the other. I stare at him for a second.

Suddenly, tears fly down my cheeks like fighter jets taking off.

Pop sighs and drops his stuff on the floor. I bolt into his arms, breathing in his smell: soap and shaving cream and leather and sadness.

"Don't punch me," he says.

"I won't," I say all muffled, buried in his chest.

"I'll be back for Pittsburgh, okay?"

I nod into his chest.

He holds both hands on my head. "Love you, Champ. You know that, right?"

"What's going on with you two?" I ask him.

"Sit down."

I limp over to the stool, push the book and bowl away.

He joins me and says, "We're not getting back together."

I drop my head. It weighs 4,000 pounds, it could crash through the island, the floor, into the dirt under our house, through layers of rock, all the way to the scorching center of the earth.

"Dad's disappointed," he says. "There's a real wall there, and...."

"Are you not...you don't love him anymore?"

"Of course I do. Maybe we need more time. That's all I can say at this point."

"But, Pop—"

He shifts. I can tell he's having a hard time. He fingers a necklace he's wearing, a silver chain with a black stone on the end of it. His eyes fill up and seeing that hurts my heart so much. "Doesn't change my love for you at all and never will. Whatever happens, I'm always here, I will always be your father and take care of you and your brother. No matter what. Things might change, but *that* won't change."

He hugs me and says he'll call me tonight wherever he stops on the road.

He slips out.

Soon as the door clicks closed and the sound of his motorcycle fades into the distance...it feels like...all the gross feelings from before return.

Even stronger than before. Is that even possible? I *can't* feel that way all the time again.

I clomp upstairs.

I find Dad in bed, sitting against the headboard. Bax is curled in his lap like a toddler. He's still wearing that old cowboy hat, and the rim is so big, it covers half of Dad's face.

"Hey, Nate," I say. I try to be cheery, which makes no sense, 'cause I know I sound sad.

Dad nods. He and Bax are flipping through our family photo album. Bax is dozing off. His epilepsy medicine makes him sleepy. Dad pats the bed beside him, and I scramble onto it, settle beside his shoulder, and look at the pictures in the album.

"I see you managed some magic," Dad says, referring to the photo book.

"Sorry," I say, remembering an evening last year, right before *The Curious Incident of the Dog in the Night-Time* opened, when I rearranged all the photos in our family album by color.

"I actually meant to put them back the way they were, but I forgot."

"It's definitely more interesting this way," Dad says.

Most of the pictures from our earliest years are from when we lived in Texas and the pictures themselves look dipped in a kind of yellow glaze. Most of them Dad and Pop had taken on their phones but had printed on photo paper. I like the yellowish glaze, though. We almost look like a family from the olden times.

"I just said bye to Pop," I say.

"I know, I heard."

"How?"

"I was listening," he says, and adjusts his glasses.

"Nate."

"Did you really think I wouldn't witness that? You know me better than that."

"It's an invasion of privacy," I say.

"Oh sure."

"It's a federal offense and I can report you to the police."

"Please do. I'd like them to come to this house so we can offer them some purple food."

I don't have a response to that. I do have a fistful of blueberries, though, so I offer him one and he pops it into his mouth.

We flip through several more pages of the photo album until it becomes obvious that Dad and Pop stopped adding photos. The last ten or so pages of the album are empty, and it fills me with a sticky dread. I feel like I'm trapped under one of these pages, the plastic cover suffocating me, the gluey layer on the pages themselves choking my skin. I take the album from Dad's hands and close it with a slight THWACK and place it down on the bed beside me.

I lean on Dad's shoulder. He smells like fabric softener, powder, and waffles. "Nate? After Pop left, I felt...all filled up with all that anger again, like, I started hating on him all over again, and I don't want that. But then I realized that I don't think it's him that I have those feelings for." I lift my head from his shoulder, and we look into each other's eyes. "I think it's you," I say.

"Good to see Kirby is feeling like himself again."

"Nate."

"I mean that in the best way: The meaner you are—to me, anyway—the closer to your own heart. Welcome back."

"Fine." I skitter off the bed.

"No, no, wait. I'm actually proud of you, Kirby. I taught my boys to be honest and always tell the truth, to always find a way to express how they feel. You do it, you do it in droves, and you do it well." His eyes are watery. He blinks. "You've gone from fourteen to twenty-one in the span of about three months. You're stepping into your power."

I walk over to his dresser and open the top drawer where all his socks live. He has dozens of pairs, and they all have wild colors and patterns and designs, but would you expect anything less from a graphic designer? I *don't* want to take them out one by one and begin arranging them colorbetically. But, I absorb the colors. They bleed together, and my brains fizz, so I close the drawer. It clicks shut.

Rain falls. The droplets sprinkle the windowpanes like a watery lullaby. Outside, the sky is October-colored, the clouds hanging low and close to the homes. I think about Pop heading down the highway on his motorcycle in the rain and hope he will be okay.

Dad looks out the window at the rain for a few minutes, then says, "Let me know what you want to do. You can go talk to someone—I've mentioned this already—a counselor at school, or a therapist downtown. Or we can go as a family, if you prefer. It's up to you."

"I'm gonna go eat and read," I say.

Dad turns to the rain again.

Bax stirs and squints at me through sleepy eyes. He studies me for a few seconds, then grins. "Look at *you*," he says. "It's happening." Then he nuzzles back into Dad, who wraps his arms around him and snuggles the top of his head.

THE GLOWING

I can't stay away. I go every night. Even though Krasinski told me that a director goes away after a show opens. They come back during the run to check up on the play, its evolution. It depends on the director. It's the Stage Manager's job to ensure that everything runs smoothly according to the director's vision and that the actors don't start running off the rails with their performances and stuff. But, there is no way around it—I need to be here.

I stand in the back where no one can see me. That's okay, it's not a long play, only 55 minutes, a good amount of time to stand in the back in the dark with your heart beating, watching your own play you wrote and directed and that's being produced and presented by a professional theater in the big city. Well, it's a mid-sized city, really, but it's a famous city, and it's a city full of very important theatre, as Krasinski reminds us.

The coolest thing is that Mel and Niccup worked with the Technical Director of Playwrights Bridge (his name is Benjamin) to create the same setting as the backyard. They removed the seats from the audience and laid down fake grass, then arranged folding chairs like the ones we had in the yard and strung the outdoor lighting in the same zig-zag pattern above everyone's heads. They built a new platform and stage (it's bigger and deeper) and a giant tree that looks exactly like Ori, with leaves and branches. There's a slight rise behind the stage that leads to the gray fence and a projection of the forest on the back wall. You're *kinda* getting the same experience of seeing this play in a backyard in Weirville in mid-October. They even placed space heaters, though they don't turn them on, but Niccup had the amazing idea to light them up so that they glow that same warm orange, even though no heat comes out.

Then, the *sound.* The whole theatre vibrates when The Seizure arrives, same with The Lightning People. When the symbols appear on the surprise glass panels, they burn so super-glowy-dayglo-green. We added more blacklights. It gives me goosebumps every time. My arms shiz with tingles and the tiny little white dots poke out of my flesh. I asked the team to give me more purple light, as much as possible. When the audience walks into the 'backyard', the haze fills the space like vapor, and windchimes clink from back in the corner of the theater to make it sound like it's coming from somewhere deep in the forest.

Purple light everywhere. Purple food in the lobby. Purple T-shirts and hats that say

THE LIGHTNING PEOPLE PLAY. Dad made them. I mean, he did all the graphic design. They have the symbols on the back, but you can't see them unless it's dark because they are printed there with invisible glow-ink. They cost $25 and most people buy them and that makes us more money for Heddy. We also set up an Insta account and Ellie and Roc post reels with the cast. Cotter did his interview dressed up as Ed and Lorraine Warren from *The Conjuring* films. He's so weird, but he nails them both, pretending they are doing a séance and the 'ghosts' are telling people to see the play, ha ha. He's brilliant. It was the best idea to have him play me and be a part of this.

We only have ten performances: Thursday, Friday, two on Saturday and two on Sunday for two weekends. There are 289 seats and one ticket costs $29, so if every seat is sold on every night, we will make $83,810.00. The theatre takes a chunk of that to help pay their rent and staff, but they said they would deduct a lesser percentage because they know what this is for: Heddy. Dad says realistically to expect about half of that, maybe less, because we may not sell out every night...but even if we make $41,905.00, then that will be a huge difference. I can call them and say, 'Hey Doggo-peeps, we raised the mighty greengold for your group, here ya go, can we have the magico-doggo please.' I wouldn't say it that way, though, 'cause they'd hang up on me.

But we do *almost* sell every ticket for each night. I know this because I don't go away (like I'm supposed to). I stand in the back, happy in the darkness, to watch my three favorite moments of the show: When Bax's/Mara's bed levitates upwards then forward toward the audience like a hovering door, the way she slides down with the blankets and Ellie crawling through, emerging as the seizure, and the dance they do together + When Roc wriggles down from the tree like a black snake and does the Lightning Dance all over the stage + When the symbols materialize and the audience goes 'Oooooooooohhhhhhhh' all at once, and it gets quiet as everyone stares at them for the short time they are lit up.

I take my shoes off. I am barefoot because I like the feeling of the blades of fake grass in-between my toes. I don't think you're allowed to be barefoot in a public theater—unless you're on the stage and it's part of the play, like it is for Mara and Cotter—but here I am, toes as bare as a baby's butt.

It's the penultimate (that means one more before the last) performance, and Izumi and Holt are hosting a post-show talk-back after today's matinee. Holt brought some of his directing students, and the theatre company's community outreach program paid for four schools to bring students, mostly 7^{th,} 8^{th,} and 9th graders. I step onto the stage after the applause dies down and the bright lights come up. They're so bright, they hurt my face. Ellie, Rockford, Mara, Cotter, Holt & Izumi join me on stage. Mel and Niccup aren't here today because they are building the set for the Weirville High autumn production. They told us to come by and see them anytime. The lights rise on the audience, and we can see all the kids out there. Most of them have pulled their phones out and are staring down into them. Some are snapping photos of us up on stage.

I take some deep breaths. I'm in my suit, but less tucked in, and wearing my Vans.

Izumi calls out, "Phones down, please," and like a wave, a sea of phones lowers into laps. The kids look the same as the ones from Weirville, mostly. Their style is more urban. They look tougher. There is a group over on the side who are dressed in all black with T-shirts that show emo icons or horror movie maniacs. A lot of cool hats and caps on top of colored hair. They look older, maybe 9th or 10th graders but I don't know. They look like artists, skaters, and the only ones here who might actually be into theatre, but again I don't know.

Izumi introduces us and asks if anyone has any questions. A younger kid in the center pops up suddenly, his hand raised. Izumi nods to him and he yells out, "IS THIS FAKE." I look at the group of us lined up on the stage, sitting in black chairs. I feel so weird. This is so weird.

"Sorry," I say. "What are you..."

Izumi calls out to him: "Can you reframe that question?"

"IS THIS NOT REAL."

The audience laughs.

Then: "DID YOU MAKE THIS UP."

"I didn't make it up," I say. "It really happened." Should we have put that in the program? The kids in the audience whisper and stir. "I have a little brother who has epilepsy, and he told me what he sees when he has seizures."

"Yeah but can *he* be making it up?" someone calls out from the back.

Ellie says, "He's not the make-things-up type."

A girl in the front row stands up. She's wearing black jeans, a red hoodie, a black skull cap and the whitest, brightest sneakers I have ever seen. "What do the symbols mean?" she asks.

"Well, we don't know," I answer.

It gets quiet.

Then someone yells out from the back, "That's stupid." Everyone laughs. "This whole thing is stupid. You're dum-dums."

Eels swim in my intestines. The eels are not happy. I look at the floor.

Ellie calls out, "Thanks! That's what we were going for! We dum-dums up here."

Everyone cracks up.

Then she says, "It's up to you to figure out the symbols."

"Cheugy," the same kid yells out. Someone lets out a loud fake fart. His teacher finds him, the one who farted, pulls him up, leads him out of the theater.

"Why us?" the girl in the red hoodie asks. "The symbols came to *you*."

"But they're not *for* us," Rockford says. "They're for the people who watch the show."

She says, "My therapist showed me Rorschach images, and I told her what I saw. Is it like that?"

I nod. "Yeah. Like that."

"Well, I saw *warnings*," she says, and sits back down. I am not sure if she's talking about the symbols or her Rorschach images.

Another girl, all the way over on the side stands up. She's colorful, like an American Girl doll who came from a book of Lisa Frank stickers. But she seems sad. She steps forward and says, "Can you tell us what you *think* the symbols mean?"

"What do *you* think they mean?" I ask.

Several kids crack up. I feel like I could crap my pants.

She looks down. "My dog Mindy got hit by a car last week and her guts were all over the street. I had nightmares for four nights in a row. I think it's her saying hello to me. She liked snakes."

I swallow. The audience stirs and whispers.

Mara bolts to the lip of the stage, jumps off, runs to the girl, and gives her a huge hug.

The belly eels slow down a little.

A girl stands up in the center section—she must be one of Holt's directing students because she is older, and the people around her are, too. She's wearing an Irish cap backwards on her head, a green military jacket, huge gold hoop earrings, and Doc Martens. She says, "I'm in awe that a bunch of twelve-year-olds managed to pull something like this off, but I have to say that I think this play is irresponsible. It refuses to address crucial social issues that directors, playwrights, actors, and designers have a responsibility to address through the theatre. You're all, y'know, clearly talented youngsters, but the whole point of this is to say something vital about the state of the world. We are saturated with issues that need addressing. So what *is* this play? What makes you think it's okay to just thrust this on us? Why write a play if you have nothing to say?" She sits down and a lot of people applaud. For a long time.

The eels start speeding up.

Cotter goes, "Whuuuuuuut."

Some kids chuckle uncomfortably.

"Well," I say, "I wrote the play to get a seizure dog for my brother."

It goes quiet.

Ellie pops up suddenly, walks downstage, and holds her hand up to shield the light. "Hey," she says. "I'm Ellie Abrams. What's your name?"

The girl stands up again. "Bailey Libra."

"Thanks for what you said, Bailey. We're not 'twelve', but nice try."

The audience goes 'aww snap' and hisses and boos, but I can't tell if they're for Ellie or for Bailey.

One of the teachers stands up and says, "Knock it off!"

Ellie continues, "I hear you. But, this is a play about caring for someone. It's trying to help, like, solve a huge problem. So, okay, it's not *The Miracle Worker* or *Radium Girls* or the gay scene in *Almost, Maine* that so many high school productions love to leave out...but it meant something to the girl over here who lost Mindy—I'm really sorry, by the way—and needed to receive a message from her."

Rockford stands. "My mom and dad think it's entirely agricultural and meteorological."

Someone yells out, "Save our URF!" and everyone laughs.

Ellie continues, "All I mean is...maybe writing a play about trying to care for someone you love who developed a sudden terrifying disability is a social justice issue, too? I, for one, think it's crucial for people to see love in action. For me, that is a huge social justice issue." She heads back to her seat, then stops and turns and faces Bailey Libra again. "And okay, we'll all write better plays as we get older, but this one already made it from a backyard in Weirville to a professional theater in Pittsburgh—who knows where it goes from here." She steps backward toward her seat. Before she sits, she says, "Bailey? Can we talk about this? After the talk-back? Come find me."

Bailey raises her eyebrows, but I'm not sure if she's impressed or annoyed. She sits down. When Ellie sits back down, she looks over at me, and I exhale. I feel so small and weird and full of eels, oily and black and squirmy. I feel scared. I feel confused.

It's hot under the lights and droplets of sweat slide out the pores on my forehead. A teacher stands up near the back and raises his hand. "Hi," he says, "I thought this was very powerful. I have a question from a student here who has laryngitis and can't ask herself. Stand up, Casey."

Casey stands and waves. She seems tired, but she looks like one of us. A theatre-doer.

The teacher continues: "Casey loves theatre and wants to know what advice—"

"I have to do this with my life," she calls out, cutting off her teacher. Her voice is so hoarse, we can barely hear her, but she is trying hard, making sure we do. "I need to be where you are. I'm so moved by this. Please," she croaks, "Tell me what I need to do. This seems so...um, I don't know, complicated, I guess, and, like, I have no way to do this, I have none of these things you have." She coughs. "How can I get there? What do I do?" I see her wipe tears away from her eyes.

Cotter calls out, "Casey, you are all of us!" The audience laughs.

I hop up. "Wait one sec. Wait wait wait," and I dash backstage, but check myself, because of the ankle. I still feel sore and have to be smooth. I sprint carefully down the hallway to the dressing rooms and find my backpack. I unzip it and rummage through until I find the Bogart book. I fly back onto the stage and hold it up. The light is so bright and hot. "Hey!" I call out to the booth above the back of the theater. "Can someone lower the lights? Are you trying to fry us up here like eggs?"

Everyone laughs.

The lights dim down to a warm glow. I instantly feel calmer.

"So," I begin, "I got this book from our theatre..." I face Ellie, Rockford, Cotter and Mara. "Um. What is Krasinski? Is he our theatre *teacher*?"

Ellie says, "Theatre...counselor?"

Rockford says, "Theatre...mentor?"

Cotter yells, "Theatre DADDY!"

The audience cracks up.

Mara stands up and shushes everyone with her arms. She looks to the sky. "Theatre Leader!" she says, over pronouncing it—'Theat-err-Leed-err'—as if anointing Krasinski to the Gods or something.

I turn back to the kids. "Our theatre leader gave me this book because I did not want to direct this show, but he really wanted me to direct it. It's called *A Director Prepares* by Anne Bogart, who runs a famous theatre company in New York City, and it's...I don't...it's like pretty grown-up, but also really not that much. Anyway. Um. I want to read you the last paragraph of the book, okay Casey?"

She nods.

I open the book to the last page and read it out loud: "'Do not wait for enough time or money to accomplish what you think you have in mind. Work with what you have *right now*. Work with the people around you *right now*. Work with the architecture you see around you *right now*. Do not wait for what you assume is the appropriate, stress-free environment in which to generate expression. Do not wait for maturity or insight or wisdom. Do not wait till you are sure that you know what you are doing. Do not wait until you have enough technique. What you do *now,* what you make of your present circumstances will determine the quality and scope of your future endeavors.'"

I close the book.

"Look at what's around you and start from there. We have a pretty amazing theatre program in Weirville—'cause of our theatre leader—"

Cotter says, "He's totes Zaddy," and the audience laughs.

"That's where I started, Casey. That's my advice. To all of you. Don't wait." I look over to where Bailey is sitting. "Bailey, whatever you have to say, get your friends together and say it."

She stands up. "Listen, I appreciate the sentiment and all, but, like, we're in *college,* we don't have time to put on little plays in our backyards."

The audience laughs and some kids go, "Whoaaaaa whuuuut."

"Every minute I'm not swamped with work or in class I'm working three jobs because college is so expensive, and my parents can't afford it, and the scholarship money they give to people like me ain't as much as it is for the people who ain't like me and who can afford it without needing a scholarship."

So many kids roar.

My face is on complete fire. "Cool. I guess that's what *your* play will be about," I snap back. "When you find the time. This one up here, meanwhile, this one's mine, and I'm doing it now. Oh, and, by the way, I did the play to get money we need. To keep my brother safe from something that can kill him. Hope that's not too irresponsible for you."

More roaring. Someone from the back yells, "He ate!"

I sit down and look at Ellie. She grimaces, shrugging.

Izumi stands: "Thank you. We need to wrap this up. We can take one last question."

One of the emo kids sitting over on the side says, "I have a question," and Izumi gestures to him. He stands and says, "Why are you all glowing?" His hair is bright green, and his eyes are lined in dark circles. Kinda *Suicide Squad.*

I'm stumped. I don't see anything. Maybe he can see some leftover haze on the stage and in the bright lights it looks like we're glowing?

"I snapped a picture of you guys on stage 'cause the ninja dude's hot," he says, and everyone laughs. Rockford shakes his head, smiling. "And in the pic, you're all glowing purple."

My eyebrows shoot upwards.

"Then I took some of my friends' phones and did the same thing thinking maybe it was my phone, but it's in all the pictures. Same thing."

Chills. Eels.

Everyone in the audience suddenly lifts their phone and snaps shots of us. There's a cacophony of 'Ohhhhhhh snap' and 'WTF' and 'Howjoodo dat' and 'Gimme back my ice.'

"Someone show us," Rockford calls out.

The guy grabs some phones and scurries down the aisle until he reaches the stage. He lines six phones up next to each other, upside down so we can see them right side up when we walk over there. Six photos of the six of us on the stage sitting in the black seats beside one another. And, the goth-guy-don't-lie: a purple halo glows off each of us, except for Izumi at the end. The shades of purple look different: mine's dark like an eggplant, and Ellie's is pale like lavender. Mara and Cotter are more blue-tinged, and Rockford's purple is swirly.

Ellie and Rockford get down on their hands and knees and bring their faces as close as they can to the photos. They take out their own phones and snap pictures of the pictures. Cotter stands looking down at them. Mara wrings her hands and squeaks like she is seeing something holy. Or *unholy.*

Izumi cocks her head at the photos, shakes her head in awe.

"Must be all those blue corn chips I've been eating?" Cotter says.

And we laugh, but...I never told them about the food. So it happened to all of them, too? I can tell by the expression on their faces that it did. Each one of us. Purple food. And now, we're glowing. I step back and look down at my feet. I feel very alive, also very tired. I close my eyes and concentrate, wondering if I can feel the glowing.

All I feel is my very sweaty pits.

AURA

I limply bolt back to the theater's Green Room after the show and sit on the big, velvety green couch. The walls are colored mustard yellow, and the space smells like hairspray, make-up, flowers in a vase, a bleachy smell like they just cleaned the bathrooms, and Ellie. A big bowl of candy and fruit and small bags of chips sits on the oval-shaped 1950s table in the center of the space. I grab my phone and call Mel. She picks up. "Where are you right now?" I ask.

"The barn. We just left the school. What's up? How was the show?"

"I need you to do me a favor."

"A *what*?"

"Har har. Where's Nicholas?"

"Up in the loft, I think. Why? How was the talk-back?"

"Grab him and stand next to him and have someone take a picture of the two of you and send it to me. Take like ten pictures. Now."

"What?"

"Mel," I say. "I'm not kidding. It's important. Just do it." I realize I'm shaking. My body is trembling. "Please."

"What's this about? What happened? Are you okay?"

"Yes. Ask your dad to take the picture so I can see your entire bodies."

"What?" she laughs.

"Mel, I mean it. Send it to me when it's done." I hang up.

I stare at the wall across from the couch. Large, framed posters of past shows gaze down at me. All the productions, all the artists: *Fences, Fun Home, Eurydice, Oedipus El Rey, Dutch Masters, The Wiz, Cambodian Rock Band, HAÏR, A Bright New Boise, Ruined, Intimate Apparel, And The Band Played On, Yellowface, Proof, The Winter's Tale, The Cripple of Inishman, Porgy & Bess, The Walworth Farce, Angels in America, The Crucible, The Flick,* and *Macbeth,* (which you're not allowed to speak the title of out loud in a theater. Ever. You say 'The Scottish Play' otherwise you will bring down a black rain of death and everyone will perish dreadfully).

Whoa. I have a lot of plays to read, and to study, and to see. To be a part of.

Krasinski's name appears on so many posters, either as an actor or mostly a director. It's like I know someone famous. Ellie and Rockford walk in and sit down across from me. I don't know where Cotter and Mara are, but they probably went out exploring with Mara's parents, who come to see every single performance. They love to explore together, Cotter and Mara.

My phone dings and I pick it up: It's Mel, and she's texted me the photographs: she and Niccup stand in the big entrance to the barn, under the frame of the doors that loom above them. I inhale. Mel's purple is almost maroon, rich and deep, and Niccup's is like neon or something. Pale but bright. I hold the phone up to Rockford and Ellie and they stare at it for a moment.

Roc whispers. "I don't feel different, or afraid, or anything. Everything feels normal and okay? Right? Is it like that for you?"

I say, "What about when we all got sick?"

"But we're okay now."

Ellie says, "I can't sleep as good, but I thought it was just the show...the excitement of doing the show here. But, I don't know."

We are quiet for a minute, looking at the pictures.

I say, "Bax said that when he was in the hospital in his...mystery sleep, he went to Lightning World to meet the lighting people's family members. There are eight of them total."

"And eight of us," Ellie whispers.

Rockford says, "But I'm not scared. I mean...it's *Bax.*"

I nod. I'm not scared, either, but I feel confused. I'm still shaking.

"Maybe it's their aura," Roc says and stands and slides his hand through his blue-black hair. It's so long now. He starts moving around the room.

"What's an aura?" I ask. "Isn't that like a rainbow?"

"Kinda," he says, "It's an invisible color field around people that's their energy."

"Who *are* you?" Ellie asks jokingly.

"I listen to this martial arts podcast, and they talk about that a lot."

I flick open my phone to look that up. The first thing I see is it's usually associated with seizures. *Aura is often utilized to describe symptoms before a seizure. An aura is usually the first sign you will have one. It can last from several seconds up to 30 minutes before a seizure. Most people who have auras have the same type of aura every time they have a seizure. Symptoms include:*

- *Visual alterations, ie*
- *Bright lights.*
- *Zigzag lines.*
- *Spreading spots.*
- *Distortions in the size or shape of objects.*
- *Blind or dark spots in the field of vision.*
- *Hearing voices or sounds (auditory hallucinations).*
- *Strange smells (olfactory hallucinations).*
- *Feelings of numbness or tingling on one side of your face or body.*
- *Feeling separated from your body.*
- *Anxiety or fear.*
- *Nausea.*

I show the screen to Ellie and Rockford. They read it.

Roc says, "That's a way different kind of aura than what I was talking about, but it's kinda the same I guess?"

Ellie says, "What if we all start having seizures?"

I say, "Uh. Then we'll need eight more dogs?"

"That means eight more productions?" Roc asks. "Dawg, I'm butt tired. My parents will disown me. My mom's YouTube show is taking hits already—she's not great at editing."

I put my phone away. Mara and Cotter walk in. We stand up and they walk over and we all embrace in a group hug. It's over after tonight and I can't believe it. Bess walks in next and says, "Gross, don't make me feel things." Her head-set squawks and the guy from the theatre, Luke, who works up in the booth, asks her something, but we can't hear. Bess takes off the headset, places it down, and joins us in the hug. Bess feels things!

I find a box of little coffee pods in the pantry. I take the pods out, flip the box upside down on the table, and balance three phones on it: mine, Ellie's, and Cotter's. I start the timer feature on each, 10 seconds, step back into the group, and we all stand in a line.

Cotter goes, "Freakwitch face, buttnuggets!" and we make ridiculous faces.

The pictures are funny, but we're not laughing as we look at them. We're looking at the purple glow around each one of us.

Mara says, "It is so the pretty."

"It's like that Simpsons episode," Cotter says, and starts moving around the room with his arms spread wide open, as if he's flying. "*The X Files* one. The one where Mr. Burns is running through the woods glowing from radiation treatment? But at first they think he's an alien? And he goes, 'I bring you LOOOOVE', so of course all the townspeople try to kill it."

We crack up.

Roc says to Ellie, "Play that CHVRCHES song we danced to in Walshy's yard. Let's hop."

Ellie dashes to her dressing room to grab her little purple Bluetooth player. We walk into the theater, into our magic space. It feels like it is waiting for us. The stage haze still lingers. Ellie returns, sets up the music. She blasts it, and the six of us fling ourselves all over the space. Dancing, spinning, flailing, and hollering. Mara jumps up and down on the bed (not the movable bed, thank God). Cotter runs around the tree, arms out like's he's flying. Roc does front and back walkovers slick as a slice down the aisle on the fake grass. Bess stands at the edge of the stage, her arms up to the sky, shaking her head back and forth, stomping her foot. Ellie moves like water all over the place. Like the mermaid from my dream. When the song builds to the super-jumpy part, I throw myself in, up and down, flopping all over like a fish or a human pogo stick.

It's possibly the best four minutes of my life.

* * *

Later, I walk into the lobby of the hotel, admiring the chandelier suspended from the ceiling. It's massive. A floating upside-down city. I see Mara's parents, Tinta and Arno, sitting on the beige couches. When they see me, they stand up and walk over.

Tinta, Mara's mom, says, "Hi Kirby. It's always nice to see you."

Her dad says, "Young man, you look even taller than this afternoon."

I look at my feet. "Can't seem to keep shoes that fit for more than a few days."

They glance at my feet, nodding. Then they look up at me and smile.

Tinta's voice is shaking. "We wanted to thank you for how you've changed Mara."

"She has blossomed most excellently," her dad adds. He shakes his head in awe.

"She loves theatre," I say. "I knew I wanted her to be part of this."

"Many other people don't see Mara that way."

"She has her own way. That's why I wanted her for my play."

"Her own way," Tinta agrees, "She's evolving because of this. She's moving through the pain of her sister."

Don't know what that means. Mara has a sister?

Behind them, an old man walking across the lobby drops his suitcase. It pops open, and his belongings fall out. Everyone turns to look at him, but no one moves to help him. I watch him, looking down at his stuff.

"Her sister?" I ask. I move toward the old man to help him. He looks sad and surprised.

"Mara had a twin sister who died when they were a year and a half."

"Oh," I say. My heart jostles. "That's so sad. I didn't know. I'm so sorry."

I make it to the old man and kneel to his things, gently placing them back in his suitcase. He looks at my face with bloodshot, watery eyes, the bluest I have ever seen in my life. Maybe not blue. Maybe purple. He looks like a Miyazaki character.

I nod to him, and he reaches his papery hand out. I take it, and he shakes it firmly, maybe saying 'Thank you?' I don't know. He smells tangy, electric. I pick up an antique clock, heavy and delicate, too. Looks like it came from the 1700s or something. But it has no face. No numbers, no hands. Just a blank white circle encased in glass. Weird.

The old man takes it from my hands and slowly brings it to his heart. Then he moves it to his ear as if listening for its ticking. There is no ticking, but he seems to hear something. He nods and smiles, then stands up shakily. I help him. He gazes into my eyes, and slowly blinks. I swallow. The upside-down city chandelier overhead starts flickering. We all look up at it. My hand tingles, the one he shook. A concierge comes over to escort the old man away. I watch them go, feeling a fizz in my chest. The way he looked at me. His violet eyes.

Mara's parents are talking, "...the doctors always believed it is why she communicates the way she does. Because of her twin."

It makes me love her more. Mara drops love all over the place. I just see her, in my mind, shushing everyone earlier during the talk-back, standing up, raising her hands to the sky and declaring, *Theat-errr Lead-errrr*. "There's no one else I'd want to be playing Baxter," I say.

"We can't thank you enough," Tinta says. "You mean everything to her. She never stops talking about you."

My eyes fill at that.

Arno says, "It's just...strange things are happening. Beautiful things. You kids are growing up so fast, and it feels so sudden, and we are mystified, wondering what it is."

I nod.

Tinta says, "What is this? This magic. What could it be?" She and Arno look at me.

My eyes dart down to the blue-green sea-swirl of the lobby rug. For a second it looks like it's moving, like the ocean itself. I'm suddenly remembering, as if remembering a strong dream, this one night in June that Pop and Dad took us into DoWe to eat at Den of Dragons. It's the awesome Chinese food restaurant with the giant red-velvet booths we could all fit into. Music played, and dark red light glowed on the golden objects on the walls and windows, glowing paper lanterns swinging from the ceiling like hovering airships. We loved that place. That was the night they told us about the separation. I never finished my meal.

I still see it: half eaten Sweet and Sour chicken smothered in pink goo on the big dark blue plate that looked purple in the red light. Little gold dragons ringed the plate, breathing tiny lightning bolts out of their reptilian snouts. Three Chinese symbols snaked between the dragons, like a strange kite-train.

I swallow. I think that was the same night that I woke up at 3:00am because I heard terrifying noises and padded across the dark room in my bare feet to turn on the light. Bax was convulsing in his bed and calling out weird words. But, I thought I was having a nightmare because of what had happened earlier that night, what our dads had told us. I saw a witch standing over his bed, cackling. The witch Dustin Brisco had drawn for me in school in Texas, because we didn't have a mom, only two dads, and that we'd burn in hell. I padded back to bed, sure I was dreaming. But Bax was having a seizure, maybe his first one. He could've died.

Will I be able to save him?

How many plays will we all have to do to save one another?

I snap back to the present, clear my mind of chicken, dragons, and witches. I look at Tinta and Arno, who are looking at me, waiting for an answer to their question about this strange magic they mentioned. I'm pretty sure I know, so I say it.

"Theatre."

UNPOPPABLE BUBBLE

Through the window of my hotel room, I can see, across the street, a small public park lit in Pittsburgh night-light. I want air, maybe pizza, so I go down. I cross the watery lobby, remembering the old man from earlier, his faceless clock. I step outside. The night is warm for November. I cross the street and enter through the gates of the park. A couple sitting on a bench huddled into one another argue, even though they're snuggling.

At the opposite end of the park, exiting through the opposite gate under the rimy amber glow of the city streetlamps, I see two people walking briskly out of the park together.

It's Devika and Dahlia.

I sprint after them. I make it to the other gate, look left, look right, look across the street but see nothing. I head right, booking down the block to the next corner. Nothing. Then I go the other way, to the opposite corner. They're gone. But, I saw them. Why do they keep showing up?

"Hey," I hear, and I yelp. I look to my left and see someone sitting on a bench. It's Krasinski, sitting alone, wearing a thick denim jacket with a big white furry collar on it, like sheep's fur. I instantly relax.

I walk over and sit down. "Are you seeing the show tonight?"

He nods. "Meeting some friends for dinner first. I like to come to this park."

I look in the direction of Devika and Dahlia, wondering if I am losing my mind.

"Whatcha up to, Kirb-waffle?" he asks.

"Oh, I wanted pizza, but then I...." I look around. "Anyway, thanks for coming."

"Wouldn't miss it."

"I like your jacket."

"Yeah, I still got it," he says. "For an old dude. Actually, Helena bought this for me. She keeps me looking stylish. Thought I'd give it a whirl tonight coming out to celebrate you young hipsters."

We look out into the park. It's quiet, not too cold, and mostly still. Shadows appear. The sounds of the city lull us, and everything feels calm, a feeling like I'm exactly where I am supposed to be. It's sort of like déjà vu but way better. Across the park, and on the opposite side of the street, the marquee to the theater pops on, its bulbs smoky bright, and inviting. That's where we are doing my play, right there, and I still can't believe it. We look at it for a minute, neither of us saying anything.

"Coming to the end of this thing," Krasinski says. "Or at least this *part* of it."

I nod, wondering where it all goes *after* this.

"How does it feel?"

"We danced today, all of us, in the space, and it felt so right."

"Aw, that's great. That's when you know it's right, when you dance with your friends. Feels like the world can't get to ya, you know?"

I nod, remembering the feeling from earlier. "We're gonna get the money for Heddy."

"You did right by yourself, your friends, and your family. Good on ya."

I feel that in my feet, in my legs, a slow rushing of blood that feels like a warm bath. "But, some of the kids today at the talkback were mean, and acted really dumb, some of them. Just, like, obnoxious, and, uh...I don't know..."

"Jealous?"

I shrug.

"Better get used to all that uncool stuff if you choose to do this for the rest of your life. And I don't say that to sound cynical or pessimistic. I say that to sound judicious. Relationships can be mercurial and tempestuous when it comes to art and artists. But somehow you always find your strongholds." He glances over at me. "Something tells me you already have."

I flash to Rockford and Ellie, standing in the shadows behind me in the doorway to the kitchen the night Pop came back, and the love I felt coming off them like mist off a lake. I flash to them dancing in the wet grass of the yard, before the theater got built back there, and the way their dancing made the 8 Hugging Snakes. All our time together. My heart waxes over and it's a good, gooey feeling. Krasinski is right.

Will we three always be friends?

He stands and crosses the little walkway, sits down on the bench opposite me. The park's tall standing lamps pop on. He clasps his hands together and looks at me. Underneath this city light, he looks like a painting. "Hey. I read your report on the Anne Bogart book. I thought you did a nice job of elucidating the ways some of the things she said manifested in your process, and in your play."

"I can tell there's a big 'but' coming."

He grins. "But you didn't mention what you've learned. How are you different now?"

I flash to the kitchen drawer the day Pop left. I didn't manage my magic. I haven't gone back to the drawer, or the linen closet, or the books on the shelves. I mean I don't feel cured or something, and I wonder if I even need a cure. And, is this what Krasinski is even talking about? "Something about directing the play has made it so that I'm not organizing stuff so much anymore. Like I don't feel the need to *fix* stuff the way I did."

"Logically, what is that telling you?"

I think about the night not too long ago when Bax came home from the hospital. Even though he had a bad seizure, and it lasted a long time, I felt calm. I laid in bed beside him, and protected him, and did what I had to do, even though I couldn't stop the seizure. I can't make any of this go away. Even with a dog. I clear my throat. "That I can't fix everything?"

"Good. You can't. And things will constantly *change*, and that'll drive you nuts." He looks at me. "So, what are you going to do?"

And I know, again, so I say it.

"Theatre."

"Good. You're going to be creative."

"But how? It's *hard*."

"Vulnerability. It's the great human irony: the thing that makes us feel the weakest and the most exposed in the face of all the madness and chaos of the world, and yet it's our greatest weapon in moving through it all with grace."

I think about weeping into Pop's chest. And a second later, punching him in the jaw. Is that what vulnerability is?

A wind picks up, breezes through the leaves in the trees above us. I close my eyes and see purple. A swirly, electric lavender swimming behind my eyelids like amoebas beneath a microscope. The gust lifts refuse and swirls it around, swooshing through the dried brown leaves that have fallen and collected in piles under the benches. Something moves, bumps along the ground under Krasinski's bench. I see it near his feet, some small object in the shadow of the light. A toy? I point to it, and Krasinski bends over, finds it, pulls it out. "What is it?" I ask.

"A kid's lunch box thermos," he says, turning it over in his hands. "Got all the superheroes on it." He holds it up, a colorful blur of capes, tights, and masks. So many of them, I can't even tell them apart anymore.

Krasinski stands and stretches, holding the thermos in his hand. He turns and looks across the park at the theater, its marquee sparkling in the dark. People are walking the streets, walking past us in the park. He tosses the thermos. I catch it and place it on the bench beside me, but it's dented, so it topples over. The scratched-off faces of Iron Man, Spider Man, Superman, Batman, and Aquaman look up at me. I don't feel anything coming off these guys. I never did. Bax loves them, Roc loves them, Cotter, too. Ellie likes that the female characters are increasing, though none of them appear on this thermos.

"Hey, I want to thank you, Kirby Renton."

I panic—that's the first time he has said my real name in full without adding something to the end of it, like food or something else.

"Because...hey if I tell you something, you promise not to tell anyone?"

I see myself immediately telling Ellie and Rockford. I nod emphatically.

"I was about to throw in the towel on all this."

"All what?"

"Teaching, theatre, acting, directing, the whole pierogi."

The warm rush of blood in my feet and legs from earlier turns cold. "Why?"

"After thirty-five non-stop years of it, I lost the thread, Kirb-sky Renton-walker."

Whew, I'm back.

"But that's art, and artists. It's not a science, it's more of a shapeshifter's dimension."

Music. Jazz. We hear it. I turn my head to the right and see a small band at the gates to the park, playing together, a guitar case open on the ground in front of them, so that theater patrons can toss them coins and bills. The sound fills the air, a familiar melody riding the breeze.

Krasinski snuggles his hands into his pockets, nodding his head to the music. He glances at me and says, "Have to go meet my friends, but what I wanted to tell you was that your play—the lightning people, the symbols—altered the course of my journey. I owe you a debt of gratitude for the re-blooming of this withering part of me."

I gaze at the leaves that have gathered around my feet: brown, dark red, fading yellow.

"I know what the symbols mean now," he says.

Chills spill. I look up at him, blinking.

"They've communicated their purpose."

"What is it?"

"Don't know that I can tell you, young Jedi."

I stare at him, chewing my bottom lip with my upper teeth.

"It has something to do," he says, "with the way people like us make our way through the world. That's what it is *for me.* It might be different for others. Probably is. Hope it is. I got the message I needed about the life I have."

He says 'people like us' as if I'm on the same level as he is. I shuffle my feet back and forth. He checks his phone and taps at it, answering a text.

"Maybe I'll tell you in like fifty years," he says, sliding the phone back in his pocket. "I'll be withered in a wheelchair, you'll be about ready to retire, and we'll talk about it."

"Okay," I say, shrugging, wondering what the world will look and feel like in fifty years. I mean will we all be on Mars? Will I be directing Red Plays on the Red Planet?

"I gotta cut, Kirb-jazz, but I'll see you after the show. Break legs, buddy."

"Nearly broke an ankle," I say. "Does that count?"

"It all counts," he says. "Everything counts." He walks off toward the music and when he passes the band, he leans down, tossing several bills into the guitar case. The musicians nod at him, and Krasinski nods back.

I leave behind the dented thermos of scratched heroes, and make my way toward the hotel. As I'm crossing the avenue, I spot Ellie and Rockford coming around the corner, holding a huge pizza box. Pizza! Their faces light up when they see me. That their immediate reaction to my presence is happiness, and that I can see it on their faces, chokes me up so hard. I hug them both, right there on the street, and they hold me, too.

I can smell the pizza, the cheese and sauce, and Ellie's shampoo, and Roc's pomade. I feel a warm bubble form in my heart, a bubble of hopefulness that for the next fifty years, we will all be this close, a pizza pie between us, outside a theater doing our own show, while a jazz band riffs in the park in the half-light.

It's not a poppable bubble.

ACORNS

After we have closed the show, Izumi and Holt call to say that after extracting Playwrights' Bridge's cut, we have raised $48,407.50. After the government takes their cut, we'll get around $38,000.00. It doesn't feel real to me. How could we have done this? I feel eels slithering through my veins and brains, giving off electric shocks of joy. Standing in the kitchen near the island, I whoop and holler. Dad clasps his hands happily, and Bax, eating syrupy waffles—for dinner—smiles and lifts his fork slowly to the sky, like an offering to the gods.

Izumi and Holt tell me they want to talk about starting a new summer youth theatre program at Playwrights' Bridge. They would like for me, Ellie, Rockford, Mara, Cotter, Bess, and the Santini twins to propose a series of six-week-long workshops we can each run for kids, aged 13-17. Directing, movement, design and management, acting, improvisation, and writing.

My forehead buzzes with joy, but with nervousness, too. "Seriously?" I ask. "You want us to do that?"

"Yes," Holt says, "And we will pay you each, as well."

"Pay us *money*?"

"No, acorns. Pittsburgh is known for its oak trees."

I chuckle. "But, why us? Don't you have people there already?"

"We sent out surveys to the schools Monday morning and started to get them back today, and based on the responses, we need to do this because the younger minds are craving it. If we can stop the doom-scrolling for even a few hours a week, it will be worth it."

Izumi says, "You inspired these kids, and we want to utilize your skills. We also found out today that we were offered a major grant for summer programming we never thought we would win."

"Congratulations," I say.

"What's interesting," Holt says, "Is that the email was written in purple."

I swallow.

I don't know who they are or what they want or whether we really have anything to do with them at all—maybe they just hitched a ride on Baxter's seizures and on the back of our show—but they are here now, and stuff is happening.

"But, just to be clear," Holt says, "This is on you. We can provide an opportunity, but it's up to you and your team what you will do with it. Is that clear? Ball's in your court here."

"Yup." I chew a fingernail.

"We'd love for you to talk to the others and get back to us," Izumi says, "Maybe early spring the latest, with a kind of *program* for how you would run a...well, imagine it's like a mini theatre school and you run it the way Thaddeus runs YOUTHEATRE, though in your own way."

A shizzle rushes down my spine. "I'll talk to them about it." Then, "Thank you both so much. Because of you, we're going to get Heddy."

"Kirby," she says, "Heddy, dear sweet Heddy, is entirely on *you*. Thaddeus told us everything about you. And it was clear, from meeting you, that this operation, this celebration, is entirely as a result of your will. We're happy to have helped, and to be witnesses to this magic we've all seen and felt. But, listen, for God's sake, young one, take a bow already, will you?"

I nod.

I don't know how to do that.

All I know is that if I take away the play, the lightning people, the symbols, and my friends, all that's left is me and my family. Bax, and my dads.

BIGGER THINGS

Last time I wrote a letter, but this time, I called them on the phone.

I wanted to talk to them. Out loud. I wanted them to hear my voice. I told them everything. I started with my dads and the witches of Freakcity, finding the symbols in Bax's sketchbook, and later how they came into our world: Devika, Dahlia, Roc & Ellie's dance in the grass. I told them about Lucius, too. I needed him, and he turned out to be an adversary because of his parents' beliefs, but in the end, were it not for him, I never would have directed the show, and that was the thing I needed to fix all my fixing, so he became my biggest ally. I talked about the barn (that day still doesn't feel real), their set and lights and music and Steven's magic glass, too. About Baxter's visit to the Lightning World and how they arrived as a family to help us move the play from my backyard to Playwrights' Bridge in Pittsburgh. I told them we know the dog's name, Heddy, and that I raised $38,000 to get her. I said that I hoped to meet Anne Bogart who wrote the book Thaddeus Krasinski gave me to 'understand' directing, and that when I looked her up, she reminded me of the woman who first ever started me on this journey years ago when we were still in Texas. How Krasinski cried after he first saw the play because he really thought he was losing a battle to being 'phone-owned'. I explained how I'm no longer arranging purposefully messed up drawers, closets, and shelves so that they can fit into a pattern that my mind seems to need in order to feel okay. Instead, I'm arranging other things, bigger things—and that, for instance, was when I went on to arrange our visit and coordinate the whole process of us getting Heddy. Finally.

And I did. And so we did.

And now it's happening.

AFTER

School starts in three weeks. Ninth grade in three weeks. High School, in three weeks.

We are scheduled to be back home just in time, but for the next few weeks, we are here, outside of Washington D.C., staying in an Air B&B that's close to Snout Power (that's the real name of the organization that trains the service dogs, I swear). Why didn't anyone tell us about Washington D.C. in the middle of August? It's pittfloods. It's swampbutt. It's the sweatiest place on the planet. I'll never visit again. Unless it's winter.

We are ready for Heddy. We are meeting her today. I'm so excited and nervous. Heddy is fourteen months old now but has been trained since she was a puppy. Her official *seizure* training, though, began at ten months, and will continue for several more. But now we have to train *with* her, because she needs to get to know us, and we need to get to know her. She is a Golden Labrador, a cross between a Golden Retriever and a Labrador Retriever. According to Snout Power, these are excellent seizure dogs. Her eyes are warm, dark brown, big, and in pictures they have sent us, she always looks like she is glowing, furry and gold and smiling.

We're all here, including Pop, who moved back, but is staying in Shadyside, in a house that looks like a small ancient castle with a turret and lots of dark red brick. He purchased it with money he received after Granbuela died in Texas. It wasn't a ton of money, but enough for him to make the down payment and buy a small house for me and Bax to visit him every other weekend or whatever Dumb Deal he is working out with Dad in the Divorce. Yes, I said the 'D' word, and it stands for these very D-ish things: disappointed, dismayed, deathfart.

But at least he's here and at least he and Dad *seem* to be trying to talk about maybe eventually hopefully one day being future friends? Dad's the really sore one, Pop's just ready to forge ahead. I love them both, but they pluck the feathers off me. My counselor at school, Gilda Allednac, helps me feel thankful. To look at it differently than what my feelings might be pointing me towards. My feelings point me toward a big, dark ditch. But feelings are only one way there. Other ways exist, too. Alter your perspective. Yup. And, I gave it a name: ALTERSPECT.

Earlier this summer, we did our youth *workship* at Playwrights' Bridge. We called it workSHIP instead of workSHOP because of all the bridges and boats. I led the class on Directing, Ellie and Rockford on Movement, Cotter on Improvisation. Mara did not want to lead her own class this time, but she participated in all of ours. Mel led a class on set design (Niccup went to visit his mom, but popped in over Facetime), and Bess about Stage Management. It lasted six weeks, with seventy-seven students total, and we each got paid $1,250.00 for our time. BUCK$, dawg. They asked us back next summer, too. Most of the students had seen our show and took every single opportunity they could to corner me and talk their faces off telling me what they think the symbols mean. So many things come up. So many.

I still don't know what they mean, or what they are, only that they make people feel curious and want to do important things. I even get letters sent to my house. A lot of kids draw the symbols and send them to me. I keep them in a small box that lives under Baxter's bed, where it's even messier than it used to be, but, I think the symbols need to live there, where I first found them. The bed where he has had so many of his seizures.

As we walk into the building, the sun peeks out through the low gray clouds, and a breeze rustles our faces and hair. I stop and close my eyes, letting the coolness dance across my face and neck. It's hot and Washington D.C. smells strange. Bax hops over to me suddenly and grabs my hand hard. He's excited. We are greeted by staff. They will take us in to meet Heddy, and after we spend some time bonding with her today, Bax and Heddy will begin some of their training intensive tomorrow.

They train the seizure dogs to smell a seizure. Scientists gathered chemicals that the body releases before it happens. I've watched vids that show you the way the whole thing works. What I know is that dogs' noses are like superheroes' powers and just as you wouldn't grab Ironman by the face and be like, "Tell me how you DO this, IronFreak," you don't grab a seizure dog by the snout and go, "Reveal your powers, SeizurePooch!" I mean I guess you could, but you might get snarled at.

Heddy will be trained in all kinds of ways, but one way is to come and find me and Dad or Pop when she smells a seizure coming on. We sent along clothes we had worn but not washed, and other personal items like a hairbrush and sneakers and things for her to know our scent. She is also trained to just alert anyone who is around if Dad/Pop and I aren't, like if Bax happens to be somewhere where we are not.

I can't believe we are finally meeting her.

Heddy's trainers, Will and Fran, are excited for us to meet her. They walk us down a hallway that smells like wet dog and apple shampoo to a room where Heddy is waiting to greet us. My heart feels like a moth. Dad combs his beard with his fingers. He's nervous but also relieved, I think, hopeful this will help us out, help Bax, hopeful things could return to normal. Whatever that means. Pop's beside me, hands burrowed into his pockets. He smells like nutmeg and mint and a little bit like leather. Today, he is quiet.

A door swings open into a big room with a gray floor and light green walls. In the corner, piles of little identical buckets line the wall, like the ones I've seen in the videos I've watched about how they train seizure dogs. I hear a noise, a swishing, a flapping, and I look to my right to see Will and Fran standing on either side of Heddy. The sound is Heddy's tail flapping happily against the floor. Oh God. She knows it's us. We are her new family. She is happy. My heart-moth bursts forth in a fury of bliss. She's wearing a Seizure Alert Dog vest—it's purple. Of course it is. I wish Ellie and Roc were here with me right now.

Bax kneels and opens his arms and Heddy strolls over to him. They look into each other's faces for a moment, eye to eye, snout to nose. Bax leans forward and hugs her. She rests her head on his shoulder. Dad is sniffling. He lets out a quiet sob, and snaps pix with his phone. He wipes tears out of his eyes. He and Pop kneel to meet Heddy. She moves to them, sits, and puts her paw up, *FWOP,* right onto Dad's shoulder, and he laughs, and he cries, too. She does the same to Pop. Tears slide down Pop's face.

It's my turn now to meet her. I'm shaking, and something's...weird, wait...I think it's my eyes, and I take a few steps backward, shake my head, trying to un-blur my vision. Something is...but they're there—I see them, forming, like smoke or mist, right over Heddy's ears. Like a *halo.*

The symbols, swirling around.

I see them.

No, wait. Maybe I'm imagining this? I shut my eyes tight and breathe, inhaling the scent of dog fur and dog food and dog toys. I open my eyes and find Heddy at my feet, looking up at me.

I don't see the symbols. Whew. Jeez.

Her tail fwomps happily on the floor. Dad and Pop and Bax smile as they watch me kneel to say hello. I place my hand out and she lifts a paw into it, then sticks her tongue out, panting—more like smiling—as we gaze at one another. She lets out a few high-pitched whines, as if she recognizes me.

"Hey Heddy Renton, nice to meet you," I whisper. She licks my face, then hurls herself on to the floor and rolls over, showing me her pink, furry belly, paws up and bent. I gently pet her, fur soft as a Beanie Boo. My whole body fizzes.

She'll be Baxter's companion for the next fourteen years or something? He'll be 25. I'll be 28. Where will I be then? In graduate school, working towards my Masters in Directing? Or will I shift into something totally different and new sometime during the years I am in high school? What if I decide to become an Astronaut? And Ellie and Rockford and Cotter and Mara and Mel and Niccup and Bess? Where will we all be? What will we be doing? How weird to think about it all, how the world might be different, or the same, fourteen years from now when Heddy dies. Wherever and whoever I am in the world and whatever I am doing, I will fly across the globe to say goodbye to Heddy before she goes.

Wait—why am I thinking about Heddy dying when we just met her and I'm stroking her belly? Rat pole, retreat.

Will and Fran come over and say it's an excellent sign that she did that—it means she trusts me and she recognizes I am Baxter's older brother. Fran calls Dad and Pop over to pet her on the belly, too. After a few minutes, she scrambles up and leaps over to Baxter, poking him with her snout as if saying, "You're it!" She gallops across the space and Baxter screams and gives chase. I watch them frolicking in the opposite corner. She's so playful. Baxter, wow. This is the happiest I have seen him since before Dad and Pop split up. He drops to his knees and throws his arms around Heddy's neck and nestles his head into her fur.

Wait.

I see the symbols again.

C'mon, what? I see them. They're swirling around Heddy, purple, glowing, but not as close to her as before. They're hanging back, as if...giving them space? I shut my eyes tight like before, take a few deep breaths, open them again and watch as the first three symbols multiply like cells under a microscope and suddenly there are three more of them, hovering, like little dragonflies over the surface of a pond.

The new ones move to Baxter and settle just over his head.

I run over to them and start waving my hand through them, through the space in the air where I see them. They're there, but invisible, or like holograms. I whirl around to face Dad and Pop, Will and Fran. "You see this?"

Pop says, "What are you seeing?"

They don't see. My heart beats faster. Feels like my bones are liquefying inside my body.

I watch Baxter and Heddy, wrestling on the ground, having the best time. I can see so clearly that they each have a halo of rotating symbols, like planets in the solar system, rotating and glowing slightly right above their heads. I'm waiting for them to split again and form another set, which will zoom over to me and settle over my head, right? But that doesn't happen. Still, I can tell that the symbols know that I can see them. I can *feel* that they know, feel it in my face and neck and stomach. A feeling like knowing something others do not know, not in a bad or secret way, but like in a superhero way, I guess. Like X-Ray vision, when you can see things other people can't see.

Baxter clambers up and comes hurling over to me, a joy bomb.

He slips his hand in mine and grins happily.

"Do you see?" I whisper. "Do you see them?"

I look into his eyes; they're so full of light.

"Do you see them? Bax, answer me."

Dad and Pop look at me all weird, and Will and Fran seem uncomfortable, and look away, like 'What's up with this freak?'

Bax claps his hands and squeals. It echoes through the space. He gestures to me, and I lean down. He's a little out of breath, and he murmurs in my ear. "You did it, Kirby," he whispers. "I knew you would."

He touches my face. He looks into my eyes. I feel like I can see tiny lightning bolts flickering in his irises, like storms in wide open fields in the distance. He blinks, and the flickers fade. Now I just see the flecked hazel of his irises. He hops back up, pats me on the head, grins, and he and Heddy bolt across the room.

THE END

AUTHOR'S NOTE

The book you just finished reading is fiction and also very real.

I worked as a professional actor for 38 consecutive years before taking a sabbatical. I performed in over 200 projects during that time, mostly theatre, but also film, TV, dance, voice over, and other uncategorizable miscellany. I've always wanted to write about being a thespian, share tales untold from deep within the theatre fold. Tales of lived stories, inhabiting a myriad of characters, of meeting soulmates, of peerless bliss. Of being an artist: battle scars and victories, discoveries and defeats. It's a mercurial life, rife with elation and melancholy in equal parts, but it has suited me.

I grew up with a severely epileptic brother. His name was Matthew. We shared a room growing up. The seizure scenes in this book between Kirby and Baxter are drawn from real life. Matthew succumbed to epilepsy in the summer of 1997 when he died of complications caused by a grand-mal seizure. He was 26. With this story, I manifested a different destiny for him, and for my heart. This is what one can do when one is a storyteller; fiction is a gateway, a wormhole, a shaman pointing to fresh and gladder dimensions.

The symbols are everywhere.

Life is theatre.

Seize the day.

ACKNOWLEDGMENTS

I wrote this book beneath the aurora borealis (simulated via light projectors) in my home office in Silver Lake. Close to the reservoir, inundated by hummingbirds and coyotes, roof rats and peregrine falcons, lizards and marbled orb weavers, crane flies and rattlesnakes, grasshoppers and owls. I wrote it in Lake Arrowhead as well, at Brian and Emily's with The Glowworms. At the UCLA Writers' Program's annual mountain retreat, too, Smoosh and The Meg by my side. I wrote it at Bricks and Scones coffeehouse in Larchmont Village where I discovered the Narnia Drawer in one of the desks, and left messages for other visitors/writers. My writing playlist included Max Ablitzer, New Constellations, Weval, Washed Out, Bat For Lashes, Chvrches, Cranes, Dead Can Dance, The Bird's Companion, Baywud, and Max Richter.

I first started this book in the fall of 2019 during Francesca Lia Block's Saturday morning, in-person writing workshop. I had a great group of writers' eyes, minds, and hearts on it then. I stopped during the pandemic because...what a weird time. I picked it up again for NanoWriMo 2021, made it deeper, weirder, enigmatic-er. I finished the first draft in early 2022.

My agent at the time disliked it, so I moved on. My first publisher was...let's just say I also moved on. A major Big 5 publisher *nearly* acquired it, but decided it would have a better shot at success in the indie realm. I concurred, but also knew it existed in a realm beyond populous classifications. We're all susceptible to this stuff, it's okay. I say all of this only to remind you to trust your instincts—and keep moving on. I kept this thing nestled in the huddle of my hands, warmed near my heart. What's most important is that it's in your hands now, and, I hope, in your heart as well.

I owe a debt of gratitude to the great Gayle Brandeis whose editorial prowess sculpted the book before it went into the publishing machine. Thank you to Reagan Rothe, Dave King, and everyone at Black Rose Writing. Thank you Francesco Sedita at Penguin Workshop. Thank you to my MFA friends, Meg and Ari and Mireya, who were early readers and champions of this book. Thank you beta-readers Sarah Innes, Lisa Curatola, and Mary Ann Regan. Thanks Oscar Rodriguez for the visual worldbuilding. Thanks to my friends, to my students, and to my bosses for keeping an artist employed. Thanks to Jessica Hanna, theatre-purveyor extraordinaire, who passed along my letter to the luminous Anne Bogart, a force of nature I have long admired, who provided me with permission to use her name, title, and any quotes from her monumental book, *A Director Prepares.* Thanks Dot and Jen, my forever besties. Thanks Paul and Gertie, my beloved family. Thanks to all the kids who dare to do theatre, and those with whom I did theatre for years as a teen. It lives on! Thanks to service dogs everywhere, the unsung heroes of society, for the loyal and loving work that you do. You help those in need to live better lives.

Thank you to the lightning people.

Lastly, thank you, reader. I appreciate, admire, and respect you.

ABOUT THE AUTHOR

Tim Cummings is the author of the award-winning, best-selling coming-of-age novel, *Alice the Cat.* He holds an MFA in Creative Writing and has appeared in well over 200 projects across theatre, dance, film, television, voice-over, and new media. Tim teaches writing, runs private workshops, and coaches authors.

In addition to his passion for storytelling, Tim is an octopus and spider enthusiast. He goes wild for anything with eight legs. He recently discovered he is a masterful hula hooper and can whirl non-stop for eons. Of course, Tim loves reading and writing, but he also possesses enviable collections of stickers, labradorite, night-sky projector lights, vintage vinyl, and rare first-edition hardcover copies of some of his favorite novels. Lastly, no one has ever made a better vat of chili, and his lasagna is infallible. Learn more at www.timcummings.ink.

NOTE FROM TIM CUMMINGS

Word-of-mouth is crucial for any author to succeed. If you enjoyed *The Lightning People Play*, please leave a review online—anywhere you are able. Even if it's just a sentence or two. It would make all the difference and would be very much appreciated.

Thanks!
Tim Cummings

www.ingramcontent.com/pod-product-compliance
Lightning Source LLC
Jackson TN
JSHW020954200625
86402JS00008B/37

* 9 7 8 1 6 8 5 1 3 6 1 9 2 *